FLASHES & LIES

Flashes

Lies

A Novel

Claire Vedensky Korn

CREATIVE ARTS BOOK COMPANY
Berkeley • California

FLASHES & LIES is published by Donald S. Ellis
and distributed by Creative Arts Book Company

For information contact:
Creative Arts Book Company
833 Bancroft Way
Berkeley, California 94710
1-800-848-7789

Thanks to Carol Haraburda, RPR,
of C & H Court Reporters,
for text transcription.

ISBN 0-88739-392-6
Library of Congress Catalog Number 2001097459
Printed in the United States of America

Tell all the truth but tell it slant—
Success in Circuit lies
too bright for our infirm delight
The Truth's superb surprise

As Lightning to the Children eased
With explanation kind
The Truth must dazzle gradually
Or every man be blind—

Emily Dickinson

FLASHES & LIES

INTRODUCTION

Teddie Waterford made up her mind when she was six.

It was a November afternoon. The babysitter they'd lived with this month had herded the two sisters out her front door, their possessions stashed in the same two brown paper bags they'd arrived with. Her own suitcases waited in the taxi. "Your mother has to be here soon," she murmured, turning the key in her deadbolt lock. "I can't miss my flight."

A horn blew.

"Thea knows I'm going to Paris. Your mother helped me plan. She's special, you know." With a backward glance, the woman who'd been putting food on the table, telling them to dress for school, and tucking them in bed was gone.

It wasn't that they didn't know how to make fun. Teddie and Aurora fingerpainted with blue toothpaste on the cold concrete stoop until the tube went flat. Then they created new fashions from their old clothes. Aurora draped herself in the entire contents of her bag. Teddie crowned her auburn curls with a hat of intertwined underpants. The laughing sisters bounced down the stairs.

Thirty minutes later their fun was finished.

Two hours more had to pass before they heard the familiar squeal of their mother's brakes. "She's here," ten-year-old Aurora said from beneath her own underwear hat. "Tell her I'm not coming."

IX

Teddie hesitated, scowled, then bolted for the car.

"Right on time," Thea, their mother, lied from behind the steering wheel, but her welcoming smile faded into the lift of an eyebrow. "What's wrong with you, Theodora?"

Only her mother called Teddie, Theodora. Big Thea and little Theodora. The child bit her lip in silence as she crawled into the back seat.

"Answer me. Heaven knows I don't ask much of you, but I insist on the truth. What's Aurora doing? Is she staying here? What a picture!" Thea raised the camera she carried like a shotgun in the passenger seat. "Forlorn. Sullen. Alone. Beautiful."

"No!" Teddie jumped out of the car and ran back up the walk. "Come on!" she begged her sister, pumping her limp arm as if she could restart life. Minutes later they sat together on the cracked plastic backseat of their mother's car. Silent tears rolled down Teddie's cheeks. Aurora's stony eyes stared ahead.

"What a splendid picture, Aurora. Everything's fine," Thea proclaimed. "Let's go home."

Yes, six-year-old Teddie promised herself. Never, never would she be like her mother.

CHAPTER • I •

Forty-four years later Theodora Waterford Olds was a dutiful professional who arrived at the Hanford Tower five minutes before her one-thirty appointment. Day in and day out, Teddie Olds faithfully converted attorneys' questions and objections and witnesses' responses, well over 280 words per minute, into twenty-four phonetic symbols. She was reliable and accurate to her bones, a court reporter who recorded spoken truths to produce one-and-only true and official transcripts.

Wind-whipped snow clung to her tweed coat as she unloaded her recording equipment from the trunk of her blue Saturn. The checks she must deposit, if their joint account was not to be overdrawn, were safe in her handbag, but the entrance to the bank that held Howie's and her accounts was at the distant end of this oversized office tower. She looked at her watch. No, not now.

Regretfully she whirled through the revolving door. Someday she'd have time to stay there, spinning, spinning, until she'd had her fill. This high-rise building surrounded by freeways fleeing Detroit often felt more homelike than the office she'd set up in her son's vacated bedroom. "Mr. Sullivan just got in," the guard told her as she signed in. "Knew you'd be right along."

"Like clockwork, Fred. Thanks." She punched the elevator button. On the exact minute she opened the door to the eleventh floor suite where paralegal Lisa Greenstein was handing Jack Sullivan a steaming mug.

"You're a sight for sore eyes," the silver-haired man flattered, "but the name doesn't fit."

"Oh?" Teddie sighed.

The lawyer took an appreciative sip and waited for the full attention of his invisible jury. "Young, Ms. Young, not Olds. Young, that's what we are. Right?"

Wrong, she craved to blurt. Not me. Not you. Fifty is not young, she ached to add, but experience had taught her tricks to stay her compulsively truthful tongue. "Well, you think so," she mumbled, integrity intact.

"Get yourself set up, young lady." Jack opened the conference room door. "Hope you don't feel squeamish so soon after lunch. It's a malpractice."

Teddie assembled her stenotype and audophone in a polished, book-lined room where the brush of a finger was enough to mar the tabletop. Squeamish? For three decades she had recorded mayhem, deceit, theft, libel, discrimination, injury, harrassment, even rape and murder. The words slid easily off her fingertips but not their intentions. At first she'd believed in sworn oaths, but eventually she'd come to recognize the false statements, the lies under oath, so like Thea.

Jack Sullivan ushered in a jittery woman accompanied by her legal counsel. "Treacherous out. Slippery. Good of you to make time for us," he said. "Like you to meet Ms. Teddie Olds. Fancy name's Theodora, but we call her Teddie. Ms. Olds runs the show. Okay? Good. Let's get to work."

Teddie shook the woman's clammy hand. "I only keep track of what people say," she explained. "Makes it official."

The witness's shoulders softened. "I've never done anything like this," she said. "I have to tell it right. What he did was wrong."

"Well, now," Jack murmured. "We'd like to hear all about it. Your own words. Ms. Olds here is a notary public and a professional court reporter." His smile took in everyone. "She's going to ask you to swear what you're telling us is true and then we'll get to work. Do you need to get back to the hospital any time soon?"

The woman shook her head.

"Well, then, Ms. Olds, will you administer the oath?"

Teddie did so. Words poured in her ears, out her fingers. She liked to watch the speaker's lips to corroborate the record she was making, but sometimes shutting her eyes improved concentration. Often she found herself in a limbo between sleeping and waking, her fingers flying, mind absent. ". . . tubal cauterization . . . ," important words penetrated the dream state and her eyes popped open.

"Would you repeat that?" Teddie asked.

"He wasn't supposed to. . . ."

"No," Teddie interrupted. "The exact words, 'tubal' something."

"Tubal cauterization, that's what I said. Sterilized her. Shouldn't have. Wrong." Teddie nodded and mouthed the words she translated. The witness was twisting her ring-bare fingers. Perspiration glistened through her makeup.

"Tell me about you and the doctor," Jack Sullivan urged. "Where do you see him? Work and where else?"

"Nowhere. Work. I never see him." Teddie recorded, but her fingers did not stop with the spoken words. "Liar!" the heiroglyphics read, her own alien opinion.

"I am always professional," the witness added and to which Teddie added, "False." This woman's legal complaints were more than a terrible tubal cauterization, perhaps the romantic mistreatment of a nurse.

"Go on," he said. "Tell us about Dr. Gardner's technique."

Teddie closed her eyes and let her fingers have their way.

o o o

The sky was darkening when witness and counsel departed, either more bad weather or the natural end of Michigan's meager winter daylight. "When do you need it?" Teddie asked.

"It'll keep. Remember, we've got an appointment tomorrow. Your mama's will. Let's us have lunch Monday."

"Jack! Take this?" He shrugged and turned to the phone Lisa held. Teddie worried as she packed her old-fashioned equipment. She'd never understand the computers she should be using. Only Jack and a few other old-timers, many of them transplanted southerners like Jack, men who called women like Teddie "ladies," would put up with her prehistoric ways. Instead of simply pushing a small plastic disk into a printer, she had to go home and transcribe, and, what's more, clean up those unnerving opinions her fingers had taken to producing. No. She refused to truck with computers. Change wasn't worth the effort. She might make dangerous mistakes.

"So late," Teddie moaned to the guard as she signed out in the lobby, "and I have to make a deposit."

"Why don't you use one of those machines?" Fred asked.

"I don't. I just don't."

"Okay, okay. Leave your things. Shortcut here, just you come back." The security guard selected a key from his heavy ring as he approached an inconspicuous door. "Takes you right there, where you wait for loans."

The hinges worked soundlessly. An empty desk and a row of empty chairs waited between her and the distant tellers' counter. A lone customer paused at the single open window. Most people with a choice would be home on a night like this. The rest would be using ATMs or marking time in traffic jams.

Quietly Teddie crossed the beige carpet, same blah color as her coat, she observed. She paused to dig deep into her handbag and heard something. A cry? Where were those checks? Another shout brought her head up. The customer had turned towards her, his features hidden beneath a multicolored ski mask. It's not that cold out, practical Teddie mused.

"Freeze! Now! Down!" she heard, but his words did not make sense. If you froze in place, you couldn't move, so what did he mean? The masked man waved a piece of pipe. How odd. A gun? Surreal. "I mean it. Don't you want to live? Don't you want to see your hubby again?" His shrill voice cracked.

Which question to answer first and how, she asked herself, then, aware of real danger, Teddie stifled a laugh. Energy tingled down her spine. With cool clarity she knew that the bank teller with kinky, wet-looking hair was paralyzed with terror. The bank robber's blue eyes were pleading, his dirty green parka frayed and worn. "Yes. Of course," Teddie agreed, and she'd done it again, accepted words as reality. The crotch of her pantyhose ripped as she knelt next to her handbag. Where were the bank officials? Where were the guards?

"All the way down. Flat," he ordered. She could see the teller carefully lower a skinny hand. Gun leading, the robber swung away from Teddie.

"Yes," Teddie said agreeably to his back. Sensing he'd discounted her presence, for everyone ignored women like her, she slung her purse around her neck and crawled backwards. If he threatened again, she might lie flat, but she'd feel like a beached whale. Retreating, she retraced her path across the scratchy carpeting. The wool jacket and silk blouse she'd scarcely been able to button this morning acted like a straitjacket; her skirt gripped like a vise. Her waistband burst and she could inhale. Rip! Her blouse was destroyed, but her arms liberated. Her skirt rode up her thighs in wrinkles, then folds.

Teddie suspected the robber and teller were arguing when she reached the first chair. The teller's eyes had rolled heavenward, as if she knew there was an emergency procedure she should remember. The robber moved his gun arm. The teller was bending over her cash drawer when Teddie cornered at the desk. Almost there, which way? The Loan Department personnel had dimmed the lights as they left, a small blessing. Her heel clanged on metal. She held her breath. The file cabinet. Eyes glued to the robber's back, she wriggled slow motion until both feet made contact with solid wall.

Inch by inch Teddie raised herself. Her fingers found the handle, and the door gave way. Tattered, entangled, she collapsed onto the floor of lobby she'd left minutes before. The hidden door swung closed. A pair of tassled Italian men's loafers, like the ones her husband wore to impress judges and juries, retreated towards the elevators.

"911, call 911," Teddie croaked.

Fred's head rose above the counter. "What the. . .? Ms. Olds?"

"Robber. Gun. 911."

Fred spoke into the phone while she worked herself upright. Then he was waving a revolver. "What are you doing?" she exclaimed. "Where are the police?"

Gun steady, Fred shuffled out the emergency exit. The chill air blasted Teddie as she trailed him into fading daylight. A figure was running blindly towards them across the near-empty parking lot. "That's him!" she hissed. "Careful!"

"Halt!" Fred intoned, his command so firm, so resonant, it was as if a god had spoken. Only yards away, the robber not only stopped, but skidded headlong on the icy pavement, masked face to the ground. With adrenalin-aided vision, Teddie scrutinized his white bony ankles. The robber wore no socks beneath his black leather dress shoes. Wool wrapped his face, but his ankles were bare. He was struggling for footing, soon would escape, so she lunged forward to press his padded shoulders into the snow. Wriggling, slippery, the thief twisted and heaved. Dutifully she dropped her whole self, full length, face down, onto the robber's back. Now he could reach neither his weapon nor the bag of money sinking into gray slush.

"Ouch," he complained. "Let me go."

"Get up, Ms. Olds," Fred's bass voice ordered. "I've got him covered."

Teddie stayed where she was. From her vantage point on the robber's back, she whispered, "Why?" into his wool-covered ear. "You don't know what you're doing. You don't know how to rob a bank."

His thrashing slowed. The green shoulders shuddered. Sirens, flashing red lights, then Teddie and her quarry were spotlighted by powerful police headlights. Car doors opened, a hand tugged her armpit upwards. "Some help here," a male voice said. Forces on two sides jacked Teddie to her feet. She was cold away from the robber's warmth, her clothing ripped, wrinkled.

"He assault you, lady?"

Fred snorted. "Her? She done assaulted him."

Pained eyes caught hers as the police twisted the robber's arms behind his back. A heavyset cop yanked the Peruvian mask from his head while another frisked him. Early twenties, he could be her own Zach. The boy's face was wet with tears, blood trickled from his nose and hands. His flattened dull brown hair stuck up in patches like a fevered child's. In a latex-gloved hand, a policeman displayed the water pistol he had pulled from the robber's pocket.

"What will you do with him?" she asked. All the officers wore latex gloves. One cradled the robber's soaked paper bag against his chest. She studied her own bare hands. A few scratches, a torn nail, a little blood, nothing serious, ice can rip you up. Sharp stings made her think her right knee was pretty raw, like a kid's after a playground fight. Reality struck. Could the boy have it? Whose blood streaked her hand?

"We'll take him in, but first we need statements all around." Two more squad cars had emptied into the bank.

"Oh no," Teddie said aloud. Spiderlike prickles crawled up her arms and legs, swept from her chest to her neck to her cheeks. Her menopausal furnace roared. Rivulets of sweat rolled down her face, trickled behind her knees. "The deposition!" A hand touched her elbow.

"Things are locked up, Ms. Olds," Fred's voice reassured. "Don't worry. Got to get back. Ask if we all can go inside. Don't need no more nonsense."

Teddie asked politely. Two officers escorted them. Most of the lawyers' and accountants' offices had emptied early. A police-woman's latexed hand held the swinging door open while her part-ner ushered them into the Hanford Tower lobby. Again Teddie eyed the revolving door with longing. Once around and she'd be free.

Leaving work for the day, Lisa Greenstein happened on this scene. "My God, what happened?" she squealed.

Teddie's muscles went into meltdown. She collapsed on a lobby chair. Tears overfilled her eyes. "Need Jack," she mumbled.

Encouraged by police nods, Lisa rested her hand on Teddie's shoulder. "Are you in trouble?"

"Not me. Him. He's going to need a lawyer. He shouldn't have done it. He didn't know how."

"What's she talking about?" Lisa asked.

"Bank robbery. She caught him," the policeman said dryly. "Stick around a few minutes? Calm her down? You know, women her age. . . ."

"Fred? Did she?" Lisa's mascaraed eyes were wide.

Teddie studied her reflection in the pretend-old mirror wall. Graying ginger hair, face cracking or was the crack in the glass? Was she grinning? The woman in the mirror looked insane, mad. Her image's smile broadened.

A gloved police hand held out a paper cup. "Drink this. We'll need a statement. Anyone waiting for you?"

Sister Aurora, visiting this week from Chicago, and husband Howie must be going about their business, whatever it was, on the white couch in the Olds's white living room.

No, she shook her head. No one was waiting.

CHAPTER • 2 •

After she'd washed her hands and face, dabbed her knee, combed her hair, applied fresh lipstick, when she'd completed a lucid statement, Teddie was allowed to take herself home. An officer recognized her from court. "Olds," he mused. "Know someone else with that name. Oh, yeah, Dr. Olds. Knows all about the crazies, that post-stress stuff. You related?"

Teddie hestitated, shrugged. "Married," she said and departed with her recording paraphernalia.

Her headlights filtered through snow-curtains, white flakes dusting dark suburban hedges, as she turned into their driveway. Fences here were both forbidden and unnecessary. The days she chose to work at home passed without human contact, yet Howie was adamant when she proposed moving to a condo or smaller house. Life in the gray center of nowhere was convenient, he said, close by his well-heeled patients and within easy reach of the courtrooms where he brandished his expertise.

They'd met in a courtroom. What luck! Teddie, as always, was transcribing spoken words into those twenty-four symbols when the young clinical psychologist, Howard Olds, was summoned to jury duty. After his service was finished, he'd returned to the courthouse, and over cups of weak coffee her husband-to-be confessed that the murky practice of clinical psychology paled next to the shining facts

of evidence, guilt, and innocence. He was so highly educated, so
darkly handsome, and her single post-high-school degree came from
the Eva Martin School of Court Reporting. For that moment Dr.
Howard Olds lifted her loneliness. Of course, it took only a come-
hither look and a magical touch for her famous, charismatic mother to stake her own claim on meeting him, an event Thea had long
forgotten and from which Howie was yet to recover.

The garage door rose on electronic command.

Excited, alive, Teddie bore her tapes into the kitchen. So late,
almost seven, no work tonight, what matter.

"That you?" Howie called.

What if it wasn't me? What if I were a real thief, a desperate
criminal? She limped into the white room where, wrapped in
strains of Cole Porter, her husband and sister sipped drinks on the
couch. "We were about to toast Thea, but you're late. What happened? Get mugged?" he joked.

Her excitement went flat.

"My God! She *did* get mugged!" Aurora jumped up.

"No, bank robbery. Sorry. Couldn't make the deposit. I have to
clean up."

"*You* were in a bank robbery?" Howie exclaimed.

"Why not me?" Teddie snapped.

"I'll come," Aurora said. "You shouldn't be alone. What happened?" Round eyes flashing, taut cheeks pink and mandatory
manhattan secure, Aurora grasped Teddie's scratched hand to lead
her upstairs. No one offered the victim her own nightly drink.

"Ted," Howie shouted from below. "Thea's been calling you.
Won't tell me why." And the phone rang.

"Say I'm not home," Teddie groaned. "Say I got stuck in traffic.
Tell her to. . . ." Her voice crescendoed. She pinched her lips closed.
Something terrible was wrong. She was bad. She asked him to lie for
her. But what did she have to say to her mother? She was unhinged.

"It's your lawyer buddy," Howie reported. "Talk to Jack?"

"Take it upstairs."

"I answered the first time," Aurora said. "She wanted you.
Wouldn't talk to me. What is it?"

Teddie shrugged as she listened for Howie to hang up. On the
king-sized bed Aurora snuggled into a flea market quilt named
Solomon's Puzzle. Many Sundays Teddie searched the discards of
others in an attempt to anchor her own floating past.

"What's this I hear about a robber?" Jack's voice asked. "You okay?"

"If you check on the boy. He needs help. All I need is a good night's sleep. Thanks, Jack."

Eagle-eyed Aurora watched Teddie peel off her jacket, her skirt, the shredded blouse. Any movement hurt, especially the scabbing knee. "Seems like a kid thing. Did Jesse and Zach get them?" Teddie asked, then answered herself. "No, they were too protected, too car-pooled." As she peered closely at her raw flesh she saw the bank robber's blood-stained young-old face.

Would she have to be tested?

"You've been beaten up worse," Aurora mused. "Remember? When we stayed with those terrible people, Thea's Last Resort we called that place, those artsy people who never cleaned their pig sty house." Like her mother, Aurora invented memories, but this one was real.

"Yeah. Everyone called them crazy, so we were nuts, too," Teddie added. "Our names didn't help. Remember?

Aurora 'n' Theodora, Robbed the candy stora.

Caught by the coppers

They went bonkers. . . .

Diddle, diddle, diddle, diddle da," she chanted. "I always cried. That boy with braces. Stuck his stinking breath face right in mine. Ugh. Punched him."

"Yeah. Cut your hand. Lucky you didn't get blood poisoning along with your black eye and bloody nose. Stains never came out." Aurora laughed. "I buried your coat in their tire heap. Told those two you'd lost it, that you always lost things."

"Liar!"

"You lost *that* coat," Aurora smirked.

"She got me a gray gabardine at Salvation Army. It stunk, too."

"Ancient history. What about today?"

Teddie outlined the events at the bank, concluding with, "A water pistol! Probably didn't know how to load it. Terrible," before retreating to bathroom privacy. The purifying hot shower stung her scraped hands and skinned knee, but still she soaped and rinsed, soaped and rinsed. A far distant phone rang, then Aurora was shouting from the dry side of the steamy door. "The home." Teddie opened a crack. "Thea, the Carleton, whatever."

"I'm busy."

"What do you think I said? They want you to call as soon as you can. Maybe it's important."

"Maybe." Teddie turned off the water. "Hand me that towel." For once she was thankful Howie had insisted on these monstrous bath sheets that took forever to dry. "Could be worse," Aurora observed. "Oh well. Wait til you see what we bought for you. Howie will die when he gets the bill."

"No, he won't. You don't understand. I pay, *if* I keep any."

"How rude. Any *civilized* person would thank me." Aurora flounced off.

This day had been impossibly long. Was it only seven hours ago that she and Aurora had lunched with their childhood friend, Marla, at the Garden Grille? It had been their first time together for ages, just the three of them. Marla made the arrangements after Teddie invited her to Rossotti, Ltd's celebration of the golden anniversary of Thea's first book of photographs. Marla always claimed to love photography.

o o o

Walking to lunch, glimpsing the three of them reflected in a store window, Teddie had felt like a cow.

"Should I say it?" Aurora asked just as Teddie started to wolf her lovely, creamy strands of fettucini Alfredo.

Teddie would have answered that she did not know, but Marla had stepped in with a brisk, "Of course. We don't have any secrets."

"It's not nice." Aurora studied the plate of Caesar salad she and Marla were sharing, a leaf for you, a leaf for me, slow nibbles like a pair of anorexic rabbits. "You're piggy, sister," Aurora smirked. "Look at yourself."

In the nick of time their waitress materialized to ask how everything was. "Delicious," Teddie answered in relief. Then Marla insisted that the overworked woman snap a Polaroid to preserve the scene, and, yes, the seams of Eva Martin's School of Court Reporting approved work outfit were stretched to the limit.

"It's the change," Marla stage-whispered. "My doctor can fix anything. Hormones. I'll make an appointment for you. Look at me." Marla was immaculate, trim, every dyed black hair in place.

"Time's up, sister. You're about to explode. What size? Sixteen? Eighteen? Not twenty!" and Aurora laughed without crinkling her surgically-improved eyes. "I take a four, but we could find something while you go to work or whatever it is you do."

"I do work," Teddie told them, "and I have an appointment. Buy something for me if you want. Go on." It was easier. She would not take responsibility for change.

o o o

Politeness versus honesty. No contest.

Honesty was her support, her pride. She'd slipped into her blue bathrobe when Aurora returned with an armload of boxes and shopping bags, none she noted, from the Special Shoppe, the mall's polyester haven for oversized women.

"Look! See?" Aurora begged as she dropped her booty on the bed.

"No. I caught a bank robber. I'm hungry. Did you start dinner?" Really, she needed a drink. Never too much. Perfect control. One, two, sometimes more, and the irritated edges dissolved. A land of temperate lucidity awaited, a place of comfort and understanding.

"I'm a guest," Aurora huffed. "*Some* people take care of their guests, but *I* have to take care of *you*." Teddie dammed her flow of precise, contradictory memories, all those times she'd saved Aurora from one horror or another. The sisters went down, one to the kitchen, the other to the man. Teddie poured herself kitchen scotch over ice, slid frozen dinners into the microwave, and shuffled her fluffy slippers into the living room. "Sit," Howie sang out from the white couch and reached for her hand. His own pink manicured fingernails shone like the insides of sea shells, rising half-moons clear and clean. "Listen."

Aurora's story-telling was transforming her sister's experience. No longer had Teddie been part of a sordid scene in a dull building surrounded by a tangle of roads rimmed with dirty snow. This woman had risked her life, she had deceived the robber, escaped, and captured a dangerous culprit. She was interesting, brave, courageous, so much more than a middle-aged female, holes in her pantyhose, purse slung around her neck, crawling backwards away from a water pistol-brandishing child. Howie placed his soft manicured hand in Teddie's fleecy blue lap. She should set the record straight, give the true account, but she was drinking in words and scotch when again the phone rang. "I can't talk to Thea," she whispered. "Can't." The truth.

Howie patted her knee as he rose. Teddie winced. She'd reinspected her scab-sticky wound by the time he returned to say no one would bother her tonight, and how about dinner? The stove timer buzzed, and, glass empty, Teddie limped back into the kitchen. The phone rang yet again as she was replenishing. "Hello!" she snapped into the mouthpiece.

"Theodora!" Her mother's voice drilled into her skull. "I have to do everything myself. Those caretakers," Thea said, scornfully twisting her words, "pretended you weren't home. Of course they didn't try." Teddie breathed deeply. "I need you. Now."

"No. I'm getting dinner. Won't it keep?"

"No. It's important."

"I'm exhausted, Thea. There was a bank robbery. I captured him. Tell me tomorrow."

"Nonsense. Speak up. Say you don't want to see me. Bank robbery. Tell me the truth. I can't say anything now. They might be listening."

"Stop it. You're bored." Teddie's head was spinning with the effort of making her mother hang up. She crossed her fingers. "I'll call when we've finished eating. Talk to you later," and she jammed the phone into its wall-receptor. Her mother could not make her run to the Carleton. Her mother could not make her phone. The thought of speaking to Thea again tonight was unbearable. But how had her lie happened? She must call back, call to make it right. She would say straight out, "Thea, Mother, I'm sorry I won't call you later tonight. You'll have to wait til morning. Good-bye." No, that would lead to worse unpleasantness. Leave the lie. A small lie, a white lie, a lie nonetheless. A thunderbolt, a force field, threatened from above, punishment she couldn't escape, unless, unless. . . . She gulped scotch and found three plates for the once-frozen dinners. Dinner and drink and straight to bed. With a good night's sleep she'd be able to cope, but there was that deposition waiting and tomorrow Thea's will. No, she'd have to call back after dinner. She'd be strong. She'd promised.

"What are you doing?" Aurora had left Howie for the kitchen. "Was that her? What did she say?"

Three questions. "Wrong number," Teddie said and a second thunderbolt joined the first. "Nothing important. Set the table."

"In here?" Aurora asked.

"Why not?" The dining room with its Chinese carved carpet and mahogany sideboards didn't fit a fluffy blue bathrobe, matching slippers, and TV dinners, even if served on china. The breakfast nook, that's what it had been called when the realtor first showed them the house. A cosy place for family mornings, essentially unused except as her standby office, though once Teddie, hearing noises, had discovered her partially undressed daughter and a near-naked young man grappling in that corner of the kitchen.

Teddie's husband drifted in. "Howie," she said shakily, "you said no one would call. What went wrong?"

"You answered. Who was it? You're upset."

Aurora rolled her eyes and wrapped her arms around Howie's shoulder. "Only a wrong number."

"It's been a rough day," he reflected in his warmest, most therapeutic voice. Her husband's understanding filled Teddie's eyes with tears. "I'll ask my service to take our calls." He patted her back. She stretched to kiss him, but Aurora's body sinuously blocked the path to her husband's lips.

"My sister doesn't know how lucky she is," Aurora crooned. Howie peeled her off to make his call. After dinner he insisted his wife go straight to bed and the two of them would clean up. "No calls, that's an order." Teddie's knees wobbled as her shaking hands poured a nightcap. "Think about the calories," Aurora said. "Spring water, even white wine would be better. Brandy for me. How about you, Howie?"

"I should call her. She's still up." Teddie sighed.

"I told you. I took care of Thea."

"But you didn't. . . ." Teddie started, then hazily recalled the second thunderbolt. What had she said? Wrong number? Now she couldn't tangle with the truth. What would they believe? What about trust? "Goodnight, then. Thanks."

Aurora's shopping had not moved. Teddie tossed boxes and bags clear of Solomon's Puzzle. Out of one flowed something soft and brightly colored. "Trustworthy clothes. Wouldn't you know," she complained.

For the second time that day she brushed her teeth, but now her chin was uncomfortable, tender. Perhaps it had been hit when she fell on the boy. Better her chin than a black eye. The mirror reflected not a bruise, however, but a hot, rising, red pimple, boil, zit. Adolescent acne at fifty. Menopausal acne. Not a little spot, but a deep volcano with a buried heart that would take days to mature and rise to the surface. A headlight shining through her hormonal storms.

o o o

At the first anxious electrical charge her body stiffened and her eyes opened to the night. Her husband's half-snores were not reassuring. With the jolt came the reality, her deceptions. Her heart pounded. She was flooded with heat, she must be incandescent, glowing red hot, a light. Slipping into the bathroom, she splashed herself with cold water and, without pausing to dry, gulped two Tylenol. Twice more she drifted back to sleep and twice more startled awake. In her dreams her unburied mother was dead. Teddie was responsible for something—for her death? For disposing of her body? She must do something, but whatever, she was guilty. When she was trapped, when she was choking, strangling (had she strangled Thea? Had she fatally twisted that wrinkled chicken neck with her own hands?), her eyes snapped open to darkness. The electrical current surged and she threw herself out of bed. Howie snorted twice. How could he sleep? How could he not sense the violent forces loose in this room? In a moment lightning bolts would flash from wall to mirror, from closet to ceiling, over their bed where he lay. One might strike him dead. Barefoot, body boiling, she fled downstairs in her nightgown. Ice. Snow. Perhaps she'd melt them and force spring. She unlatched a living room French door and stepped into moonlight, her feet sinking into the snow carpet on the brick patio. "Ahh," she sighed, rubbing handfuls of cold on her face, neck, arms, on the backs of her knees. The night was clear. She tossed snow offerings to the moon; tiny flakes soared and twisted, returning the light they had captured. She held her white nylon gown away from her heated flesh to tempt the crystals to caress her sweaty breasts.

The night silence embraced her, held her enthralled.

Snow angels. Why shouldn't she strip, throw herself flat on the silver surface, and make her angel wings real? Because you'd have to get up, she answered herself, and besides, they'd see your impression in the morning and you'd never hear the end of it. She wasn't ready. "Shhh," she said aloud. The earth beneath her feet spun; the heavens shifted. Cleansed, purified, and getting cold, she reentered the commonplace. The snow feathers that fell from her feet melted into the carpet as she found her way back to bed.

CHAPTER • 3 •

As she stretched in her warm morning bed, her muscles twinged, throbbed, ached, but she felt good. Strong. Clear-headed. Her husband was in the shower, Aurora asleep. Outside a growling, clanking snowplow was clearing their driveway. She had time before, before . . . before she had to call her mother, before she had to see her mother. Phone Thea, who'd assumed she'd lied with the truth but who accepted the lie. The first lie. There was a second, but to whom and about what? These details were shrouded in fog. Never mind. It would come. This morning she felt oddly powerful. Perhaps she should rehearse:

"Good morning, Mother. How did you sleep?" Don't pause. "Jack Sullivan and I are on our way with your papers. Are you ready for your party tomorrow? Do you remember the time? Aurora's here already. Zach and Jesse promised they'll be there." The truth. The truth and patronizing. "I could get there early if you still need to talk. Let me know." Compassion. "Have to run now, don't want to be late." Half lie. "See you soon." Hang up. There.

She smelled coffee. Her husband had switched on the automatic maker she always left prepared in their bathroom. Howie, scrubbed and rosy, cheeks shaved, beard freshly trimmed, silently handed her a steaming mug which she carried two-handed into the bathroom. She wiped a blob of hair-studded shaving cream from the sink before washing.

"Hey, Ted, I'm going!" Clean and robed, Teddie opened the door to be caught in her husband's arms. Coffee and toothpaste mingled in a deep, exploratory kiss. His warmth filled her. This was their moment, the high point and singular instant of closeness, their passionate farewell kiss, the summit of their relationship. For these nostalgic seconds their life together held meaning.

Howie extricated his wrist to read his watch. "I'll be late," he said, and he drew her close for another kiss.

"Remember Thea's reception tomorrow," she whispered.

"You know I'd never miss a Thea-bash," and he was gone.

Teddie heated a bran muffin and swallowed orange juice; that and the coffee would fuel her. Thea did not answer her phone. Teddie left a message with one of the office caretakers. "Don't worry. Mrs. Waterford was just here," the voice told her.

"Complaining?" Teddie could tell.

"Your mother's full of herself," the voice continued. "She wanted to talk to you last night. I'll see she gets your message."

Perfect. Teddie refilled her stoneware cup and shuffled to Zach's bedroom, her office but still his space. He'd promised to stay the night after the reception. Precious time. She'd be happy to remove her equipment.

A framed triptych hung over his bed, three photographs together, not Thea's images of humans in joy and despair, but abstractions of corn and wheat fields in winter. A friend's work, he'd said. Zach was neat, everything in order, so why did Jesse live in crumpled chaos? How had she slacked off in child-rearing after the first?

Machines working, Teddie drifted into the nirvana of routine. In federal court she'd recorded stories that could have fueled even the most sluggish cocktail party conversations. "How exciting! You were there? The whole time? Was he awful? Was she guilty?" they'd chime after she'd answered their questions about how she spent her days.

"What was it about?" she'd ask.

"But you were there!" they complained. There in body, perhaps, but not in mind. Under her mother's tutelage she'd learned how to split herself, but all court reporters were adept.

"THE O DOR A!" Angry syllables returned Teddie to West Bloomfield and an irate Aurora. "I've been trying to get your attention for hours!"

"Not hours. Fifteen minutes. That's all I've been working."

"You know what I mean. We have to get started if you're to get a real makeover. It's time to schedule."

Had she agreed or only avoided the subject? Whatever, this morning she felt fine, no matter how she looked. The rising mound on her chin had cooled. Snow and moonlight, a treatment for menopausal acne.

"Look, Sis. I'm terribly busy the next few weeks," she said, although her calendar was entirely blank after the delivery of this transcript. Another one. Astonishing. This wrong felt so right. "How long does one of those things take?" she asked.

"For you all day. Wraps and soaks, and you do need coloring. My touch-up's nothing, a couple of hours at most, but you are a self-abuser. Your self-abuse is outrageous. Maybe a spa, say two weeks?"

"A spa—what a good idea. Just not now, thanks." Teddie forced a smile. "Make an appointment in three weeks. I'll schedule around it once it's in my book." It was getting easier. "I have some business this morning," she added accurately. Cancelling should be simple. She would cancel Marla's menopause doctor, too. "Get yourself some breakfast. It's late." Patronizing. A little hostile. "I have to go."

The multi-colored dress, swirls of blue, green, and dusty rose, still hung on a hanger hooked over the door, when Teddie returned to make the bed and prepare to leave. The boxes and bags were piled in the overstuffed chair overlooking a sea of trees. When they were in full leaf, she could sit in that chair and be in a treehouse. Other months gave her abstract art, today shades of gray, brown, and black against almost-pure white.

She had not considered yesterday's damage to her Eva Martin School of Court Reporting's approved working wardrobe. The dress on the door would have been better for crawling. It was clear that Eva Martin had not anticipated her professionals being involved in bank robberies. The dress looked expensive, but bore no price tag. She slid it over her head and let it settle. The zipper whispered closed. The image in the mirror made her gasp, for she was transformed, a Wonder Woman alteration.

"Not bad! Now what do you say?" Aurora was leaning on the door frame.

"You're right. Okay?"

"Little doors
Open with ease
With two keys
Thank-you and please," Aurora chanted.

"Sickening. Doggerel to teach us manners because our mother couldn't do it by example." She slipped out of the dress. "Well?" Aurora raised her eyebrows.

"Thanks. I hope the rest are as good." Give in, threaten, add a dash of self-importance and mix. "Have to get to work," and she pulled a gray suit from the closet where her ever-tighter wardrobe hung. She'd add the antique gold earrings Howie had given her recently, a reparation payment for one of those amorous adventures they never discussed.

o o o

In daylight the Hanford Tower looked solid and safe, not a place where a fifty-year-old woman had held a bleeding boy bank robber pinned to the icy pavement in winter dark. That bandage on her knee, required if she were to wear stockings, was her proof. Oh God, that and what might be coursing through her blood. She'd have to ask Jack if the boy had been tested for HIV, but perhaps she didn't want to know. Wouldn't they tell her? Wasn't it their responsibility? Do you ask your family doctor or do you have to go to a public clinic? Impossible.

A young stranger had replaced Fred at the security guard's desk. "Good morning," was all Teddie said.

Wordlessly Lisa Greenstein studied Teddie.

She can't figure me out. Is this figure before her a meek, mild-mannered court reporter or a hormonally imbalanced madwoman?

"Let me take your coat. Do you want coffee?"

As if I'm a paying client and she a fawning receptionist, not an overwrought paralegal forced to work on Saturday.

"No thanks. No coat. No coffee. Is Jack ready?" Lisa still stared. "Last night was pretty shocking, wasn't it?" Teddie needed to help the child cope with reality. "I mean, you were only going home and there I was, bloody and battered, surrounded by police."

The girl looked at her nails. "Oh, it's all right, Mrs. Olds," she said, fingers now flying over the keyboard.

Why, she's afraid. She's afraid of me. Yesterday I was safe and discountable. Today I am dangerous. I menace someone young, vital, and attractive, if not exactly brilliant.

Jack Sullivan burst out his door. "Look at you! Our lady who catches bank robbers."

"Are you ready? We can't be late for Thea's scheme-of-the-week." Teddie rested her handbag on the desk. "Oh, and thanks for calling. Did you learn anything about the boy?"

He checked the contents of his briefcase. "You won't believe it, Teddie. He could be one of our neighbors, good schools, graduated in goddamn architecture, and you saw him. Looks like a bum."

"How did it happen? What are they going to do to him?" What a relief that the bleeding robber comes from a good background.

"Park him in jail a day or two, feed him, keep him warm. Then, depends on what we hear—he's got parents somewhere. He says no, but maybe they'll take him back. And the shrink has a say. The kid says robbing a bank is the best thing he ever did. For once he was taking control of his life."

"Oh!" Self-recognition jarred Teddie. "I'll drive. I know the way."

The Carleton was a tall gray building surrounded by three-story wings and winter-killed gardens, a retirement home where eighty-five-year-old Thea laughed at the joke she was playing on the management. Not only had she signed a suitably amended real estate agreement with the extended care facility, but also, the previous week, a contract with Rossotti's for a photographic study of the aged.

"I can't wait to get to work," Thea had said. "Never did understand them."

"Who?" Teddie had asked.

The wrinkled woman answered with exaggerated patience, as if she were lecturing the hard-of-hearing or slow-of-mind. "Old people. Senior citizens. You have to be one to live at the Carleton, you know. As different as Africa."

Today her mother was waiting behind her blue door. Thea had explained the rainbow colors of the apartment entrances were not a decorator touch, but rather a scheme to help the age-befuddled find their way home. "Imagine!" she'd said.

o o o

"You're lovely!" Jack exclaimed. The old woman was enthroned in her high-backed, green plush wing chair. "Isn't she beautiful, Teddie?"

Perhaps once before and perhaps once again, but not at this moment. Possibly it was last night's unmentioned trouble, possibly this ceremonial signing of her Last Will and Testament, but every second of Thea's four score and five years appeared carved into her scanty flesh. Mute, Teddie bit her lip.

"Now tell me. Just what *were* you doing last night?" Thea demanded. "Not a bank robbery. Not you." She then flashed a conspiratorial smile at the attorney. "My girls were rascals, but they always behaved for me. It's true. Aren't I a magnificent mother, Theodora?"

Teddie's face burned. Wordlessly she displayed her nicked and scraped hands, then raised her skirt to expose the bandaged knee. "See?" She begged for her mother's belief, this woman whose career had been fired by her jump-starting lies that set two previously disinterested galleries into competition for her artistry. The very first exhibit generated enough critical acclaim to propel her photographs into private collections. Later the museums clamored for her.

Today the old crone had the gall to remake motherhood.

Don't be ridiculous, Mother, you don't know what maternal means, Teddie would have to answer. Thankfully Jack interrupted before her tongue could form the first word.

"I know you appreciate how special this daughter of *yours* is," he said, resting his hand familiarly on Teddie's gray wool shoulder. "She did catch a robber. Visited with the boy myself. She's the best court reporter in the state of Michigan. We've worked together more years than I can count. How many's that, Ms. Olds?"

"Twenty-eight, Mr. Sullivan." An old vaudeville team.

"That's what I mean, Thea. Your daughter is accurate, precise and faster than the speed of light. She records everything just as it is. All us lawyers agree. This woman's a jewel, a real jewel." The little brass plaque Teddie had won at the Eva Martin School rested on the bottom of her underwear drawer. The school's fastest and most accurate graduate, Theodora Waterford, a genius at breaking speech into phonetic fragments.

"When are your children getting here, Theodora?"

"Not to worry, Thea. Nothing for them to sign," the lawyer said. "Just your daughter and you and me. Your Living Will, your Last Will and Testament, and the Power of Attorney for Teddie if anything should happen to you."

"Your idea, not mine. I'm indestructible. I'm steel." Thea did not insist Teddie agree.

"They'll be here for your party. Don't you remember, Mother? They're busy. Zach's teaching ninth graders at that prep school in Kalamazoo," Teddie responded, while the unanswered question rankled, her magnificent mother, her know-nothing mother. "Jesse's in school in Ann Arbor and doing something in theater, a gopher, but not burrowing underground she says, just running errands. But shouldn't Aurora be here?"

"Not at all, Theodora. Your sister's good for some things, but she's fragile. I want this to be our little secret."

What secret? That their mother's making a will? Or that she's made of cold metal?

"Thea, my love," Jack said. "You put me in mind of something. I went through your papers. Came across a birth certificate for a Maude Slote. Mean anything to you?"

"Nothing," Thea said.

"This Maude Slote person, she was born in South Dakota. I had a feeling you might be familiar with her. Where was it you hail from?" From ancient hiding places on different occasions little Teddie had listened while her mother regaled admirers with conflicting accounts of her many auspicious beginnings, her birth deep within a Colorado silver mine, her birth aboard a ship transitting the Panama Canal, her birth in the back seat of a New York taxi. As far as she knew, Thea had been born on Venus.

"It doesn't matter." Thea shrugged dismissively.

"What doesn't matter to you could matter to the law. The law wants proper names on papers. I've got me a hunch you changed your name somewhere along the line."

"Wouldn't you? Maude Slote, indeed." Teddie's heart smiled. "The farm, freezing, suffocating, dust between the sheets, grit in the food. South Dakota." Thea shivered.

"Did you change your name legally, Thea?" Jack asked as Teddie's fingers danced over her imaginary stenotype.

"Of course. I married him, Theo, Theodore Waterford, Aurora's father. Yours, too, Theodora. A good name. I kicked the little man out, no more use for him," her mother declared.

"You and this Mr. Waterford get a proper divorce?" Teddie's fingers recorded on air.

"What do you think, Jack? He took care of the details. I was busy. My career, you know."

"You'll have to tell me everything, Thea, but for now we can sign these papers. No lollygagging," and Jack Sullivan handed Thea an old-fashioned fountain pen. "You sign here, and here, and here, both names, see like it's typed out, and now you, Teddie. . . ."

Teddie's thoughts rolled like worn beach stones. This stranger professed to be her good mother, the woman she'd yearned for in vain. The woman here today was replete with power, power Teddie could not dare to dream of possessing. Without prospect, she felt no envy. Fear. Yes, fear. Fear of Thea's power, power achieved through lies, but this woman was Maude Slote. Maude Slote indeed! Teddie contained her laughter and signed her one and only name where indicated. Theodora Waterford Olds once, twice, and once again.

CHAPTER • 4 •

"Isn't she wonderful?" Marla trilled, her too-black hair gleaming beneath the chandeliers of the Carleton's largest reception room. "Look, Teddie! Aren't you proud?"

Flushed and radiant, Thea was holding court in this room crowded with sycophants, some sucked dry and brittle by the years, others stranded soft and boneless. "You mean Thea?" Teddie mumbled evasively.

"You're a stitch!" Marla giggled. "Of course. Imagine! Fifty years of art!"

"A half century. Just like me." Closing her eyes, Teddie willed herself away, elsewhere, anywhere.

"My dear, are you all right? How are you?" Marla ran on.

No, I am not all right. How am I? My varicose veins ache, my knee stings, I can't fasten my waistband, my job's immoral, my husband's a tomcat, my mother's terrifying, I've got a hot flash coming on. . . .

But Marla's elastic attention was bouncing across the room. "Isn't that Aurora? Wasn't our lunch darling? Like the old days? Need more girl talk? Coming?"

Five questions. Teddie long had understood that those who ask most listen least. "No," she answered the air, for Marla was gone. She stole a look at her sister, four years older and still half a head shorter.

Museum posters, compelling images frozen by her mother's camera and her unerring eye, were mounted on the room's washable wallpaper. Stacks of commemorative books awaited both the photographer's signature and new owners. By Thea's side a young man with golden curls and tight jeans lifted, opened, and smoothed each volume for the age-spotted hand.

"I did it!" a welcome voice penetrated the babble. Jesse. Tall, slender, in black from her 1920's cloche to her 1940's basketball shoes, wisps of blonde hair over her eyes, gold earrings rimming her left ear. "What do you think? What do you think *she'll* think?" Jesse stroked the new gold ring embedded in her previously perfect left nostril. Teddie had to fight down the urge to wipe her child's nose clean.

"What will happen when you get a cold?"

"Oh, Mom."

"Look, it's your body. You're of age. I'll never get used to it. Maybe Thea will think you're one of her exotics. Should we beard the lion in her den?" Daughter at side, Teddie at last could abandon the security of the wall, only to witness Howie's kissing lips approach Thea's claw-like hand.

"Isn't that sweet?" Jesse asked. "Dad's a real romantic. Is Zach coming?"

Two questions. Sweetness was untouchable. "Your brother said he would. I told him he didn't have to, shouldn't in bad weather."

Jesse shook her head. "You never change. Only snow. I'd want to escape Kalamazoo."

"In Santa Fe last winter someone claimed Kalamazoo was a funny name invented by a comedian. Poor Zach." Mother and daughter shared smiles at the edge of the book-signing table. Thea's gaze passed through them as if they were empty air; her target was in the crowd beyond.

"Aurora! My breaking dawn!" the old woman crowed. "Come!" Teddie's sister shrugged as if to tell her companions she had no choice.

"You look wonderful, Thea." Aurora bent down to kiss the old cheek. "This place agrees with you," she added, as if any mere place had options about agreeing or disagreeing with a life force. Aurora barely glanced at her sister before her eyes fastened on Jesse. "Your child's mutilated herself!" she exclaimed. "But you did it first, didn't you, those holes in your ears, claiming you didn't want to lose the earrings your sweet husband gives you. So lower class, so third world."

"And here *you* are!" Thea's tardy acknowledgment made Teddie feel at fault for something. Howie's fingers didn't miss a beat as he massaged Thea's bony shoulders. "You know how to care for woman," she purred. "You're privileged, Theodora."

Howie beamed at his wife, who felt her chest fill with molten lava. Her face was crimson; she was sizzling. "You've been into the punch, Ted," Howie observed with a little smile."You're positively glowing."

"She's always had a weakness for drink," Thea crooned as if sharing a little family secret. Teddie stood rooted beside her ring-nosed daughter.

"Mom? A boozer?"

"Oh yes, I know. I remember the first time," Aurora said. "You were away, Thea, Mexico maybe, her thirteenth birthday. My little sister and her little friends broke into your liquor cabinet. Got stinking out-of-mind drunk, that's what they did. Impulsive. Thoughtless. As always."

Teddie's mind replayed her always picture-perfect memories: Aurora in a white flannel nightgown strewn with blue forget-me-nots leading the charge; Aurora goading Teddie into breaking the lock; Aurora clutching bottles like a victorious boxer; Teddie sipping the sour, burning liquid only once before gulping a plain Coke to kill the taste; Aurora drinking, drinking, drinking.

"Mom didn't encourage me. She hates these." Jesse ran an index finger from one gold ring to another.

Teddie yearned to be able to tell her daughter she didn't hate the holes in her face, but wasn't she forbidden to speak false words?

"Anthropology, is that what you're studying, child? African cultures, must be. I have a picture here, reminds me of you. She's just slaughtered a chicken." Jesse bent close while her grandmother's gnarled fingers leafed through her book. "There!" Thea stabbed a glossy red fingernail on the black and white image of an ebony-skinned young woman. Jesse stroked the photograph, touching the half-circle of earrings, brushing the twin star-shaped nose ornaments and the ring that pierced the center of the smiling lower lip, before sliding her fingers over the patterned scars on the nubile, near-naked body.

Teddie sucked in air. Upside down, the photograph's power struck her with physical force.

"How primitive! Barbaric!" Aurora snorted. "Thea, you're giving her ideas. Don't let her ruin herself. Knives. Scars." She shivered.

Jesse's thin lips curved upwards. "That's wonderful, Grandmother. No wonder you're famous." Thea plucked Howie's hand from her shoulder and resettled.

The tide of guests turned; sandalled, polished, and spike-heeled feet pressed close to congratulate Thea. "Pretty as a picture. Famous photographer with lovely family," Marla crowed. "Teddie, next to your handsome husband; Aurora, over there. Don't move," and they obeyed the woman who clutched the latest in foolproof autofocus instant cameras. Once a teenage Marla's Brownie had snapped photos until its owner passed out from too much gin. "Say cheese!"

The swirls in the darkening air beyond the windows could have been swarms of agitated white flies, but really were snow. Snow. Hazardous driving, danger, but Zach stood beneath the entry arch, Teddie's own pink-cheeked, red-haired son. Relieved, she waved. Marla's shutter opened and closed with a grating electronic whir. Like a naughty child's tongue, a blank photograph reeled out of the machine. Marla plopped it on a page Thea had labored to sign.

"Zach's here," Teddie said. "Can you take another?"

"My last shot. Stupid little me."

The ghosts on the treated paper solidified. Handsome Howie looked flatly blank and Jesse caressed her nose ring while Aurora glittered with a prearranged smile. Thea became a slack-jawed harridan dwarfed by a pile of books. Teddie's own green eyes, amber earrings, and tight beige suit took form, her arm reaching beyond the photograph's white edge.

"What is this thing?" Impatiently Thea brushed the chemically treated paper from her open book.

"Isn't science wonderful? You could get one of these, you know," Marla lectured while stroking the image the professional had tossed aside. "Don't you love it? Take it, darling," she insisted. "For you on your special day."

Zach exploded with a noise between a sneeze and a laugh. Teddie hid her smile.

Thea capped her fountain pen so she could cradle Marla's right hand in her two. "I couldn't," she replied softly, earnestly, her faded eyes intent on Marla's. "Too precious," she said, charm as cloying as warm butterscotch syrup.

Precious?

Oh, the interminable slide shows Howie and Teddie had suffered with Marla and her husband, Dick. Legless, headless bodies pointed at mountains leveled by distance, at churches without steeples, at monuments without magnificence. Later they laughed in the safety of their own bedroom.

Was it possible Marla had preserved her Brownie prints in old-fashioned paper and cardboard albums? She needed proof to clear her name. Not drunk. Not irresponsible. Documentation of that birthday party would force them to acknowledge her true sober self.

Thea's young assistant chatted with admirers as he shifted the books. The old woman returned to smiling and signing while Marla herded the rest of the Waterford women toward refreshments. Teddie refused the alcohol-kissed candy pink punch for sparkling mineral water

"Not drinking, Mom? Aren't you a lush?" Jesse teased.

"Why do you tell those lies?" Teddie snarled at her sister.

"Aren't we having fun!" Marla proclaimed. "I have a wonderful idea. Let's get together again tomorrow."

"She says she has to work." Aurora answered for Teddie.

"Oh, no! How awful! Another time, then. Must fly. Kiss Thea for me." Marla set her punch glass on a passing silver tray and, lips pursed, brushed her pancake-soft cheek past Teddie's chin and Aurora's forehead. With a "Bye now," she bounced into the dwindling crowd.

Zach and his father joined the punch drinkers just as Jesse was saying good-byes. "Have to hit the road. Midterm tomorrow," she said, "but Mom, do we have her book at home? I need to look at it."

"No," Zach answered, "but Dad does, in his office."

"Ask her for another," Howie said.

"Can't wait. See you sometime. Give me a call, Zach." The slender black whirl threw a kiss at Thea and was gone. Thrice-divorced Aurora linked arms with Howie.

Thea's helper was stowing the remaining commorative books in boxes hidden beneath the green-skirted table as Teddie approached, one limping step after another. Never had she asked favors of Thea, but this request was not for her. It was for Jesse, for her daughter, although she had to admit she, too, yearned to study that elegant scarified body. Of course she could buy her mother's book, but didn't she deserve better?

Signing finished, Thea braced her hands on the table top and struggled to stand. Instinctively Teddie took hold of her mother's arm, her fingers recoiling when they reached the bone beneath the old woman's nonresistant, parchment skin.

"Don't touch me, Theodora!" Thea croaked. Teddie jumped back. Thea rocked until her assistant dropped his book to balance her. Teddie bent down to retrieve the heavy volume and stood before her mother.

"Would it be possible?" she started, ". . . oh, don't bother." Silence. "Would you?" she tried again. "Probably not. Could you? Never mind. . . ."

Thea shook off her assistant. "Out with it!" she commanded. "Young man, this girl is just like her father. No backbone. Never could get to the point."

"I want a book," Teddie blurted. "Howie has one." She sounded peevish.

"Can't he bring it home? I don't have enough. Rossotti's is stingy."

"My dear, how can you say that? We're all in this together. Now we must pack up." The senior publisher's representative, returned from stroking the guests, added, "Thanks for helping."

"She wants a copy. That's her daughter," and the junior curly-haired book handler swiveled his chin from Thea to Teddie. Teddie was grateful for his assistance, for his making the request for her. Perhaps he was sticking up for himself, making his own statement.

"Of course, of course. Take it, for you. What a marvelous mother. You must agree. So vibrant. So talented." The older man patted Teddie's shoulder. "Would you excuse us? Thea dear, we must talk business."

The bank robber's pleading blue eyes and dirty face took shape in Teddie's mind. Wasn't there something else she must say or do? She'd always acted as she should, honestly, truthfully. The boy claimed he was taking control of his life, but he didn't know how. Pathetic. What if she could transform herself? What if she had power? Impossible. But she had to change. First things first. A step at a time. She'd done it twice yesterday and again this morning. A difficult task, but she had to try. Yes, she would learn to speak false. She would steer her own life.

"So soon? You're leaving?" Thea asked Howie.

"Darling Thea. Pay attention to me," Rossotti's rep insisted. "We'll need one or two more signings, then up-dated reviews. Imagine, fresh acclaim, the sales. And the new book? How is it?"

Thea smiled easily. "As planned. Best work yet," she said.

Dumb onlooker Teddie struggled to recall any pictures Thea had taken, any work she'd done, but found nothing. Thea was lying. How simple. How comfortable. Why couldn't Teddie explain how busy she was, how much she wished she could be available whenever her mother called? "No one on earth's more important to me than you," she might start. Mentally she contemplated her empty calendar. "But right now my work is impossibly demanding, Jack Sullivan and all those lawyers. I'd give anything to be able to be there for you whenever you call, but I know you understand." Dare she add, "You're the most understanding person in the world"? No. Not yet. None of it now. Lying would take time.

"Good night, Mother. I'll phone tomorrow," Teddie said. Thea wiggled her fingers in farewell.

CHAPTER • 5 •

Monday morning. Almost nine. She'd overslept, Howie had gone to his office, and her head was painfree. Weakness for drink? Never. Not her, no matter what they say. The sky outside was a bright leaden gray, but no snow was falling. Speculating about where and with whom she actually might be lunching, Teddie stared into her closet. Over the the years Jack had issued innumerable invitations, only a few of which had taken place, those mostly shared office sandwiches.

Aurora's boxes of fancy clothes were piled up in the tree-viewing chair, all unopened but the multicolored dress hanging before her. Aurora's voice floated up the stairs. What! Her sister had the audacity to lecture her son. Hurry. Once again the dress slipped over her head to rest easily on her body. Eva Martin would frown on this unprofessional garment. Teddie smiled at her reflection.

They were in the kitchen, next to the breakfast nook where Thea's anniversary book and Teddie's recording equipment and deposition were stashed.

"Just when are you going to settle down, Zach?" Teddie heard. "Get someone to take care of you." Aurora poured herself a cup of herbal tea. "It's time you married and started a family."

"Who are you to. . . ?" Zach started irritably, then swallowed. Teddie squinted at her son in this strange, snow-reflected light.

Fine lines marred the delicate skin around his blue eyes. Wrinkles. Her child?

"Mom, you look great! I have to get going. Thea's fame was enough only for a morning off."

"Look! Don't I have good taste?" Aurora chortled. "Almost a new person, little sister. Still fat, but. . . ."

Hand on his coat sleeve, Teddie told the puzzled Zach, "I'll explain later, but do you have to go?"

Her son's frizzy beard tickled as he pecked her cheek. "Unfortunately yes," he said. "Teenagers don't wait. We've got to talk, Mom. Later. Tell Thea it was a good party."

Teddie followed Zach to the front door where she watched him scrape the snow from his windows and will his battered car to life. "Drive safely," she pleaded too softly for him to hear. A trail of gray exhaust swirled and settled on the snow.

o o o

No paying customers were waiting in Jack Sullivan's reception room. Teddie shrugged out of her coat, surprised at her dress's swirls of color.

"There you are! Look at you!" The attorney burst through his office door and opened his arms. Confused, Teddie stood stock still as his eyes roamed up and down her body. By the time he'd rested both hands on her shoulders, her face was radiating heat, her body warmth rising, not a hot flash, but an old-fashioned blush.

"Never seen you look so fine, Ms. Olds, a treat to these old eyes. You're different this morning."

"Thanks." She slipped from his grasp and opened her briefcase. Next to the deposition was a copy of the Power of Attorney her mother had signed. Power over her mother, how ridiculous. Tingling from approaching hormonal flames, she excused herself. "Right back," she promised.

"Sure. Then we'll grab a bite."

She breathed deeply while icy water ran over her hands and wrists. With chill fingers, she brushed her temples and forehead. There, it was fading. The person in the gold-framed mirror looked younger than yesterday. What a miracle of lighting! No flat fluorescents here. Her eyes were bright and rested, her cheeks smooth and rosy. She'd noticed something similar at the Carleton. Professionals knew how to shape light, to shift reality. Pain-free plastic surgery—how much did they charge? She imagined Aurora basking under an enormous hat battery-wired for beauty lights, and smiled. What if someone pulled Aurora's plug?

Wrapped in his overcoat, Jack was tapping his fingers on Lisa's desk. "I've got us reservations. Come along young lady."

"Where are we going?" Teddie asked.

"You'll see. It's a surprise."

Chez Nicole was secreted at the rear of a combination mall and office strip, its gray concrete exterior livened by a modest red awning. Almost before Jack's white Cadillac Seville had halted, two attendants opened the doors. "The usual Mr. Sullivan?" one asked. His partner bowed slightly as Teddie's legs slid out of the car in easy, full-skirted freedom—no need to press her knees together to keep from revealing something she shouldn't. Provocative Thea could never have been the model for this fearful habit, Eva Martin perhaps.

With much smiling and scraping, the host led Jack and Teddie through a maze of winter-defying floral arrangements, past carts heavy with shimmering desserts. Such fruits had not grown in snow-sleeping Michigan fields, although Teddie had picked fall raspberries for the family while snowflakes fluttered earthward. "They seem to know you here," she observed.

"Yeah, well, nice little place. Now, what would you like? Or how about me ordering for the two of us?"

"Please," Teddie said, wallowing in Jack's care. He's going to order oysters, she predicted, a dozen on the half shell to share from a single plate. Champagne arrived unordered.

"We deserve this," he said. "Why haven't we done it before?"

"Jack, nothing to drink for me, not during the day." Teddie smiled.

"Afternoon appointments?"

"No, general practice."

"Well then, we'll demote the general." He nodded to the waiter who filled her glass with gold liquid studded with rising bubbles of light. "Here's to private practice!" Jack brushed his glass against Teddie's. They sipped.

The glistening oysters rested in shimmery shells bedded on crushed ice. She'd swallowed such plump living mollusks only on rare occasions, the first at age twelve at the gallery opening of Thea's Maritime Series. She'd watched guests, many of whom attended yesterday's reception, squeeze lemon juice onto a wincing oyster, lift a shell, suck it dry, and reach for another. Did they chew or swallow whole, she had wondered. At the final moment, when the shell's rough edge touched her own lower lip, she closed her eyes and her mouth filled with a slithery piece of ocean: salty, sweet, strange. She swallowed. Thea found her after she'd raised the sixth to her lips. "Put that down," she'd ordered. "Oysters are for guests, Theodora." Teddie's terrified arm jerked the oyster in its lemony juices directly into a punch bowl.

"These are good. Here, try one." Jack held a half shell before Teddie, a silvery, heart-beating morsel waiting for her.

"Yes," she said. So distant from the seas, an unnatural pleasure, oysters and champagne for Monday lunch. "The young architect, I didn't ask, was he badly hurt? He was bleeding."

"The report said he had a bloody nose or something. Nothing serious."

"He looked so thin."

"Said he hadn't been eating. Out of money, living in doorways, claimed he couldn't find work. Got down in the dumps. The folks at that church shelter fixed him up with a doctor. Got some pills, started to sail, decided robbing a bank would finance him until his career took off." Jack raised his fourth oyster.

Someone replenished her bottomless glass. Roast squab with wild rice appeared, then a salad. The table was cleared once more, a cast of two assembled a chafing dish, cherries, ice cream. Jack nodded. The meal from a time warp was to conclude with Cherries Jubilee. Throughout Jack had regaled Teddie, first with legal gossip, then, without mentioning his wife, tales of exotic travel. Teddie repeated her story about the New Mexican who thought Kalamazoo was a stand-up comic's joke.

Her foot. Something was touching it. Without thinking she pulled into neutral territory. Perhaps Jack needed to stretch. Maybe he was prone to leg cramps. The touching continued, now up her leg. "Paris, you've been there?" Jack continued without a pause. "Beauty, wherever you go, lovers. What it's like on the river bank. . . ." Being touched was not totally unpleasant, she decided, but what did he want of her? How much did she have? It had been so long. Jack's stockinged foot reached her knee, her painful skinned knee, and began to stroke. She rose in pain. Bolt upright, she could see through the branches of forced spring blossoms and convoluted hickory that made their privacy screen. Two alcoves away, in three-quarter view, her husband was holding her weeping sister's hand.

"It's late, almost three," she said, swallowing bitter agitation. What was she to do? "I said I'd get back. My sister's still visiting." Should she go home to an empty house and wait to confront her husband and her sister?

"I was thinking a cognac. . . ."

"I've had enough. Please, Jack." Her tongue felt clumsy, thick.

"Something I did?"

"Not you." Teddie lowered her head and looked into Jack's eyes. She did not want to see the people beyond the flower screen. "You've been wonderful." What if they should see her with him? Teddie and Jack were sharing a simple mid-afternoon working lunch of champage and Cherries Jubilee, that's all. Likely Howie and Aurora had consumed the same, Chez Nicole's lover's feast for midlife assignations.

Jack's rheumy brown eyes gazed earnestly at Teddie. "The lady knows best. Can't remember when I had such a charming companion for lunch." He signaled the waiter; they conversed briefly, faces averted. "Put it on my tab," Teddie heard. The waiter eased back her chair. She stood, stealing a look at her sister and her husband. Aurora was dabbing a now-winsome face. Her weeping had been for effect—to good effect. Howie leaned forward, past his melting vanilla ice cream and fancied-up cherries. Her knees shaking, she took Jack's proferred arm and allowed him to lead her away from the family scene.

The toasty warm Cadillac purred beside Chez Nicole's crimson awning. She let Jack stroke her hand on the return to Hanford Tower, but fended off the grab for a kiss after they'd parked next to her car.

"If you won't let me take you home, we could get you a cab," Jack offered plaintively. "You sure you'll be okay?"

"Just fine, Jack," Teddie lied as she struggled to open the locked car door. "Let me know what else you find out about that boy. Lunch was delicious."

The attorney pushed the button that freed her door, and Teddie slid into the frigid, grime-scented air. The darkening sky threatened more snow. "We'll do it again," Jack said. He waited for her to start her engine, then left for his parking place close by the tower's revolving door. Lisa Greenstein waited above.

With her motor running, Teddie's thick tongue and dizziness were less demanding. She was fine. She switched on her headlights and bumbled into traffic, only to turn off the main thoroughfare at the first opportunity. Too many moving vehicles. She remembered the lake-studded suburban byways, from Karen's house to Nathan's, from Stacy's to Mark's, the multiple routes of carpooling. There, where that turreted, oversized house had sprouted, she remembered a small, hard-scrabble farm where she bought eggs until the owners cashed in on their only money crop, land. She could cope with thoughts of real estate, but not with Howie and Aurora. While she'd been driving Karen and Nathan and Stacy and Mark to ice skating and Little League and school, Howie had been getting to know their mothers intimately, if briefly, along with what then were "stewardesses" and today are "flight attendants." Found objects. "You know it doesn't mean a thing," he'd say when discovered. "You're all that's important to me, you and the kids."

Teddie imagined herself being undressed by Jack Sullivan, her stretch marks, saddlebags, and varicose veins, slowly, sensuously being revealed. She visualized herself slipping off his jacket, unbuttoning his made-to-order shirt from the top down, the pants button, the zipper—she laughed out loud. Not only was his hair dyed, that she'd long known, but a corset controlled his paunch. The temblors of excitement she'd felt when Jack's stockinged toes had fondled her panty-hosed leg evaporated. Ludicrous. As perhaps was Howie, but Howie was like an old shoe, now out-of-shape and predictable, once shining and tempting.

Almost home, she turned on the radio to avoid thinking about Aurora. News. O. J. Simpson. The Unabomber. A flash lit the interior of her Saturn, on off, on off. Something behind her, an emergency, pull over to the plowed snowpile, let it pass. Don't get stuck. In its own time, her alcohol-slowed body did as it was told. The light continued to flash in the dusk. It was there, behind her in the rearview mirror, in front of the Anderson's house, although five years ago they'd left for retirement in Florida. Teddie wondered if the newcomers had children. A tap on her window, and a bright beam blinded her. Another tap. "Open up. Police." The light-wielder illuminated himself to show a uniformed man, this one wearing an official-looking badge, Fearful, she did as ordered.

"Is something wrong, officer? Can I help?"

"Your license, please."

"Of course. What's wrong? Did something happen?"

"You notice anything back there?"

"Well, no. What do you mean?"

"A stop sign. The one you drove through." The hand that took her license was wearing a leather glove. Was latex beneath? And hadn't she stopped? The sign was useless, a relic from the past, erected at the neighborhood mothers' insistence so their children would be safe. The cop was shining his light on her license. "You live right here," he said.

"Yes, and I helped get that sign put in. I'm sorry officer. I must have been dreaming."

"Drinking?" he asked. "Alcohol?" Questions out of the blue.

"A glass of wine with lunch, that's all. It was a business lunch." She was in control, but the two-bottle truth was clamoring to be heard.

"I'll be back. Stay here. Close your window," the officer ordered. Teddie watched the car clock. Three minutes. Four minutes. The tap returned. She opened a crack. "You're Dr. Olds's wife. Didn't know he lived here. He's helped us. Remember when Johnny Martin thought he was back in Nam and. . . ."

Teddie stared, open-mouthed.

"All right. You can go. The computer says this is your car. But be careful. I'll remember. Next time I won't be so generous." He returned her license through the slitted window.

The darkened police vehicle waited for a taxi to pass before pulling out in front of Teddie. Her hands trembled as she tried to remember how to operate her car. Scarcely had she finished navigating their driveway when Aurora climbed out of the taxi.

CHAPTER • 6 •

The garage door closed. What now? How had she handled it when her funny, beautiful psychologist had first danced attendance on Thea? She should be used to these family scenes.

Aurora burst through the swinging door as Teddie warily entered the kitchen. "Where have you been? Why did the police stop you? Do you have money? My driver's waiting."

Two to ignore, one to go. Howie didn't pay for her trip? At least *her* good old boy had offered. "How much do you need?"

"Give me twenty."

The still-undeposited checks accused Teddie from her purse. Tomorrow. She would go to a different branch. She found a neat ten-dollar bill, and, after rummaging, two crumpled clumps of ones. "All I have."

"Messy." Aurora smoothed the bills.

Her sister's criticism brought normality. Aurora securely outside, Teddie closed and locked the front door. Minutes later she heard scratching, then tapping, perhaps long fingernails, then knuckle knocks. The Olds's doorbell chimed once, twice, bells seldom heard in these parts except when the religious were selling magazines, cleaning products, or salvation. Aurora's voice rose above her pounding and ringing, headlong, tumbling words, "Help! Let me in! Someone! Help me!" Teddie stroked the winter-warped door. She smiled through another "Help! Help me!" In no hurry, she leisurely opened the door.

"What are you doing? You locked me out!" Aurora studied her sister. "Not like you. Here," she said, thrusting out a fistful of change. "I'm going up. I need rest."

No one would need much dinner after their respective Chez Nicole love feasts. But what if she could get a few dozen live oysters at the Seven Eleven? What a treat to watch their reactions! It was clear she hadn't been seen. Aurora was not one for hoarding ammunition.

The answering machine's red eye was blinking. Taking a clean glass from the dishwasher, she punched the button to retrieve the disembodied voices trying to sound as if they were holding up their ends of conversations.

"This is Margie at the Carleton, Mrs. Olds. Your mother didn't want me to call, but I thought you should know she had a fall. She's all right, nothing broken, but you've been so concerned. We'll take dinner to her tonight. Let me know if I can do anything."

Teddie sipped her drink and shivered.

"Dear, tell me! Weren't we wonderful? I can't wait to see you. Give me a call." No name, no number. Marla, unless it was a wrong number. The machine clicked and beeped. The mechanical voice, which had informed her the first call came in at two oh seven, a little before Jack's leg had gone wandering, and the second, the unascribed Marla, at three forty two during handpatting, announced the time as five seventeen.

Teddie entered the number and counted the rings. Thea answered on the sixth. "What do you want?"

"It's Teddie. What happened? How are you?"

"What are you talking about, Theodora? Have you been out with bank robbers again? Or you've been drinking. I'm fine."

"I got a message you fell. I was worried."

"You said you were busy. I don't want to bother you. I'll be better in the morning. Good night."

The dial tone buzzed and Teddie tried again. Thea answered. "That's enough, Theodora. Good night."

"Listen, I'll be there after lunch," Teddie wedged in. "We can talk."

"Whatever you need. I said good night." Teddie bade the telephone to sleep well.

Perhaps *she* should lie down. Upstairs the contents of the boxes and bags had migrated, under Aurora's hand no doubt, from the chair to the bed where unfamiliar clothes covered Solomon's Puzzle. Teddie shook out a heavy natural silk skirt and found a matching top. She slipped out of her dress and systematically tried on the pile, one after another, most quite miraculous, nothing she would have brought home for herself. Still no price tags. The top and sweater she felt had to be returned went back to the chair, the rest onto hangers and into the closet.

Beneath them all were two filmy garments, the kind a twelve-year-old once upon a time dreamed of for her wedding night. Silk, a rosy coral, tawny lace, cut to conceal while it revealed. She'd tried everything else so she stripped to her skin. The silk slithered sensuously over her bare body. Deep within she felt a stirring, an almost forgotten longing, a need. She closed her eyes.

Arms encircled her. She inhaled Howie's combination of scents. "Ted, you're irresistible. You're, you're. . . ." He spun her around and pulled her close, exceeding the ardor of their morning parting kiss, his tongue caressed hers, her moist inner cheeks, moisture between her legs. Always holding her, one arm, then the other, he slipped out of his jacket, kicked off his shoes, unfastened his pants. Teddie's fingers nibbled at his shirt buttons; one after another they slid open. His chest was smooth, well-muscled, his hands stroked and enticed and lifted the silk from her body.

"Close the door," Teddie whispered.

"I did," her husband answered, and tumbled her onto the bed. The unexpected didn't take long. Afterwards Howie rolled over, his back resting on her quilt, his breath still coming hard. Some mechanical need had been met in her, but the stirrings had not. The swirling colors of that dress, the blue, green, dusty rose, were inside, spinning, dancing, asking for recognition, a seal broken to free forgotten storms. Pandora's dress.

"Why don't we do this more often?" Howie asked. Is that what he says to them all? She was a possible Aurora substitute, even wearing Aurora's silks, but Howie was not a Jack Sullivan stand-in, or was he? Maybe it's only animal, doesn't mean a thing except for those moments of merging that defeat loneliness. Jesse, her precious nose pierced, what did her daughter do about her stirring emptiness? Teddie's knee bandage flopped half-off as she walked to the bathroom. Howie had closed his eyes; possibly he slept.

Condom, she wasn't afraid of pregnancy, but those latexed hands that had ministered to her the other night were a reminder of a changed world. The boy might pass his test and she fail hers. There'd been no one but Howie for twenty-nine years, although three had preceded him in her youthful confusion, yes, she knew condoms. "Like swimming in hip boots," one had said as he begged off. With her knee curing in the air, Teddie was tempted to crawl into bed, but Howie's side-to-side sprawl left only an empty edge. She pulled on faded navy sweat pants, one of Zach's abandoned T-shirts, and a sweater, and descended to her domain.

Emptying the dishwasher was the work of a minute. Getting the glass and ice and scotch to replace the unfinished drink left upstairs was automatic. She rummaged for the morning papers, turned on the little kitchen television, and settled in the breakfast nook with Peter Jennings. He used to be so urbane, such sophisticated, well-informed company telling her about the day's happenings, always a triumph included among the many disasters, but lately he'd changed. Some nights he was judgmental, his mouth edged with prissiness. He must be tired. A vacation was what he needed. She opened last Sunday's travel section. Marla had offered her Cancun condominium for a modest fee, right up Howie's alley, built to isolate free-spending tourists from the realities of their dark-skinned servants and guides, where drinking to excess is much cheaper than at home and where everyone who serves knows more than the served, even if they don't call you by name.

Her glass was scarcely touched when Aurora appeared, face pillow-creased, eyes dazed and glassy, hair one-sided flat. "What are you doing?" Aurora asked.

"Reading, watching, thinking. Did you sleep well?"

Aurora looked inward. "Dreams. Do you dream?"

"Always," Teddie admitted. "A requirement if you're married to a shrink." Take that, big sister. She mentioned neither the dead body she had been trying to hide the other night nor the live one she'd just coupled with. Howie's dream requirement probably extended to all his contacts. Did he leave nightmare-stricken women in his wake of beds? "Can you remember what happened?"

"No, yes. I was somewhere outside, like a desert, no trees, no roads, empty. I couldn't get back, no, that's not it. I didn't know where I was from or where I had to go. I was nowhere, lost, alone." Eyes empty and wide. Aurora searched Teddie's face, perhaps seeking salvation, a child alone on a cold concrete stoop.

"Sounds terrible." Sympathy for them both. "I have to tell you, your shopping was wonderful. Only a couple of things to go back." The used nightgown couldn't be returned. Aurora said nothing. "Have you ever thought about running a shopping service? I'd be your first subscriber. Oh, yes, and Marla called." Aurora stirred.

"What's this about a shopping service? Are my girls going into business?" *My girls*, Howie's harem. Teddie's revulsion was tainted with, she admitted, a spark of pleasure. She took a long pull from her glass.

"She thinks Marla and I should do it. She liked what we picked out for her." Aurora smiled up at him.

Howie waggled his eyebrows. "That sexy silk thing one of them? You should know what hap. . . ."

"What do you want for dinner?" Teddie interrupted. "We could order out—the Dragon's Kitchen will deliver."

"No hurry. Aurora and I can pick up whatever we want, can't we, sister-in-law?" How easily Howie smothered Teddie's perverse spark.

"Oh, let me see. Do you have a real menu? I adore Chinese."

"Who's driving? Look out if you're going to the Dragon's Kitchen. They seem to be patrolling our neighborhood."

"I forgot! That was you, you with the police. What happened?"

They were looking for expert advice, they wanted me to identify another criminal, they needed me to answer further questions, Teddie tried in her head. "I was dreaming or something, listening to the radio, you know, and went right past that stop sign by the old Anderson house, the one I helped get put in centuries ago. The officer suggested strongly that signs should be respected," Teddie said.

"You finally got a ticket! How many points?" Howie prized his clean record, especially when he could witness others' failures.

"He let me off with a warning."

"Where were you coming from? Didn't you have a meeting with that pseudo-southern old boy, what's his name?"

"Yes, Jack. I gave him the deposition, and we had a bite and talked shop." Aurora rolled her eyes. "That's all. Now, have we decided?" She recorded their orders and made the call. "A half hour, they say, but their truck's on its last round. We have to pick up."

"Goody," Aurora said. "I love riding with you."

Teddie looked heavenward. "Isn't your faithful horde waiting for you in Chicago?"

"No travel for me," Howie said. "Big case. Have to be in court, probably the rest of the month. Let's get going. We can stop for wine." Wrapped in her fur coat, Aurora was rubbing against Howie like a lonely animal as they went to the car.

Teddie's solitude was short-lived. On the fourth ring she relented. "Some time we had today. Glad you got home safe." Jack.

"Me, too."

"Can't wait to do it again," he said. "Thought you'd want to know. His parents posted bail. They want your robber architect back. There will be a hearing. You may have to speak up." Teddie tried to imagine someone else transcribing her words, her words to dissect, object to, and fight over.

"Thanks for filling me in."

"Lisa will give you a call when we've got more witnesses. Don't be a stranger."

"Yes, oh no, Jack. See you soon." A stranger. A stranger to whom. She'd always be a stranger to Jack and tonight she was a stranger in the world. Everything was askew and fresh. Again she contemplated the ringing phone.

"Mrs. Olds? Detective Williams," a female voice said. "How are you? Some workout you got the other night." The voice paused.

"I'm fine," Teddie said. "I understand the boy's being released. How can I help?"

"Well, we noticed you had some scrapes and the young man had a bloody nose and all."

"Yes," Teddie said, drawing in a breath.

"I don't want to make you nervous," Detective Williams said delicately, then paused. But you have, you've accomplished exactly what you didn't want to. "You know there are some bad diseases out there."

"Of course." Neither spoke its name. "Well?" Teddie thought she was play-acting well, the calm little lady of the house.

"Well, we wanted you to know he's clean. At least now."

"You mean he's not HIV positive? No AIDS?"

"That's right." Then the detective added, "Not so far." Teddie breathed deeply but felt deflated, as if she'd been stripped of a special status. "We'd still recommend you get tested now and twice more during this coming year. It can take a while to show up." The detective sounded clinical as she finished the formalities. "We can arrange it for you."

"I'll let you know." Teddie tried to imagine herself going to police station to have blood drawn.

"Well, we'd appreciate your giving us a copy of the report. Nothing official. Part of our service."

"Certainly, of course, I will," Teddie said, not knowing what she'd do. "Let me know if there is anything else." Do they think I could have infected him?

"We'll stay in touch," Detective Williams said. "Good night now."

She'd muted the sound on the television when Aurora brought up dreams, but undersized colored figures still gestured between flashes of made-up faces and trumped-up machinery. The camera tracked the game show's victorious while the defeated smiled bravely. There was no room for compromise, for dividing the spoils, although night after night the commercial sponsors and master-of-ceremonies and his sexy sidekick won big.

Teddie moved to renew her melted ice and the phone rang once more. She let it go, heard her businesslike answering message, then, "Mom, where are you?" and grabbed the receiver before her son could get away.

"Sorry about that, Zach." The machine bumped and ground and they were alone on the line. "I'm here, where are you?"

"Where do you think? Enjoying sophisticated pleasures with Kalamazoo ninth graders. Everything's relative you know."

"And I'm in the kitchen waiting for your Aunt Aurora and your father to come back with Chinese food. When will we see you?"

"That's why I'm calling. Can't make Thea's dinner. Guess she isn't famous enough to get time off twice in a week, even if it is after school. I have to take over—would you believe it—the photography club. Their regular guy's sick, you know, Bob, the one who did those landscapes in my room. Actually he's in the hospital and pretty bad, and the boss doesn't want the kids to get too upset. So I'm it. I thought about bringing them in on a field trip to meet Thea for dinner, but she isn't exactly fond of anyone under the age of reason."

"You remembered right. Over either," Teddie said. "I'm sure

Aurora will be back, and we'll do it again. Oh, the Carleton called to say Thea had fallen."

"Anything serious, Mom?"

"Thea says she's fine. She seems fine. She hung up on me."

"I won't do that, but I've got to go. Look, I need to talk to you, but not on the phone. Any chance you could get out here? Wait a minute." Teddie heard shouts in the background. "Sorry. They need me. Regrets to Aurora. Bye."

"Bye. Take care." Immediately she dialled Jesse's number. Speaking of incense and darkened rooms, the static-larded music tinkled interminably before a young voice reeled off the list of people not at home. How many students lived in that house? It seemed like a cast of hundreds, all sexes and sexual preferences absent and accounted for. "This message is for Jesse Olds. Let us know when you'll be getting here. Call when you can." She left her number but no identity. Messages from mothers might stray or disappear. She looked forward to giving Jesse Thea's book.

She carried the volume of photographs and her still-full glass into the living room and settled on the couch. When the brown bags of dinner arrived, Teddie was in another world, in an Africa captured by Thea's magical camera and artist's eye.

CHAPTER • 7 •

Stung by yesterday's encounter with traffic law, she braked hard when the green light went yellow. Tires squealed. The bopping, gum-chewing driver in her rearview mirror must be the source. Light green, still she hesitated. Wait. These days red lights did not get respect. Horns chorused behind her. A truck pulled in on her right, Saturn and pickup nose to nose, its driver jabbing his raised middle finger towards the gray heavens.

"To hell with you!" Teddie shouted and returned his gesture. Boiling, she leaned on her horn long after after the bastard sped away.

Thirty minutes more of this to the Carleton. Jaw clenched, teeth grinding, Teddie stopped, and started. Aurora had accepted her sister's claim she was working, and so she was, just not gainfully employed.

The shopping service idea had catapulted Aurora and Marla into serious talk. Perhaps Aurora would stay in West Bloomfield and Teddie could move to Chicago. Switcheroo. But for now the present was enough to handle, her minute-by-minute life.

Once she had let herself dream. Back then life had been magic, each day a treasure. Georgio Aponopolis, dark, thick hair curling briskly from every opening of his white undershirt, made the sisters laugh while he taught Thea to make *pastitsio* and *suppe avgelemono*.

Thea foreswore travel and took a long-term lease on a small yellow house with white trim. The girls had their own private bedrooms while Georgio and Thea shared. None of Thea's visitors slept in her bedroom as long as Georgio. From seed to harvest, twice Thea's camera chronicled the garden's cycle of lettuce, cucumbers, squash, tomatoes, corn, and pumpkin. Georgio hung fragrant bouquets of oregano and thyme to dry in the kitchen while Thea developed and printed her images in her basement darkroom and Teddie and Aurora returned to familiar schools with familiar students, including Marla, as if they were a whole family.

Little Teddie savored her walk home. No hurry, soon enough she'd be biting into the fresh cinnamon cookie Georgio had promised he'd teach Thea to make. But instead of cookies in an herb-scented kitchen, she arrived at a house turned inside out. Her bed, *her bed*, broken apart, waited on the lawn for its turn to be carried away.

"You're back. Good." A transformed Thea was packing her canvas camera bag, no longer peaceful and almost motherlike, now whirling energy. "Hurry up. I'm leaving." Teddie's heart thudded. "Georgio's taking you to his mother's. I've packed your things. Hurry and see if I forgot anything. It's all going into storage."

"No!" Teddie screamed. "No! No!" Thea walked away. Georgio implored. Aurora arrived home from junior high, where she'd stayed late for the prom decoration committee meeting, and took her sister under control.

"It's no good," she said. "You can't change anything."

"No!" Teddie yelled.

"Where's Tiger Poo? Where's Blankey?"

This morning Teddie had left the worn pink blanket under her pillow, with the threadbare stuffed animal on guard. "No!" she shrieked again.

"We'll look. Come on."

Teddie let her sister pull her into their devastated home. The furniture that had anchored the simple space was gone, the tapestry of hanging photographs, paintings, and prints packed up. Shreds of paper, balls of dust, dirty footprints, and a musty smell remained. They flattened themselves against the wall as two men carried Aurora's dresser out the door. "Hurry up. We'll look for Tiger Poo."

The battered toy, Teddie's her whole life, given to her by her

father, or so Thea claimed, lay on his back in a corner of her closet almost as if someone had thrown him there. Safe, the child
rubbed the toy's ear against her cheek while her eight-year-old
thumb found its way into her mouth. Blankey was nowhere.

Aurora's doll collection, the beauties Thea brought her from
her travels, were gone, but in her room's trash Aurora found a
string of doll pearls and a pair of miniature, lace-up ice skates from
Norway. Squeezing Tiger Poo, Teddie ventured into the kitchen
and peered into the open garbage can. There, under rotting lettuce
and mildewing onions, was a piece of pink. With a claw of thumb
and forefinger, she tugged at the slimy square she wanted to kiss,
but the stench held her back. Dropping Blankey, she picked up a
bouquet of dried thyme, and went to find Aurora. To this day she
can see her Blankey in the garbage as she sees Aurora in a tight
ball, rocking herself in the corner of what had been her room. "I'll
stay with you," Teddie promised and squatting, patted her sister's
shoulder.

Georgio found them. Thea had departed. Georgio's mother,
Mrs. Aponopolis, let them sleep in the room Daphne, her daughter, had left empty when she married. Georgio's mother said she'd
been lonely until Thea's girls arrived.

Two months passed before Thea took her girls back. They
weren't surprised that Georgio and his mother disappeared entirely from their lives.

o o o

Last August the watery murmur of the Carleton's courtyard
fountain below had kept Teddie company while she unpacked her
mother's possessions. The sounds were soothing, but angry cries
erupted. Three floors below a short thick woman with an untamed
gray mane gestured and yelled at a uniformed man pulling greenery
from the earth between neat rows of baby box hedge and fibrous
begonias. Tomato plants heavy with unripe fruit, their bare roots
clinging to vestiges of soil, lay on the concrete path. "I've got my
orders," Teddie heard the professional say. Keening, mourning, the
amateur bore her destroyed crop into the opposite retirement wing.

Today the garden paths had been shoveled. Beneath the snow
the earth waited for its foreordained crop of pink, red, and white
flowers. Teddie asked herself if she should go to the central office
to get the true account of Thea's incident. Perhaps she wasn't even

in her apartment. As the residents faltered and declined, they were sucked bodily from the wings to low- and high-care tower rooms, nearer my God to thee, one iconoclast had said.

"Don't dawdle," and there Thea was on her balcony, hugging angry arms around herself. "I'm waiting!"

Teddie was breathless when she reached the blue door, open like a trap waiting to be sprung. Thea herself sat stage center in the wing chair that had been moved in and out of storage uncounted times. "Shut that door."

Teddie obeyed. "How are you?"

"What do you expect? Make the tea. There are cookie things over there." She waved her hand.

"I was worried, you know. What happened? Why'd you fall?" The tiny kitchen was open to the living-dining room. In the silence, Teddie turned from filling the kettle to watch Thea's face. "Well, what happened?"

"If you must know. I had wine with lunch, a civilized practice."

"Yes? What then?"

"I fell down. That's all."

"That's all? At your age?"

"I'm fine. Oh, I wanted to tell you. Georgio, do you remember him?" Thea gestured grandly towards a framed and much-honored photograph of furry, undershirted Georgio in the midst of his bountiful Detroit home garden. "He's joining us for dinner tomorrow."

"Of course I remember Georgio." I remember everything, she wanted to add. "I didn't know you were in touch. Does he live here?" It would be too much to expect to find warm cinnamon cookies in Thea's tiny kitchen. She ripped the paper from a box labelled Langues du Chat and arranged the cookies on a plate.

"I loved him, you know. Still do," Thea reminisced. "The only one."

Teddie warmed the tea pot with hot water. They'd all been one and onlys, all of them. Could Thea be speaking the truth about Georgio, not that she had any working knowledge of the concept.

"That woman last summer, the one with the tomato plants, she's Georgio's sister."

"Daphne? Aurora and I stayed in her room. She's here?"

"It's the eyes I recognized," Thea continued without pause, "and I asked her one day in the lunch line. You know we're forced to eat cafeteria style just like one of your elementary schools. It's shameful."

More than once Teddie had partaken of this luxurious spread. No one had to wait, selections were arranged to tempt flagging appetites, and willing hands stood ready to serve and carry. She placed the tray with tea and cookies on the round table next to her mother. "Daphne. Talk about coincidences. What about Georgio?"

"Daphne had his number. I called. He said he'd like to come."

"So you asked him to dinner. Why now?"

"Your tea is delicious, child. No one here can hold a candle to you. Have a cookie."

Thea did not explain her actions. Indeed, why should she tamper with success? Her camera thrived in her intuitive hands, always taking pefectly composed, crystalline images never in need of cropping. At exhibits Thea liked to regale listeners with tales of her creative cookery under dark light, as if she were a lighthearted amateur, but Teddie suspected that steely discipline created those perfect products.

"Where's the darkroom? Who's going to print your pictures for Rossotti?"

"My dear friend, Frederico, will be joining us," Thea announced.

"Your editor? You should have told me. But Zach can't come, has to take over the school photography club for a sick colleague."

"Good. Room for everyone." Thea reached for the teapot, but Teddie's hand was there first. The old woman looked pale and feeble in unfiltered daylight.

"What did you want to tell me? You said you couldn't talk on the phone. It must be important."

"Yes, the night of the famous bank robbery. Strange. I didn't read about you in the papers—nothing on the news."

"Well, it happened. See?" Once again Teddie held out her nicked hands and exposed her battered knee. Absurd. What was she proving? "Was there something you wanted to say?"

"Georgio sounds just the same, that deep voice. What do you think he'll look like? What will he think of me?"

After Teddie returned the tray to the kitchen, Thea was struggling to get to her feet.

"I'll get your cane."

"No," Thea barked. "I can do it," and she rocked until she achieved a shaky balance. Grasping furniture and walls, the bent figure made her way to the bathroom.

Teddie followed helplessly. At least the bathroom walls were studded with chrome safety bars and an emergency chain. She heard water tinkle behind the closed door, then rushing water, then silence, then more silence.

"Theodora," a lifeless voice murmured. "Could I trouble you? Open the door." The daughter obeyed.

Thea was leaning heavily on the white counter, her face chalky under the rosy glow. "I don't seem. . . ." she grimaced in the start of a failed smile. "I can't move." Her arms were trembling. "Help me."

Teddie slipped an arm around her mother's waist. "Lean on me. Put your arm around my shoulder," she instructed. Intertwined, she bore her mother's weight. "Where? The bed?"

"No!" Thea's voice gained strength. "My chair. It's that stupid fall."

"I don't want to hear about it," Teddie lied. She eased the light body into its chair and settled close by.

"No one else needs to know. This is between us, our secret. I can trust you, that's one thing about you." And so Teddie heard the chronicle of Thea's growing weaknesses. "It's nothing serious. Old age, that's what they say. I'm supposed to exercise, in a class. Can you imagine me with a bunch of old biddies waving their flapping arms? And they suggested firmly that I need one of those metal frames, those walking things. Some have wheels."

"You? A walker?" Teddie felt childish horror. "How would you use your camera?"

"Exactly. How would I exist?" Early evening had darkened the room. Teddie turned on the lights. "There's a room in the basement I can use for a price. It has water. I've made do with worse. Set up my equipment. That's all."

The impossible, that's all. Teddie opened her mouth to announce those days were over. Her mother simply would have to return her advance to Rossotti's and go on with living. But her mind's eye mustered up that dark-skinned, scarified beauty Thea had captured on film decades before. "I'm sure you'll work it out. You always do. If you need anything, I could help." Never had the girls been allowed into Thea's mysterious workspaces although Teddie sometimes lingered outside. When the door swung open, her eyes would struggle to adjust to Thea's satanic red-lighted room.

"Run along," her mother always said too soon, then shut the door. "What are you wearing tomorrow?" Teddie asked. She had decided on the heavy natural silk and a green jade necklace and gift earrings from Howie.

"The old red wool—everything I own is old."

"Aurora and Marla may set up a shopping service. See, they got this for me. They probably could find whatever you want."

Thea's knobby fingers rubbed a fold of the new sea green wool skirt. "Expensive. How much?" Teddie had no idea. "Aurora always was concerned with appearances. You can go now. I'm going to rest my eyes."

"That's good. Can I look at that darkroom space?" she asked, but Thea either was sleeping or ignoring her. She propped the cane against the wing chair. The Carleton's office provided directions to the basement bathroom.

Ignorant and uninformed, Teddie could only look. She'd have to get the equipment out of storage, but then how would Thea get about with a camera when she could scarcely support her own weight?

The old woman was sitting on her bed when Teddie returned. "Where did you come from?" she asked ferociously. Your womb, literal Teddie thought.

"Your darkroom," she answered, finally understanding. "The office told me where. What's your book plan? When do you have to get it done? What does your contract say?"

"Oh, contracts." Thea waved her hand dismissively. "They'll have my work soon enough. Get my bag, the canvas one, you remember. In the hall closet."

Teddie followed orders, and Thea plunged her right hand into the large, weather-stained bag. Instead of raising the camera, which always had claimed the passenger seat of the old car, her hand came up empty.

"Is it stuck? Can I help?" Teddie asked, willing but in terror of Thea's machines.

"No. You don't know how," Thea answered. "Shouldn't you go home to your sister and husband? I don't want to stand in the way of your family. You know that."

"Yes, Thea." Her mother watched while Teddie slipped her beige coat over her sea green outfit.

"Be here on time tomorrow," Thea demanded.

"In time for what?"

"Theodora! I need you to take me to that dinner thing."

"Of course. We'll be here at six. Will you be ready?"

"Not we. You are taking me, no one else. Don't be late," Thea commanded. Once again Teddie would be her mother's handmaiden, always ready to make tea, to chauffeur, to help as needed, all so Thea could live her way. I could refuse. Say no. I can't. I'm too busy. Why not? Why not, indeed.

"Yes, Thea. Of course. Tomorrow." And she kissed her mother's dry forehead.

CHAPTER • 8 •

They arrived at the restaurant on Thea's time. Everyone was assembled when Teddie parked at the London Grill, still functioning in a rare piece of intact, never-wasted, downtown Detroit. Sam Nevelson, who had nurtured the restaurant for forty-two years, helped Thea shed her coat, told her she looked better than ever, and pulled her hand through his waiting arm. Teddie, the eternal bridesmaid, followed alone.

Thea did look wonderful. She'd issued orders from her dressing table where she manipulated make-up that smoothed her wrinkles, emphasized her eyes, and put color in her cheeks. Teddie found the accessories that turned the ancient red dress into an exotic event. Those cosmetics did not make Thea over, they brought her out. The fragile old woman was a mask, a shell. The real Thea had color, strength, power.

"Capture the essence of age, that's my plan," Thea said. "No one else has done it like I will. They think if they catch light on folds of old flesh they've got age. Old is not age," and she swirled her fringed Spanish shawl around her fragile body.

The London Grill had neither flowers nor ficus, but the walls above the red leather booths were lined with striking photographs, many of them Thea's. Diners ogled the procession, but not every seat was taken, for fewer and fewer people braved the city at night.

The three men and Jesse sprang up in welcome. Seated, Aurora rocked her fork by its tines. The sisters exchanged looks of the long-suffering.

"Thea, you're splendid, as always," Howie crooned as he raised to his lips, palm up, the the arthritic hand Sam had released. Can-you-top-this time, Teddie thought, but while the waiter stood at attention at Thea's chair, Frederico Whatsis (Teddie never could remember his last name) slid his wispy self back next to Aurora, whom he studied seriously through his steel-rimmed glasses. A balding, white-haired man whose eyes looked like those of Georgio Aponopolis smiled at Teddie. "I often think of you," he said in Georgio's familiar deep voice, "of you and your sister and mother." Jesse, still in black, still in nose ring but no lip-piercing yet, thank goodness, patted what she could reach of her venerable grand-mother's arm and stood back looking bemused.

Thea's entrance had been a success. She needed no introduc-tions, but Howie, his handsomeness enhanced by his crisply trimmed gray beard and paisley foulard, assumed the task of closing the circle. "Ted, do you remember Thea's editor, Frederico Aspin? Fred, this is my good wife. Her mother calls her Theodora."

"Good to see you again." Teddie held out her hand. "But please call me Teddie. Everyone does." After the ritual touching of hands, the editor's eyes returned to Aurora, resplendent in midnight blue silk.

"And this is Georgio Aponopolis." Howie prided himself in remembering a name after a single exposure. "Aurora tells me you have a long history. Someday you should fill me in."

Georgio had kissed Thea silently on both cheeks after Howie's manicured hands had released her. Now he turned to Teddie. "So long ago. Once a little girl, now—what can I say?" and he placed small moustache-tickly kisses on her left and right cheeks. Once a little girl, always a little girl, Teddie thought to herself. "Time flies," Georgio said sadly.

An extra chair was placed between Georgio and Jesse; Teddie would spend the evening straddling a table leg. Thea was flanked by Georgio and Howie, with Aurora to Howie's left. Frederico Whatsis to Aurora's right could contemplate Jesse's multi-studded ear or, whenever he wished, gaze directly across the table into Thea's eyes. Drink glasses dotted the white-clothed surface, but before the party had settled, two bottles of champagne, a silver ice bucket, and seven tall champagne flutes had arrived.

Howie was paying court to Thea and, Teddie knew, was set to jump to his feet to toast the object of his deepest affection. She considered beating him to the draw, of getting there first, but she'd have to find the words. To my mother, whom I fear. To my mother, who shaped me and controls me but is growing weaker. To Thea, who makes her dreams come true. Georgio had risen before she'd found the right words.

"Fascinating! You edit photographs?" Aurora's voice filled the silence.

"Hush," Georgio admonished. Aurora frowned and Georgio continued. "I would like to pay homage to the woman who made my image famous, even though the honored 'Man in the Garden' did not assist my career. Stockbrokers are not valued for their tomatoes and squash. Financial managers do not appear in public in their undershirts. But Thea and her wise eye and camera plunge beneath surfaces to capture one's essence. She exposed my true farmer's heart. To success in her new undertaking! Let us drink to art eternal and the wisdom of age!"

"Wow!" Jesse exhaled into the pause. All but Thea, even Aurora, rose while Howie bleated, "Hear, hear!"

"To Thea," Teddie heard herself saying, "who always has made her dreams come true." Thea raised her glass to her honorers and they drank.

"One more," Frederico added, still standing. "To Thea's dynasty—to the Waterford women!" Teddie couldn't remember being toasted, well, maybe at their wedding but that was as a couple. If she was included in this attempt to charm Aurora and always Thea, should she drink to herself?

"To us all!" Thea proposed from her seat, and nearby diners craned their necks as seven people reached to touch the others' glasses.

"Hear, hear," Howie repeated. Teddie had decided her husband's champagne flute was too far away to be worth the struggle when his hand stretched out. He clicked her glass, then Jesse's. They drank again, then sat. The show was over.

Teddie opened her menu and turned to Jesse. "Do you know what the London Grill is famous for?"

"No, Mom." Jesse's nose ring gleamed. "It was hard enough finding this place. My friends don't, you know, exactly come here.

What's hiding in those silver things?"

"Meat. A haunch of lamb. A side of the best roast beef you'll ever taste. Sometimes, on the weekends, succulent roast veal."

"How disgusting! Sickening! Is that what everyone is going to eat? Slabs of bloody meat?"

"Not everyone," Georgio said. "They have a fresh vegetable tart and a savory bean ragout. I seldom eat meat these days. The old farmer has to be careful."

"We never did eat much meat, did we?" Teddie remembered. "I always thought we couldn't afford it."

"True. Thea had that one collection with Rossotti's, and of course those two successful shows, but her true fame was yet to come."

"Tell her artists don't make money until after they're dead. It's not a good arrangement," Thea said. "Your advice saved us back then, got me where I am today—poor but subsidized, ready to reveal the truths of age." Teddie saw her ashen mother tremble helplessly in the Carleton's sumptuous bathroom. A stomach full of fear triggered haywire hormones and her heat began to rise.

Hurriedly she pushed back her chair and excused herself. "I'll have the roast beef, rare, you know, the usual, when they take our order," she told Howie.

"I'll come too, Mom. No flesh for me," Jesse told Georgio, "you order."

After the restroom door had closed, Jesse wonderingly watched her mother flap air under her silk top. "What's going on?" she asked. It was one question with too many answers.

"What you see is your old mom in the throes of The Sea Change. My thermostat's out-of-kilter and I didn't want to eat dinner in an ocean of sweat." Teddie plunged her wrists into cold water.

"Too bad," Jesse said hurriedly, "but who's that bald man, Georgio someone? Dad wanted to kill him, and that editor's hitting on Aunt Aurora. Grandmother looks great, though."

"I haven't seen him for almost forty years, but I suppose Georgio's the closest I ever had to a father. For two years when I was little—well, life was good." Teddie held a moist paper towel against her temple. "Thea scared him up the other day. Claims he's the only man she ever loved."

"I thought she said that about everyone. What about your real father? Haven't you wanted to find him? Thea should scare *him* up. You look great. Is that new?"

"Your aunt thought I needed improving. She went shopping. She could do something for you. Starting with feet." Jesse was wearing heavy black leather paratrooper's boots. "When did you start jumping out of airplanes?"

"The pinnacle of fashion, Mom. You need to get out more."

"We'd better get back. I'm cooler, chilled out you'd say—but is that good or bad, I forget the translation. It's so hard being up-to-date. Remind me to give you that book before you leave."

"Thea's book? You got it? Could we get her to sign it?"

Had the scavenged book been signed? "You ask. She's fond of you."

"Sometimes," Jesse said.

Georgio welcomed them. Teddie wanted to know all about him, where he'd been, what he'd been doing, what she meant to him. Perhaps he could explain Thea. Jesse took command, however, and Teddie sat back. Frederico was more than interested in Aurora, but whenever they seemed lost in a shared world, Thea would steal his attention. Squeezed out, Howie struggled for a foothold. Georgio moved at his own pace, spreading his warmth among them all, but allotting the lion's share to his former lover. Teddie's fingers moved, habitually committing the conversation to her nonexistent stenotype.

"It's pheromones, Mom. That's what Thea has, but I thought they dried up at middle age or something."

Fer o mon, Teddie's recording fingers spelled out. "What's that mean?"

"Sex. And more. Chemicals she sends out to attract human animals. They can't resist her. Look."

Georgio was ignoring his bean ragout. "Tell me," he said, "where you've been, what you've seen. I've followed your exhibits, your books, of course, but what about you?" A disgruntled Howie stuffed a piece of juicy red meat in his mouth before making another effort at laying claim to the old woman. Frederico resignedly stirred his baked potato as he waited to hear Thea's tales.

"*Male* human animals," Teddie observed. "We seem immune, but then we're family. Do you know what's going on with Zach? He looked tired Sunday, then he called and said he couldn't come tonight."

"Oh, Mom, there you go again. He's probably got a friend who keeps him busy."

"Maybe a friend, but so busy in Kalamazoo?"

"Good point. But stop worrying. Zach's okay."

With the men ignoring her, Aurora turned to Teddie. "I'm not leaving tomorrow," she said. "I thought you should know."

No, Teddie wanted to scream. How long before Howie slid down the hall into Aurora's borrowed bed? More the principle than the deed, the idea was disgusting. "I thought you had a date or something."

"I cancelled. Marla and I want to develop our idea. Dick thinks we should draw up schedules and marketing plans."

My idea, Teddie thought. "Sounds like it could take a while," she said.

"Don't worry, sis. I'm moving to Marla's, at least until the initial work's done."

"You're leaving? But you're not going home? Why? We love having you," Howie said, having surrendered Thea to Georgio.

"My sister says she's scheduled solid and you have to be in court and I hate being alone. Besides, I had such a *wonderful* idea about Marla and me and the shopping business. We have work to do." Teddie pictured her own empty schedule, was amazed, and wondered what actually was recorded in Howie's Week-at-a-Glance.

"Both my girls working! Theodora does something with lawyers and courts, not exactly professional but you can't expect everything, and you're going to shop for a living, Aurora. Why, you'll be able to support me in my old age!"

Jesse blinked. "I think it's great, Aunt Aurora. If you want any help with certain things, let me know, like these shoes. Aren't they cool?"

"Tribal identification marks," Thea said, "the heart of the matter. Come spring I'll ride into Ann Arbor to catch the rites. What do you think? Would Rossotti's be interested in a companion volume, Frederico? Adolescent next to the old?"

Teddie imagined her mother pushing a wheeled walker down the Carleton's garden path and out onto the highway. Serves her right. She'd given up driving as soon as her fame allowed her to honor others by asking them to do her work. Wherever she wanted to go, her cameras could be cocked and ready at her side, her attention freed from bondage to the steering wheel. "Adolescent?

Me?" Jesse gasped.

"But do the tribal rituals fit?" Teddie smiled.

"What is your work?" Georgio asked Teddie. "Something to do with the courts?" So Teddie told him about her three decades of recording the words of others, but instead of the true, dull story of a court reporter, she larded the account with some of the well-known whose words had made news.

"Always listening," Georgio said.

Ears stuffed with words to quiet the roars, Teddie thought. "Do you know anything about darkrooms?" she asked cautiously and explained only that Thea was going to establish work space and might need help. "I always was curious, but she'd never let me in."

"She knew what she wanted. Anyone else was in her way. Sometimes I was allowed to clean up."

"Were you a stockbroker then?"

"It was the beginning. I worked in a bank. A teller." Teddie studied Georgio Aponopolis, his hands, his neck, and saw how young he was, at least fifteen years younger than once-ageless Thea. To the child, Thea and her Georgio both had appeared the same impossibly old. Today Georgio bridged the gap between the ancient mother and her end-stage menopausal daughter.

"Thea knows how to get hold of you, but would you very much mind giving me your number? Where do you live? Did you marry and have children? Here, I'm babbling. You don't have to answer."

"Maybe it's a habit with you. You want to get everything on record."

Teddie shrugged. Georgio slid a card from his wallet and wrote on it with a gold pen. "Here, my work and my home. I did marry, but she left with our boy. She claimed I always dreamed of others when we were together. I don't know. I tried. Your mother may be like a drug, a person you crave even when you know you will be gravely injured."

Jesse put in, "I say it's chemistry, biochemistry. Thea has over-active pheromones. You men can't stay away."

"Fancy words for old ideas," said Georgio. "My great grand-mother was said to be irresistible. She'd go for a walk in the woods with her maid and come home alone with grass in her hair, leaves clinging to her clothes, and a smile on her lips. Her jealous hus-band did everything he could to safeguard her, but the men never stopped. That's how she died." He paused.

"Tell us! What happened!" Jesse begged.

"It was a spring day, the sun warm, new leaves budding when an army officer in full uniform caught sight of her on her daily walk. She smiled, then he, and, like a dance, they entered into a child's game of tag, his sword's silver scabbord flashing in the light. She ran downhill, where he waited on one knee, unbuckling his weapon. Perhaps she was blinded, for she tripped and fell headlong into an icy stream. He carried her home, chilled to the bone. Never warm again, she grew ill and died. My great-grandpapa was inconsolable."

"She must have been very beautiful," Teddie said.

"I thought that too until one day my grandmother showed me her mother's photograph. She was squat, plain, and old—at least as old as I am now. If anything, she looked like a toad, an irresistable toad, a toad rich in, what do you call it, pheromones." Jesse had been drinking his words. "You know, men have them, too," she said. "You do." Teddie shared her daughter's conclusion, and in this new light also observed that her pale, blonde daughter in paratrooper boots emitted her own rich, steamy sexual attractants. She feared for her. While mother and daughter had been hanging on the words of grandmother's former lover, husband and editor were swarming over Aurora. Had Thea let them loose? Teddie glanced at her mother. Thea slept, decrepit and vulnerable, the fringe of her shawl dipping into the barely touched, congealing lamb juices on the plate before her.

"Have you finished?" their waiter asked, puzzled disappointment in his voice. Howie's platter was licked clean, but no one else, Teddie included, seemed to have had much appetite for food. Teddie knew she'd be hungry once she got home, and asked for her leftovers, as did Jesse.

Thea's confusion on waking was scarcely visible. "Who wants coffee?" she asked munificently. "And someone has to have the black forest cake. Sam Nevelson's black forest cake is the stuff of dreams."

Teddie was still tingling from tea with Thea. Coffee now would mean no sleep at all, but nothing kept Howie awake. Jesse joined him in coffee, and she and Teddie shared a piece of the famous cake. Howie dug into apple pie a la mode, while Aurora was frustrated in asking for herb tea in this old-fashioned place.

Dinner done and paid for with Howie's gold Visa card, Georgio would drive Thea back to the Carleton. "After all, I know the way," he said.

Jesse got her grandmother to inscribe the book and kissed her on the cheek. "Thanks. It's wonderful. So are you." She pecked her father's bearded cheek good-bye.

Teddie felt the cold metal of the nose ring as they mother-daughter kissed good night. "Drive safely," she incanted.

Aurora forsook Howie to travel with Teddie which gave the sisters an opportunity to wonder at Georgio, Thea, and their lives. As the Saturn entered the garage they were arguing about what Georgio raised in the garden. "Corn, tomatoes, zucchini, green beans, lima beans..."

"No lima beans. Never lima beans."

"Lima beans."

Frederico left for the airport hotel alone. "Think about doing adolescents," Thea had reminded him. "I'll need an uplift when I'm finished with age."

CHAPTER • 9 •

Teddie closed herself in Zach's bedroom while Aurora packed. Her calendar might be blank, but she had work. Thea was soaring when she answered her telephone.

"Has Georgio left yet?" Teddie asked.

"I'll move out when my work is finished. You will help me. Somewhere private. Of course he went home. Can you imagine the hurricane two hundred gossiping old tongues would make? I may not be perfect, but I do not gossip."

Two truths. Not perfect, not a gossip. Perhaps no one else was as interesting as she. Nor would her vanity allow a lover to witness her weakness, a crone in need of a walker.

"I called about your darkroom stuff. It's in that self storage place, isn't it?"

"Where else? Not in the Carleton's mean little space."

"I think Zach marked the boxes. I thought I'd see what I could find. I'll let you know. Do you have film?" Teddie flinched and waited.

"Why are you being so helpful?" Thea replied, more a heavy pat on the head than a blow.

I'm getting rid of Aurora by pretending to work, I'm tired of the words of others, I must understand you, you'll fail without me. "Do you have to ask?" Teddie tossed out. The question was nonsense.

Yes, she had to ask or she wouldn't be asking. Thea was silent. "Last night Jesse asked about my father, said you could find anyone. You *did* find Georgio." Now she had stepped over the line. "Wasn't he older than you? Wouldn't he be close to ninety?"

"How would I know? Someone's here." Thea hung up.

She'd tell Jesse she tried. It was a school morning, but she needed to hear Zach's voice, even on tape. Waiting for his phone to pick up, drumming her fingers, she studied a new snapshot on his dresser, a boy his age, but smooth-shaven and blonde. Zach's polite request to leave a message was too short for reassurance. "This is your mother. Are you all right? Call as soon as you can."

This morning Teddie had encased her body in another Eva Martin special, so constricting after Pandora's dress and heavy raw silk. Old sweatpants and a sweater went into her briefcase. Could she squeeze her walking shoes in, too? Telling lies was simpler than living them. She was hiding her costume for moving storage from her sister, who hovered in the kitchen like a waiting spider. "You're leaving," Aurora stated accusingly.

"Off to the Hanford Tower. I could shake loose for lunch." Breathless from lying inventions, she paused. "Where will you be?"

"Dick's picking me up at eleven-thirty for our working lunch. He's brilliant."

"Before you go, I was wondering . . . will I get a bill or something?"

"Oh yes," Aurora giggled. "You will."

"If you say so." Teddie pecked her sister's cheek. "I'm late. We have dinner at Marla's tomorrow night. We both have work to do."

The Beekman Storage Tower was a low-cost, scaled-down version of the Hanford Tower, surrounded by the same tangle of dry, salted roads rimmed with blackened heaps of melting ice crystals. Its stacked-up storage units reminded Teddie of the wall she'd seen in a cemetery field, each building block a convenient space for stashing your loved one's burnt remains. Purse and briefcase in hand, she punched in Thea's identification code and the electronic gate opened. Television eyes probably watched her take the elevator to the seventh floor. Live people accepted payments and whatever in a windowless command room, but alone in this dusty corridor lined with metal garage doors, her clunking heels and noisy breath were the only signs of life. The padlock of 726 responded to her key. Haphazardly stacked boxes, an old rocking chair, rusting metal tables, a lamp with a frayed cord. Were there family treasures behind other doors? A four-poster bed too large for a studio apartment, an outcast heirloom dining table with ten matching chairs, forgotten now that their single rightful owner ate with television talk shows?

Teddie lined up court reporter shoes with her walking shoes, then moved boxes until she had made a protected space. Off with her jacket, out of her skirt. The voice spoke as she was tying her sweatpants. She dropped into a squat and pulled her sweater over her head. A man.

"I said, would you like to join me for a cup of tea?" he asked again.

"No thanks, I have to work," she replied as casually as her voice would allow. Two pairs of shoes were in plain sight. She could be two people.

"How about coffee. Or soup? Good for a cold day."

The damp, penetrating cold outside had reached Teddie's bones. She'd like soup. "No. Sorry," she said.

"It's been too quiet since the storm. A person gets lonely. I could give you a hand. I'll check back later." Teddie held her breath while rubber-soled footsteps faded. Then she looked up and down the empty corridor.

Tea? Lonely? He was gone. Surveillance would find him. She tied her shoe laces and, one after another, pushed three boxes labelled Books next to the rocker. Linens and Kitchen joined them. Next to the wall Aurora's old dresser was stacked with more boxes, their contents recorded in Zach's even hand. Two read, Darkroom. She was standing on Books, stretching for Photos, when she sensed him. She spun around.

His dark, neatly combed hair was flecked with gray, his jacket a shapeless herringbone tweed. "Your shoes told me to look respectable when I came back. They also told me to come back. May I give you a hand?" He looked harmless, no, that wasn't it, he looked nice, friendly and safe, but didn't evil travel in disguise?

"I can handle it myself, thanks." Always warding off danger with those charm words.

"I understand," he said. "Would you mind my sitting here? We could talk while you do whatever you must." Across the hall he slid to the floor and folded his blue-jean-clad legs. The accent was vaguely English; perhaps he was a Canadian.

She feared the darkroom box was beyond her reach, but still she stretched and grasped until she started to sway. Stuck in space, she wavered, unable either to lie or to scramble down. He must be in his forties. His eyes were blue and full of light, like Caribbean waters. "I'm stuck. Can you help me?" At last, when a crash was inevitable, his hands took the load. Free, Teddie stepped down. "Put it over there."

"I haven't introduced myself. Michael Henderson. I live here. Are you a photographer?" he asked.

Teddie hesitated. "Yes, Liz Gutleben," and she held out her hand. His felt competent but gentlemanly, good muscles under warm, dry skin. She smiled. "I need my darkroom equipment. You live where?"

"Here. Down the hall. Let me." They communicated in monosyllables as they rearranged boxes and Teddie mulled over Michael Henderson's words. It must be an apartment, she thought.

"Do you work for Beekman?" Perhaps he was a black sheep member of that rich family.

"Oh, no, Liz. I'm afraid I don't do much work, at least not for money. I'm a historian, only one of a glut on the market. I like the quiet here."

Liz. She shuddered deliciously. Liz was light and carefree. "I think we've got it all." Their shoulders nearly touched. "I didn't know they mixed apartments with these storage units."

"They don't," the man named Michael said. "Would you like to see? I'm quite comfortable and entirely illegal, although I do pay my monthly rent by mail."

Often uncomfortable and always entirely legal, Teddie was tempted. "You have soup simmering on the stove?"

"Cans. And an opener and a microwave. Chicken noodle, minestrone, split pea, something I can't remember, but we can see. Are you ready for lunch?"

Teddie was ravenous or perhaps it was Liz who was hungry. "I need to find one of those cart things. Maybe I should close this for now."

Michael studied his stainless steel wristwatch. "Carts are on the third floor. I won't go with you. Security will check their monitors in a minute. I have to lie low. 751. Chicken noodle?"

"Perfect," she answered the tweed shadow which disappeared down the hall. Teddie slid home the bolt and stashed the key in the security pocket of her sweatpants. Her civilian clothes, briefcase, and handbag with identifying documents remained hidden in storage. The carts on the third floor were miniatures of the ones train porters used to stack with luggage and freight, and possibly still did if enough people traveled by train to warrant them. She didn't know. Except for their Caribbean cruise, she and Howie always flew or drove. Parking her cart outside 726, she walked the gray corridor to her secret assignation.

At 751 she tapped. "It's me." She paused. "Liz." The closed door raised enough for whoever she was to duck inside. The room was bigger than Thea's, five by ten instead of five by seven. Books were everywhere. Squares of woven grass carpet covered the floor. A table and two chairs stood beneath an elevated sleeping platform. Neat stacks of paper and a worn portable typewriter waited on a table. Two shoeboxes of multi-colored note cards stood tidily on top of a three-drawer file. Michael pulled a sheetlike curtain across a rope to conceal the door.

"It helps with the sound, sort of muffles, you know. Looks better, too," he explained. She should fear this stranger in his hidden apartment, but it was too much like Zach's tidy college dormitory room. Gentlemanly hands placed two blue bowls in the microwave. On what would have been Zach's window wall, she saw gold curtains around a large picture window, but no, it was a large picture of a window showing a bright winter scene, sunlight glistening on the skeletal trees and distant skaters on a frozen lake.

"I close the curtains at night. It makes life seem more regular. I'll repaint in the spring." He opened the microwave before it could beep.

"What is it you do? Are you a student or an impoverished professor?"

"Bingo. Liz hit the jackpot."

Liz, Liz, Teddie hummed to herself feeling as if her bones were making new blood, her body fresh hormones. He opened a box of crackers and pulled a hunk of cheese from a miniature refrigerator. Then he moved the papers from the chair to the floor and placed the typewriter on top. "Have a seat. I'll bring it to you. This is a treat, sharing a meal."

"Why the jackpot?" Teddie asked.

"For recognizing a defrocked academic who's failed to make tenure. Seven years I've been working on this." Michael waved his hand to take in the papers, files, and books. "They assumed I'd never finish and didn't care if I did. I began too late to play the game right. No proper professor of history should be interested in how mythology moves events and creates history. That's what you photographers do, too. The present you preserve alters the future. Sorry, I'm rattling so. How's the soup? Tell me about yourself."

Teddie finished crumbling crackers into her blue bowl, picked up her spoon, and tasted. "Delicious. Is that cheddar?" She pointed her spoon at the cheese. "I love old cheddar."

Michael speared a piece on the end of the knife. "Good. It's Canadian."

"Are you? Canadian, I mean?" Teddie did not want Liz to have to talk about photography, a subject about which both were remarkably ignorant. "Good cheese."

"Born there, my father was a Brit, but I've been in the States forever. After university, I worked in a bookstore, then opened my own. Couldn't handle the business end of things. Then I followed my desires and studied history. I'm talking too much. It's the isolation."

Teddie could have said that in her thirty years of court reporting she'd seldom heard a witness who spoke so clearly with such concern for the listener. She chased a noodle around the blue bowl. "Why history? It seems so dry. So dusty."

"Dad used to take us on driving vacations. We stopped anywhere he sighted a historic plaque. We marched through each and every local museum. Amazing what we collect, history's underbelly. I save stories."

"We went west the summer my sister got her driver's license," Teddie mused aloud, "but no museums or plaques for us. My mother made up her own stories. She had something against Norwegians, so I learned how the Norwegians killed the buffalo and massacred the Indians. My teacher was stunned when I told her my mother's version of American history."

"I'd like to meet your mother. She must have spirit—like you."

"Too late," Teddie said with simulated sadness. "She died a year ago. Heart disease." Cancer of the heart. Teddie emptied her bowl, then studied the electrical wires that snaked and split from the light socket in the ceiling of the storage room. Somehow they'd been coaxed to feed the refrigerator, microwave, and lights below, but she could find no sign of plumbing. "How do you wash?"

"My worst problem, that and keeping track of my car. I have to keep it moving. You're a good observer. There's a small restroom at the end of the hall, but I import water, along with my food, of course, like the survivalists."

"That's what you are. A survivalist." Like Thea, Teddie told herself. "How long will you stay here?" She was beginning to think about a winter of soup and afternoon conversation, then a spring, she could bring in early asparagus, then. . . .

"Until I'm done, I suppose, or until I have enough cash to live a real life. Hard to find a room with utilities for $78 a month. My agent thinks my book may warrant an auction." Michael ran his fingers through his hair and stood up. "I'll clear, then. Tea, biscuits, ice cream?"

Teddie would have insisted on cleaning up herself, but Liz asked, "What flavor?"

"Fudge nut or," he bent his long blue legs and peered into the mini-freezer, "or cherry vanilla." He appeared pleased at his discovery.

"Good! How about a little of each? No tea, but I wouldn't mind a cookie. Then I suppose I should go."

"I'd be interested in seeing your work. You're a very attractive woman, Liz." Teddie looked down at her faded navy sweatpants and blushed with pleasure. Howie's ring glimmered on the hand in her lap, but Howie's ring was not Liz's responsibility. She let her shoulders settle. Comfort pooled in her open palms, a woman waiting while she was waited upon. Michael heated water for his tea in a blue cup and scooped ice cream into red bowls. While he worked, Teddie asked him what an auction was. He explained competitive bidding for manuscripts while waving the serving spoon as if he were conducting a choir. Melting ice cream ran down his hand. "Look at that." He stopped his story to lick his hand, then apologized. "Forgive me. It's living like this. Manners go by the way— that and the effort to cut down on trash. You can't imagine, no, you can imagine the trouble I have covering my tracks."

"An urban Indian," Teddie reflected. She made up her mind to leave when they were done, but she wanted to stay. She could climb into that neatly made sleeping loft and feel as at home as in a dream. They ate and chatted about myths they knew, his living arrangements, and a few of her childhood experiences (never photography) and when the cherry vanilla was gone, Teddie stood up.

"I'd like to see you again," Michael said, rising next to her. "Here, let me give you the schedule. One day I phoned in from the outside and asked the manager the right questions for she happily explained the details of her work." He handed Teddie a paper. Their fingers touched. She pulled him into her arms and clasped him tight. He kissed her forehead. Her lips nibbled his smooth-shaven cheeks. He kissed her eyebrows, then her right ear. Their lips came together in gentle exploration, silently speaking of friendship and small possibilities.

Delight filled her as she pulled away. "I have to get to work," she said. "So do you. What can I take out?" Michael filled a plastic bag with refuse, including their soup can and the cheese rind. She would recycle the can at home. Their hands brushed as the garbage was transferred. Teddie smiled. "I'll come knocking if I need help," she said. "I'm glad I know where to find you."

"Take care of yourself, Liz. Come back soon."

She looked down the bare gray corridor lined with identical metal doors. But for the garbage bag, she might have been dreaming. The cart awaited her. She opened the door, loaded up, changed, relocked, and left the Beekman Storage Tower.

CHAPTER • 10 •

Today Shop and Save looked like a wonderland. Such a modest name and such opulence—transplanted tropical forests waiting to die in desert-dry living rooms, flavorless summer fruits from the bottom of the world, glistening lettuces sprayed on schedule to keep up weight and appearances. Teddie's habitual dislike for shopping always turned to hatred in supermarkets. Head down, she aimed her cart directly at what she needed. Fresh spinach. Small, round new potatoes. Tiny carrots—flavorless, but cute and easy and Howie liked them. A cucumber. A chicken that had lived to see the sky and walk the earth. A bottle of a middling chardonnay. Coffee ice cream as a change from her lunch fare. Her smiling face was reflected in the freezer glass doors.

At the check-out counter her undeposited checks sank deeper into the slurry of sales slips, receipts, and old shopping lists. Howie's turn. He could drop them off on his way to court, legal or tennis, wherever he was spending his Friday.

Home again, home again, jiggety jig. She and her groceries floated into the kitchen. She set the wine to cool, then nibbled leftover mu shu pork from its carton, rinsed the hidden grit from the spinach, scrubbed the potatoes, and birthed the chicken into the sink from its plastic bag. Walking vegetables is what a chicken farmer whose testimony she'd transcribed had called his product, and she drew on the farmer's excuse to continue enjoying roasted bird. The slab of red roast beef from the London Grill remained in its cold doggy bag.

Zach, she had to call Zach, but the red eye was blinking. She pushed the message button. "This is Detective Williams, Mrs. Olds. That young man's parents are concerned. Call me as soon as you can."

Why were they pestering *her*? She was the one at risk from *him*, except for Howie, but he claimed he stuck exclusively to neighbors and the like, at least for the last several years, and that's what she had to believe. He wasn't one to take chances, he insisted, and mostly that was true. That call could wait.

"Teddie? Jack. Want to chat with Michigan's champion court reporter. Call me." Teddie frowned. She wanted neither to record the words of others nor be touched by a lawyer's wandering foot.

"Mom, everything's fine, at least I hope everything's fine. Could you meet me in Ann Arbor Saturday? Bob's in the hospital there. Call with a time and place. Leave a message if I'm out."

"What's happening?" she demanded of his machine in return. "You're making your old mom nervous. Let's meet noon, Saturday, the main library, by the magazines. I need your help with Thea. I'll see you."

Shoving the insoluble out of mind, she took the mail from its box. Catalogues, ads, bills, requests for money, *Mature Living*, the magazine that had followed in the wake of warm greetings on her fiftieth birthday. Had Aurora received her own card four years ago? Surely *Mature Living* would not dare visit her mailbox.

Settled with the mail, she reached for her drink, but she hadn't made one. Oh, well, later. She leafed through ads for insurance, retirement communities, wheat germ, tai chi for seniors, and there it was. "Go anywhere, do anything, be free," the text proclaimed. A beaming elder sat with an adoring child on a three-wheeled scooter, motorized, a place to sit securely while going places. Thea might need an attachment for her working camera, the one she liked to rest on her shoulder while searching for subjects and she would have to be her own chauffeur. Many ifs, but rolling around in a Romper would beat creeping about in a metal cage. Or falling down.

Almost six and no Howie. The bills and discards were separated, the onion and herb stuffed chicken in the oven when he called. "Something came up, Ted, technical stuff. I'll grab a bite out."

"I understand." But did she care?

"Don't stay up."

She said she wouldn't. She should have invited Michael Henderson to dinner. To tell the truth, she'd been shopping for him, for him and Liz; aside from the flavorless carrots, tonight's dinner was planned for them. She'd take him his share in a basket on the way to the Carleton tomorrow. His garbage was still in the car. A good garbologist would read his discarded pages, study his bills. Where did he get his mail? So much to know. She craved more floating delight. No, spying was wrong. She retrieved only the soup can and jettisoned the rest. Clean and dry, a can can be company.

Her overused muscles ached. Court reporting was so sedentary. She ran a bath and slipped into the hot water, sighing with pleasure. All she needed were strong fingers to rub her shoulders. Lacking a masseur, again she reached for her drink, but found nothing. So she sank deep in the foam-covered water to blow little crevasses in the mountains of bubbles around her head. But the water cooled and the tantalizing fragrance of roasting chicken drifted upwards.

Potatoes.

Time only for a single kitchen scotch and soda before she sat down to her fine dinner, solitary but with an imagined companion. Childish, but the clean soup can rested in Michael's chair.

Later, in the small hours, Howie sat on the bed but she did not open her eyes. In the morning he lay on his back, eyes closed, lips open, corners crusted with white. As required, she'd been dreaming. It was something about travel, she was barefoot, waiting for a train. The station was surrounded by mountains, a milky lake was trickling down from a glacier's tongue. This morning her icy feet actually hung bare, the warm blankets kicked off in the night during a hot flash. That part of her dream made sense, and the train, waiting, well. . . .

No more Eva Martin clothes, today the Aurora collection, rose-colored skirt, matching blouse, and fuchsia sweater, a winter flower garden.

"Ted?" Howie stirred. "What time is it? You dressed?"

"Clock's right there. Yes," Teddie answered. "You got home late."

He stretched. "Not so late. You were out like a light. I missed you."

"I've got a full day. You'll have to make a bank deposit. I'll leave the checks by your briefcase. Dinner with Dick and Marla tonight. Aurora, too."

"Wow!" Howie propped his head on his hand. "Look at you." He wolf-whistled. Against her will, Teddie was pleased. It had been eons since Howie had seen her, really seen her.

"Thanks." She darted forward, and, dodging his grappling hand, kissed her husband on the forehead. "See you tonight."

"Can't wait." Howie grinned, but Teddie dashed downstairs for the phone.

Lisa Greenstein wanted her to take a deposition at one sharp and another at three, was she available? Is this what Jack wanted to talk about? Reluctantly she agreed, but first the sweatpants and sweater had to come out of her briefcase.

A chicken leg, a thigh, a piece of breast, raw spinach with a side of dressing, potatoes straight from the refrigerator—his microwave could warm their cold hearts, and the remaining half bottle of wine she wrapped and packed in a brown bag. In her rose and fuschia clothes, she was an aged, modern Little Red Ridinghood. The Yellow Pages told her of the Securimed equipment store between Beekman Storage and the Carleton, although fitting Jack Sullivan into this travel equation made her day a tight squeeze instead of one luxuriant with possibilities. Thea didn't answer, but Teddie didn't feel guilty enough to bother the office.

Michael's surveillance schedule meshed miraculously with her own. An elevator took Teddie and her brown bag to the seventh floor of Beekman Storage, where she felt like skipping down the dusty concrete corridor. A distant tapping could be heard through the metal door of 751. She knocked. He didn't stop typing. "Michael!" she stage-whispered once, then again. Footsteps, the door lifted, and Teddie slipped beneath.

He glowed with pleasure. "Liz!" Teddie startled, but didn't look for Liz because Michael's sunlit blue eyes were focused on her. "Let me look at you. How long can you stay? Here, give me your coat." Flustered, Teddie managed to tangle her beige coat sleeve with the picnic bag. Placing the food on the table, she stood before him. "You're lovely," he breathed.

She snatched up her food offering to prevent herself from pulling him into her arms. "Only a minute," and she paused on the brink of honest explanation. No, she instructed herself, Liz is the photographer and her mother is dead. "Here. I brought this for you." Their hands touched and they stood in a Fourth of July sparkler shower. "I'm afraid I drank the other half last night," she apologized when he lifted out the wine.

"All the better," he said. "But do you have to go? I've been thinking. . . ."

Teddie looked at his fake window, surprised at his painted shining sun when she'd left a gray morning outside. "What have you been thinking?" she asked him.

"About myths. About history. About you, Liz."

"I almost dug through your garbage last night to try to get to know you," Teddie said truthfully. "Instead I thought about you while I ate alone. That's why I brought your share." He pulled her into his arms and they explored each other's faces with kisses less innocent than yesterday's. Her heart rate rose. "I have to go. Before it's too late." She grabbed her coat.

"Yes," he said. "I'll get the door. There's time for us, isn't there?" She felt his eyes follow down the hall. "Your phone number. . . ?" he moaned suddenly. "Tell me," but she turned the corner to the waiting elevator.

o o o

Securimed was in a strip mall abutting St. Luke's Hospital and the Carleton. Pressure from either feet or wheels, it didn't matter which, opened the door to this netherworld. For every body organ that once ran smoothly and automatically, Securimed sold a substitute appliance. New, improved systems of pumps, tubes, bags, braces, and locomotion, all illustrated by photographs of loving families outdoors in warm sunlight. Teddie was alone, surrounded by her future, the only breathing human, although traveling tanks of oxygen and tubing were available. What a display of horrible, awesome ingenuity!

The scooters were to the rear, behind wheelchairs, motorized and lightweight, looking cheerful and nonmedical, rather like grown-up children's toys, although the padded seats spoke of a luxury or necessity not granted children.

The man who came out of a back room had the dingy pallor of a cheap gambler or a cut-rate insurance salesman. Saliva glistened on the chewed end of the toothpick he pulled from his mouth. "Didn't hear you. That one's good. This here's better."

She forced herself to look at him. She didn't want to be here, to face all this. But there's no escape. This, too, is life.

"How do these work?" and she pulled out a small notepad.

"For you?" he asked, voice drenched in scorn.

"Oh, no. My mother."

"Okay. I have to ask. The reason is what's good for you could be bad for someone else. I don't want to mislead you."

"I need information."

"Who's paying? Insurance? Her policy cover one of these babies? What's wrong with the old lady?"

She always could mail in the magazine coupon or call an 800 number for information, but instead she soldiered on. "Of course there's insurance," she insisted without any idea. "Do you have any written material, something I can read?"

The salesman looked sullen. "You pay first. That's how we do it. Insurance pays you."

"Do you want to tell me how these things work or do you want me to go someplace else?" If her schedule weren't so tight, she would have left long ago.

"Okay, lady. Keep your shirt on." After his short explanation, Teddie requested a demonstration. "It's not for you. Can't do that." Teddie turned to leave. "Okay, okay. This one. We custom fit. What the patient needs."

What I need is to run you over, Teddie thought, but with all the safety features and padded bumpers she probably wouldn't be able to dent the worm. The electric machine started easily and moved smoothly and quietly. Teddie made one sharp turn at the oxygen cylinders and swung back at the cases of canned complete liquid diet. "Take it easy!" he shouted. Satisfied, she parked the machine back in its rank. Now she knew enough to plan her approach to Thea.

"Thanks," she said as she walked toward the exit. She would not ask for his card.

"Hey, we've got other models, three-hundred-sixty-degree swivel chairs, lifting seats, up to five-and-a-half miles per hour, batteries good for ten to twenty-five miles." The information she'd wanted poured after her as she walked out the door.

The Carleton office was next. "Oh yes, Mrs. Olds. Just now the director was saying she wanted to get in touch with you. Something about your mother. Too bad, she had to step out. A problem in the South Unit."

Trapped, then saved, Teddie explained again about the bathroom darkroom that had been part of Thea's contract with the Carleton. "Can someone help me? And I need a key." The Carleton had none. It would have to be a padlock, like her storage room.

Pallid, chest hollow, moustache drooping, the man in a coverall answered the office's summons for help. "Which is yours?" he asked as they transported all but one of Thea's boxes.

"What do you mean?"

"Which one of them?" He waved at a man teetering in careful baby steps past the empty fountain.

"My mother is Thea Waterford," Teddie announced. "She lives on the third floor, up there," and she pointed at the balcony.

"Oh, yeah. She's some kind of famous. I know. Done some work for her." He surveyed Teddie up and down, and ground out his cigarette in the frozen earth before they went inside. Two boxes went in the shower, one on the toilet, and two stacked on the floor with room left over. Thea would need work surfaces.

"Do you do carpentry?" Perhaps he'd had something to do with bookcases.

"Not me. That's Joe. Tell the office what you need. My services are more personal-like." His smile bared small yellow teeth. She'd ask Thea but would not get an answer.

Teddie closed the bathroom door firmly. At the parting of their ways she handed her helper a five-dollar bill. Scarcely time for a bite before her appointments. Thea would have to wait.

CHAPTER • II •

Howie was shouting nonsense words. Fatigue had weakened her will, and an evening with Dickie Davis and his bride Marla was yet to come. Not to mention Aurora. Still in her winter coat she opened the freezer for drink ice and came upon the coffee ice cream. Michael. How many simultaneous lives was she living? No wonder she was tired.

She felt no better when they pulled out of their drive. Howie was talking, had been talking, talking since she'd stepped in the door, something about a case that had been decided so now his lips were unsealed. She heard AIDS, but perhaps it was an old-fashioned verb, not the modern plague noun. Her fingers recorded his words.

Marla and Dick's house was festooned with strings of lights, not colored, not blinking, but tasteful, they told everyone, like small flames. The Santa, sleigh, and reindeer that always won the neighborhood prize had been stored away, but Rudolph and his flashing red nose still welcomed visitors. "What are we supposed to do?" Howie spluttered. "Scratch its little plastic ears?"

Marla opened the door before Teddie could remind him of the annual Easter Egg Forest or the Giant Halloween Pumpkin Patch. One Thanksgiving weekend, they'd had to coo over plastic cobwebs, fake blood, and battery-operated skeletons before sitting down with pretzels and beer for the slide show. "Missy and Lisa loved their haunted house so much we couldn't take it down," Marla had explained. "We just added turkeys." Rudolph did not follow them inside, although the photograph of him surrounded by four small children held the place of honor in the middle of the mantle. "The grandbabies," Marla exclaimed, jacked-up eyes shining. "When are Zach and Jesse going to do you proud?"

"They are now," Teddie said. "Every day."

"You know what I mean," Marla said. "After all, the twins each have two. Does Zach have a girlfriend? He used to dote on Missy." Mothering was Marla's competitive sport, but Missy had suffered more than one scrape with the law and Lisa kept dumping her brood on Marla's doorstep, only to reappear, arm in sling or eye blackened, to claim her own.

Teddie steeled herself.

Dick's tray seemed too large for him to handle. Little Dickie Davis was what his ruder classmates had called him, but he had retaliated by becoming an IRS accountant, an official who sniffed out their monetary deceits. Aurora followed, bearing a silver bowl of guacamole dip. While the rest sank into overstuffed couches, Teddie wandered among the ranks of framed pictures. Stiff adults posed with solemn children in century-old studio portraits, black and white snapshots, fading color prints, even the color polaroid of the three of them shot last Friday at the Garden Grille.

"Your photos are wonderful," Teddie murmured. "You really capture something."

Howie looked up.

"Think so?" Marla beamed. "You never told me."

"You've been snapping pictures as long as we've known each other," Teddie began as she settled next to her hostess.

"I guess you'd have to say photography's my little hobby. Your mother's my inspiration. Remember when you lived in that house with the garden? Thea used to take me into her darkroom. It was so exciting. I mean she was famous and making time for, really, just a little girl. You're so lucky, both of you."

The sisters' bloodlinks clanked together, one deprived of speech, the other silenced by the unnameable.

"How's your business planning?" Howie interrupted. "The stuff you got for Ted here is something. She's a new woman. Or it could be love." He winked and Teddie flushed. Did he think those mechanical gyrations were love? She thought of Michael, of his curtains drawn against the dark. She feared for her children.

"That green's good for you," Aurora said, appraising the new velour outfit Teddie had pulled out of the closet. "I remember when you used to wear my emerald party dress—of course that's before you got so big. It made me look sick, kind of jaundice yellow but you looked radiant. So unfair."

"Unfair, unfair. Who guarantees fair? You have to make your own life." Was this Little Dickie Davis? "Who'd like another martini?"

"Me," Howie said. "That's just what I was telling Ted on the way over here. Fair, unfair, right, wrong—depends on your point of view. Then there's the law. It has to be evenhanded, and that's where I come in. I explain what's really happening, help the jurors see the whole person."

"Hey, me too," Dick interrupted. "Except I turn out their pockets. Nothing closer to the heart than money. You agree, partner?" What chilling business arrangements was her sister making?

"I trust you," Aurora said sweetly. Howie patted her left thigh. Dick hand-passed her a chip heavy with guacamole.

Marla's lips tightened. "I'll finish dinner."

"I'll help." The scab on Teddie's knee snagged her stocking as she rose. "How are your business plans? Howie's right. The things you picked out are wonderful—I feel like a new person." Or persons she said to herself.

Marla frowned into the oven. "It's supposed to be brown. I'm not sure about the business."

"Put it under the broiler. You know, Lisa might call to say she's leaving the kids with you tomorrow night. Aurora might find she needs to get home after all."

"You think so? I haven't seen them since Christmas. Your sister's hungry. Seems like she wants a man real bad."

"Aren't we all hungry? Remember when we were kids? The things we used to do?" Baited with living room compliments, Teddie cast her line deep into Marla's memory pool. "You always were taking pictures way back then."

"Didn't we have fun? Me and my camera got it all."

"Did you save those pictures?"

"Natch. You know me." Teddie would be the first to say she did not, that she never knew those who claimed she did. "I never threw out a single one. I mean I've got albums and albums of the early days. It's burning!" Marla snatched the casserole from the broiler.

"Definitely brown," Teddie said. "Shall I take it in?" Operation retrieval was underway.

"Thanks. Tell them to come and get it." Marla seated Aurora at the end of the big table, where she'd tear a tendon if she tried to play footsie with Howie or Dick, and they ate. "You know I work with a lot of Nam vets," Howie announced over his empty plate, "but this woman was a first. A nurse in a field hospital, helped fly the boys out. Tough work. Came back, got a hospital job, married, lived normally, kids, husband owned a gas station. . . ."

"Cut to the chase," Teddie nagged.

". . . arrested for assault with a deadly weapon. You'll never guess." Howie looked around the table. "Anyone want to guess?"

"A snake? A truly nasty poisonous snake." Marla giggled. Howie shook his head.

"Could be a spider, black widow, or a golf club," Dick offered.

"Nope." Howie grinned. "Be serious."

"Who was assaulted?" Teddie asked.

"Good question. The police!"

"Why?"

"Why? They were taking her in for aggressive panhandling. She deserted her family, took to the streets, drugs, sex, the whole scene, just like the guys, imagine. She fought. Thought she was back in Nam, flashback to a nasty scene with a colonel, hit in the face, her blood went flying. She caught a handful and. . . ."

Marla paled. "Stop. I can't stand it."

"I'll help you," and Teddie rose to clear.

In the kitchen Teddie rinsed dishes while Marla poured whipping cream. "I'll be a few minutes," Marla said. "Silly to feel faint. It's what he was saying, accidents, blood. I hate blood. You go in."

"I'd rather be with you," Teddie said sincerely. "I've been trying to remember a birthday party, either my twelfth or thirteenth. A sleepover. All of us. You took pictures. Remember?"

"Not exactly. This will keep. Let me show you. You won't believe it. Everything, I mean everything, is in order. By date. Come on." Wiping her hands, Marla marched into the adjacent family room, slid back six panels of louvered folding doors, and snapped on a light. "Voila!"

If Marla had had the imagination and skill, she could have

become a blackmailer. The closet held row after row of albums and boxes, each marked with a different date. "What year?"

Teddie had worried about rummaging through storage boxes of dog-eared snapshots and crumbling albums, and wasn't ready for such organization. "Late fifties."

"Here." The fifties didn't require much space, a foot or so. "Hurry up. It's almost ready."

The first album displayed only strangers the teenager Marla had memorialized in out-of-focus images. Their lives began to intersect in the second album. That shadow with big ears must be a youthful Dickie Davis. A party, little Teddie excluded, in someone's rumpus room, a basement with linoleum on the cold concrete floor, the mottled green shag rug rolled back for dancing slow enough for Marla's camera to catch. There was Aurora, eyes closed, glued to her partner from face to knees, swaying to the music that provided the excuse for sucking lips and grinding pelvises. "Teddie? Are you ready?"

"Right there," she stalled, pulled out a third collection, and caught a falling snapshot. This black-and-white scene couldn't be real. She had no memory. She remembered everything but not this sunny day, two people in a park, a park close by the yellow house. Little Teddie played there. Sometimes she sulked among its grass and trees and swings. Mostly she escaped there when her mother shut her out of her life, but here was a young Thea in slacks and sweater, long hair braided and twisted around her head, laughing and running, arms outstretched towards, towards the figure facing her, a small figure, a figure known to Teddie from photos, plateglass windows, and mirrors. Her mother running to her. This time Marla's camera hadn't even cut off her subject's legs, propelled as they were by the power of a mother drawn to her daughter.

"TED-die!" Marla singsonged. Teddie slipped the picture into her pocket and flipped the pages. This was it. There was Aurora in that virginal, flower-sprigged nightgown.

"Got it. Coming," The album she placed securely on an end table before closing the closet doors. "Will you let me borrow it? Just for a day or two."

"Sure. Take it. I phoned but Lisa wasn't home. I'm worried about those kids—thanks for the advice. Now give me a hand." Marla marched her tureen of cake, custard, fruit, liqueurs, sauces, and whipped cream into the dining room, where the little party sighed in obligatory appreciation. "It's only a trifle," Marla said modestly.

"You mean it's not a syllabub or a fool?" Teddie joked. "I remember something made out of suet and raisins and flour called Spotted Dick. Trifle's a treat," she finished hurriedly.

In one breath Marla asked Dick to serve and announced that Lisa was arriving with her children tomorrow for an indeterminate stay. "It was a surprise, but I couldn't turn her down. I hope you don't mind, Aurora. We've plenty of room. They're little sweeties. Jimmy's almost two and Kimberly's just over three, almost completely potty-trained, isn't that something?" Teddie gaped. And she had thought the woman simple!

"Spotted Dick!" Howie wiggled his eyebrows in Little Dickie Davis's direction. It wouldn't have been surprising if the host had counterattacked with his accounting tools, but Howie had shifted his attentions. "There was a call for you, Ted, before you got home. A lady policeman, called herself Detective Williams. Said it was important and you'd know what she wanted. What's she talking about? What have you been up to?"

"It's the bank robbery," Teddie said dismissively. "Your trifle's delicious." She bent to serious eating.

"Come on. What's this about a bank robber? Aurora told us some tall tale, but we didn't believe her. Give it straight."

"Yeah. What does that detective want?" Marla trilled.

"Not now." Teddie scooped up another bite.

"My wife's too modest," Howie said. "I had to hear about it from Aurora, too. What about Detective Williams?"

"She took my testimony. She has some more questions."

"What're you hiding? Sisters know. This is so interesting. Come on!" Four pairs of eyes watched Teddie chase invisible bits of whipped cream.

"Remember, you asked." Nothing would be the same. "We both got bumped and scraped that night, the robber and I. Did you know he's a trained architect? Couldn't get a job? He was desperate."

"All right, Ted. You cut to the chase!"

"We bled. Sorry, Marla. You saw my knee and my hands got roughed up. The police wore latex gloves."

"Okay," Dick said. "Who says we don't have the best police force? They're worried about you, aren't they?"

"Yes, that's right. They want me tested."

"Tested!" Howie exploded. "You mean for that? It takes at least six weeks to show up. Everyone knows that. Oh, God."

"His came back negative, no HIV, at least for now," Teddie said flatly. "His parents are worried. I felt insulted but they're right. They want to know whether I could have infected their son." Silence smothered the guests while outside Rudolph's nose flashed on and off, on and off. "Testing's not required. Only recommended."

"They think *you* have AIDS?" Aurora finally murmured. "Not you. Never you, but. . . ." Her whisper trailed off.

"Ridiculous," Howie blustered. "And I should know!"

"Why didn't you tell me?" Marla whined. "You *ate* here! You were in my kitchen, my grandbabies are coming."

"Knock it off, Marla," Dick said. "You don't get AIDS from eating together." Aurora's eyes brimmed with tears. Teddie served herself more trifle.

"Want some?" she asked.

Marla screeched, "How can you?" but Dick said he'd join her.

"You have to go to a secure place for that test, a lab where you're a number, not a name," Howie said. "Wouldn't want it to get out."

"Maybe we could go together. You could be checked."

"You're joking."

"I'm not."

Aurora's face crumpled.

No one wanted coffee. Now forbidden from touching food dishes, Teddie retrieved the photo album and headed for the coat closet. "You wanted to know. I did not want to tell you. Time to go."

Howie glared. Deep inside, beneath superficial fears, beneath upsetting Marla and being a bad guest, Teddie discovered a pulsing vein of satisfaction. They were afraid of her. Howie shoved his arms into his coat and shouted, "Put that damned deer out of its misery!"

Teddie murmured, "Sorry." No hugs, no kisses.

Aurora grabbed her sister's coatsleeve. "Stop! Don't go."

Teddie wrapped her in her arms. "It's all right, all right," she whispered. "I'm not going anywhere. Talk to you in the morning."

CHAPTER • 12 •

Howie asked if she wanted him to sleep in his study.
"Sleep wherever you like."
"I want to be with you." Teddie sighed. He would want to hold
her, and, honestly, she craved his warmth, the not-alone comfort.
She refused his offer of a drink and pulled out the snapshot of her
and her mother.
"What's that?" he asked.
"An old picture. An album from Marla, too." She did not con-
fess how she'd schemed to acquire this evidence of her innocence,
proof she'd never been a child drinker.
Yawning, Howie flipped the yellowing cardboard pages.
"Tennis tomorrow. Saturday. Let's turn in."
The shock was fading. He wasn't a bad person. She might ask
him to drop off his blood sample before taking to the courts. Would
Zach know about testing bodily fluids? She prayed not, that he had
no need. Her body furnace flared, set her skin on fire, burning,
untouchable.
"I'll be up soon."
She poured her first cold drink, planned on studying those photos, but instead punched the button beside the phone's blinking
red eye. "Mrs. Olds, this is the Carleton. Director Olson has to talk
to you. It's your mother. She'll phone tomorrow morning. Nine

sharp." Teddie gulped kitchen scotch, then pressed the cold glass to her temple. That was all from the Carleton. No more. Perhaps a problem with the darkroom. Simple. She was too tired. These pictures could wait.

o o o

During that last indulgent morning sleep when she should have been at work, the spell when she travelled unmeasureable dream distances, Thea came. A young, strong Thea, wearing rust-colored slacks and a tan sweater, blonde braid gleaming in afternoon sun, runs up a grassy slope towards a sullen-faced, ginger-haired girl with tear-swollen green eyes. Thea's voice carries across the gap, but little Teddie cannot understand her mother's words. The girl wants to swoop into her mother's arms, but she is rooted to the spot she has chosen for her stand. She hears someone cry, "Sorry, sorry," and closes her eyes to wait. The mother pants with exertion; the child feels her warmth, smells her perfumed presence, then nothing. She opens her eyes. She searches. Thea has passed her, running straight for Georgio who leads a pack of men. The child turns her back on them and joins big Teddie on the swings. Big Teddie turns to the naked, scarified black woman beside her, and they smile knowingly. The child is young. She has much to learn. Little Teddie pumps herself into the air, higher, higher, almost to the sky. . . .

"Ted!" Howie was shaking her shoulder. "Wake up! The Carleton!" Thin sun lit the hollow winter scene beyond their bedroom window. He was in tennis clothes, her body was in bed in West Bloomfield, and her split soul was in a Detroit park.

"Sorry to wake you," the telephone voice said. She wanted to correct the woman, for her husband had wakened her, not the caller, but kept a grip on her silence. "Director Olson is here." Another good morning and a voice announced that her mother was making problems. Teddie stretched. Thea was not conforming. She was careless, refused to use her cane, laughed at the exercise class, and yesterday induced several members to pick up their canes and walkers and go for coffee when they should have been playing catch with foam balls.

"Is she all right?" Teddie asked.

"She has not adjusted to her condition. Many of them, many of our residents, have similar problems at first, but they come around. They enjoy their physical therapy and bridge. They don't say our luncheon service is like an elementary school cafeteria. They don't lead walk-outs. They conform to their new, and I might say, very luxurious, lives. Mrs. Waterford should be grateful she lives so well. We've been very generous." Well, yes, but remember it was a trade—Thea's reputation and publicity photos in exchange for a two-bedroom apartment.

"What do you want from me? Have you talked to Thea?"

"Mrs. Waterford insisted I make an appointment. When I arrived she told me to hurry, that she had to get back to some project. She may be delusional. She *is* over eighty-five."

"I can't do much about that," Teddie said.

"Talk to her. Make her see reason."

"I'll do my best." Teddie hung up smiling, and went looking for her husband. Of course Howie was hovering by the kitchen phone.

"What are you going to do, Ted? It's a serious problem."

"You know she'll never 'fit in.' Never has, never will. You wouldn't be in love with her if she did." Teddie did not pause. "You're the professional. What would you do?"

"I'll go see her. Find out what she needs, what she wants. It's simple."

"Hah! Simple. Will you tell her you're coming?"

"No. Better to catch her off guard. She'll be more honest. I'll do it this afternoon."

"I don't know. That doesn't seem fair." Teddie hesitated. She felt angry, angry that Howie thought he had the right questions, angry that he would invade Thea's privacy, angry that Thea played him like a sport marlin, angry that she had feared Thea all her life. She listened to her thoughts and wondered what "had feared" meant.

"You and your sister keep talking about fair. You're so alike."

Teddie's jaw dropped. She pivoted to avoid their morning ceremony, but somehow Howie managed to plant a brief, and, yes, arousing, kiss on the back of her neck before he picked up his tennis bag. "Time and reservations wait for no man."

"I have to go to Ann Arbor. I may be late."

"Have a good time."

She tore the scooter ad from *Mature Living*, and called Thea. "I need your advice," she said.

"Why?"

"Humor me. Isn't that what mothers are for? Giving opinions?" How dare she be so outrageous, but Thea laughed.

"If it makes you happy."

"You might want to know. Those darkroom boxes are in your basement. Take a look if you've got time. And, oh, Howie's dropping by this afternoon to see how you're doing."

"My keepers are complaining."

"Of course. Do you make life easy for them? I thought you should know. We'll go tomorrow."

"You think I can help." Thea was gone.

On the road again, Teddie brooded about the man stashed in the Beekman Storage Tower. Liz should be there, not in a blue Saturn on a gray freeway headed towards a mysterious appointment with Teddie's son.

The library's potholed parking lot was full, but she managed to slide into the last empty spot. A good omen?

Four bundled, dirty figures chain-smoked on the icy library entrance wall. This could be where her architect-robber conceived his scheme, but these discomforting homeless were weatherbeaten, ageless, no sign of youth. Head down, eyes on her feet, Teddie walked their gauntlet. She despised her avoidance. I'm one of you, she wanted to say, an outcast. See my old coat?

The calm inside the library was comforting. She was early enough to open the card catalogue to HIV and was referred to "AIDS (acquired immunodeficiency syndrome)". She dropped her coat on a chair, but failed to find even one of the references. How could she ask a librarian to believe the preposterous truth, that the police wanted Teddie Olds tested for a fatal virus whose presence, if real, was her husband's sole responsibility—but there was that dentist in Florida and what about Michael's searching kisses—serpentine trails of truths. "I need to know about AIDS? Nothing's on the shelf."

"We're changing systems. Going computer." The librarian bent over her keyboard, nodded, and led Teddie to the Young Adult corner where she pulled a book from the shelf. "What do you need?"

"Oh, I don't know." The librarian smiled at her. "Well, when can you get a definite test, where do you go, things like that," Teddie said as offhandedly as she could muster.

"Health Department does testing. I went there." The gray librarian certainly was awesome. "They promised privacy, knew how scared I was. Waiting was the worst. They said it could be a couple of weeks before they got back to me because of their backlog."

"Are you, are you, well," gripped with curiosity, Teddie hesitated, "well, okay?"

"Yes, at least no HIV. Here, why don't you see if this book answers your questions."

"Young adult?"

"Why not? Clear writing. Let me know if you need anything more," and she left to take care of the line at her desk.

We all need information, Teddie thought as she stared at the homeless huddled outside. Six weeks for the immune response to develop. Neither she nor the boy would be in the clear for six weeks, and that would be true only if neither engaged in dangerous activities in the meantime and, anyway, they should be retested in six months. Was perfunctory sex with her husband a dangerous activity? She read about dental dams for safe oral sex, stared blindly out the window. What a world. Did her children know all this? She had not taught them. She had not known in safe suburbia and, besides, she was simply ignorant. There was Zach, greeting those homeless people ouside. What was her Zach doing? She'd almost forgotten, but here he was.

Like a school kid hiding a comic, Teddie threw her arms over her book. "What are you reading?" her son asked. Zach kissed her cheek, sat down, and lifted her arm. "How much do you know?" he whispered.

"Hardly anything," she whispered back. "What should I know? Why are we here?" He looked exhausted, his eyes red-rimmed and bloodshot, his face pale beneath his frizzy red beard. "I've been doing a lot of thinking. My friend Bob, you know that teacher in the hospital, he has pneumonia, a really bad kind. Out of the blue, no warning."

Teddie's stomach flipped. "AIDS," she said, no question in her voice. "Were—are you close? Zach, have you been tested? Are you sick?"

"Look, let's go somewhere. Do you want that book? I've got a nonresident card."

"No, yes, I don't know."

"I'll get it. I don't know much myself." Zach grabbed the book and took his place in the check-out line. Rancid body odors swirled around her. Their source, a man, watched her with eyes as much a Caribbean blue as Michael's but set in a brick red, weatherbeaten face. "He seems like a good kid," he said softly. "Good luck."

Surprised, she whispered, "Thanks. He is."

"How about walking by the river," Zach suggested. "It's a short drive."

Behind the wheel, she followed his directions to a riverside park where bridges and trails meandered over and around dark, ice-edged water. Displaced Canada geese, unwilling to migrate, hissed and clamored under signs warning the public not to feed the wildlife. A woman tossed slices of bread like frisbees into the flock from her open van door. "There are lawbreakers here," Teddie observed.

"There are lawbreakers everywhere," Zach responded. "A court reporter should know."

"There's too much I should know. I have to be tested for AIDS. Do you know how?"

"Why? Dad isn't sick?"

"The long or short story? Your dad's fine. The police want me tested."

"Something about your work? Yeah, I know what to do. I've done it."

"ZACH!"

"It was okay. Have to have another, though, six months. Still, I feel hopeful. About me."

"What about your friend?"

"Worried. He's a great person, Mom, the only one I've felt close to in a long time. I don't know what it means. We have a lot in common—like loving art and teaching or whatever it is we do in Kalamazoo. Now he may die. How soon?"

"How bad is it?"

"Not good. He thought it was the flu, didn't think he could be HIV positive. Now he's in the AIDS unit and of course the school knows and those parents are having shit fits. I wanted you to know." Mother-love overwhelmed the part of Teddie that wanted to complain, to shout, "Too much!"

"It's okay." She rested her hand on his knee while he wiped his eyes. "How sick is he?"

"Bob? He's breathing a little better. They say he'll get over this. They've seen much worse."

"Do his parents know?"

"Dad's dead. Mom knows he's sick. She lives in Maine or something."

No. You can't solve all the world's woes. Take care of your son, keep him safe, and Jesse. "Does your sister know?"

"She's got the outline. Said she'd visit him, that she knew her way to the AIDS unit."

"What?" Teddie exclaimed.

"Probably friends or something. Kids have got it, classmates, professors—one died last month. I worry about Dad and you. Everyone knows he plays around. Do you think he's careful?"

Teddie recalled their sudden unprotected encounter. "I want to think he knows what he's doing."

"Talk to him, Mom."

"I try."

"Why are you supposed to be tested?" Zach blushed bright red. "You don't have to tell me. Sorry I asked."

"It's not what you think," Teddie answered. "It happened last Monday, kind of wild. Let's walk." The sun was still high enough to light the paths. Teddie told her tale from fettucini Alfredo and a single Caesar salad to the bank robbery. Zach laughed, and they stopped walking and laughed some more. She mentioned neither Jack Sullivan nor Michael Henderson, but told of Aurora's and Marla's shopping business and Rudolph outside the door. "I'm glad we can laugh, but the boy's story is so sad."

"Imagine you tackling a robber. You're something." Zach grinned. "You said you wanted help with Thea. What can I do?"

"Let's talk over lunch. You look as if you've been forgetting to eat. Do you have time?"

"Yeah. I'm going to see Jesse tonight. I'll go back to the hospital. And I've got a stack of papers to grade. But I almost forgot. We've got to get to the Health Department. My mom needs a blood test."

"I want to forget," Teddie complained.

"Can't. All we can do is live. Bet you're scared of needles, Mom. Don't worry, I'll tell them to be careful."

"We have to take care of each other."

o o o

Teddie had a bandaid on the crook of her elbow and yet another identity when she left the Health Department. She liked her number. It came without a past, wasn't judgmental, simply existed. She was lucky to get an appointment to return next week. She and

Zach ate lunch and visited Bob who smiled tiredly through his tangle of tubes.

"I've seen you before . . . on Zach's dresser. What a way to live," she said reverting to blunt, honest Teddie.

"It's not as bad as it looks," Bob said, "and it's only temporary. For now. They've got good medicine here. I'll be out next week."

Like show and tell, Teddie uncurled her arm to expose her bandaid. "I gave blood, too. I'm number 83759. For testing purposes."

"Wait til you hear what my mom did," and Zach recounted his mother's story with his own twist. Bob laughed until coughs overwhelmed him. Zach looked terrified, but the nurse said not to worry, just come back later.

Teddie leaned through Bob's tubes and kissed his hot cheek. "Sorry," she said. "I never knew my life could have such an effect. Take care of yourself." Bob waved weakly as Teddie exited. She could not bear to watch Zach say good-bye.

CHAPTER • 13 •

She mustered all her powers to shut out the uncontrollable, the impossible, but her right foot refused to be contained. The speedometer needle had passed seventy-five when lights flashed behind her. Heart pounding, she released the gas pedal and glided into the middle lane. It was almost upon her. She blinked. A siren crescendoed, then passed, strands of sound sinking as the police car spun away. Rubbernecking drivers crawled past the two-car accident. Had they been speeding? Drunk? Plain careless or dumb chance? The encounter placed her in the here and now, not with young men in hospital beds.

She drove lawfully the rest of the way home.

o o o

Howie pressed the phone to his ear with one hand and shuffled papers with the other. A half-full glass, ice melting, had left watery rings on the cover of a professional journal. He held up his hand, thumb and index finger not quite touching. Only minutes more.

She was sorting mail on the coffee table when he found her. "How was Ann Arbor? Meet someone for lunch?"

Silently she rehearsed alternatives before settling on simple sincerity. "Fine. Yes." She held out her arm and peeled off the bandaid. "They took blood. I'm number 83759. Results next week."

"Smart to go there. Tell that detective. Next we know, there'll be a police car at the door. What will the neighbors think?"

"That it's your business, or maybe mine. The blood was simple. Those people must have seen and heard everything, even silly wives making silly requests," said the new Teddie. Never had anyone called her silly—dull, responsible, reliable, but nothing frivolous.

"Thea's fine," he said. "We had a good talk. Got her to compromise. She took me to see a bathroom she's making into a dark-room—the Rossotti book, you know."

"She told me. What sort of compromise?"

"Well, I pointed out research proves exercise makes people like her stronger and steadier, but she said I can't imagine how stupid the class was."

"I bet." Teddie laughed. "What else?"

"Wait. I told her she could always work out alone or she could get a personal trainer. She said I had wonderful ideas. She'd do that. Someone on the staff, helped her before, provides personal services. She wanted me to get drinks to toast the new, physically fit woman. Ted, do you know if the Carleton provides booze? We drank sherry, but she's got a well-stocked bar in a cupboard next to the stove."

"Not when I was there. I'm sure Director Olson wouldn't approve. Do you think she's running a geriatric speakeasy? No. Thea may do everything to excess, but she doesn't like people enough to be a bartender."

"I think she's lonely. She's never had time for a lot of friends. She should come here more often, spend the night. Anyway, I solved the exercise thing." Teddie could not remember a single night her mother had spent in the Olds's house. Instead she saw the image of the nicotine-stained, hollow-chested worker with the drooping moustache. Cigarette in one hand, drink in the other, he sits in an overstuffed chair across from Thea. When he says, "Up!" they raise their glasses, at "Down!" they lower them. Personal service to her mother.

"Are you going to interview her trainer?" Teddie asked.

"Don't treat her like a child. I told the office their problem was solved."

Oh Howie. I add exercising my mother to my list? "Remember that colleague of Zach's? The sick one? I saw him today. He's in University Hospital."

"The photographer? What's wrong with him?"

"Pneumonia. Zach's really concerned. Bob's in the AIDS unit."

"Did they run out of regular beds . . . or is it . . .?"

"It is. Full-blown. Zach says the school parents are pretty upset. I guess it's frightening if you don't understand, like Marla. Bob didn't know he was infected." Shored by a lifetime of practice, Teddie ignored the threatening storm.

"Okay, Ted. I'll get tested—prove everything's okay."

But is it? Where are we headed?

"Should I get the phone?" Howie asked.

"I will," Teddie said, and there was Aurora in Chicago.

"We got our planning done," she reported, "and I came back here to work on our mailing list. Dick says that's first. Would you give us a testimonial? Like how we changed your life?" Aurora's laugh had silvery edges.

Teddie swallowed. "Did Marla's grandbabies come?"

"I thought I wouldn't wait, so much work to do. How about that testimonial right now, over the phone."

"Do you have a name?"

Aurora giggled. "Fancy, high class. As You Like It."

"As You Like It has brought color and style to my life. These tasteful time-savers are worth their weight in. . . ."

"No weight," Aurora interrupted. "Never that word."

". . . are well worth their commission—you fix it up. What's your fee?"

"Dick figured your bill. I don't bother with numbers. I'm the artist."

"I guess so. I was thinking. Thea's been complaining that everything in her wardrobe was too old."

"That's fitting. So's she."

"You could find her a few good things. She's starting a new project. Probably size six, like you."

"Remember, I'm size four. Okay. I'll send you the bills. You get her to pay up. I have lots to do, just thought I'd let you know where I am." Aurora stopped. "How are you, Teddie?" she added so softly Teddie wasn't sure she'd heard. "You're all I have."

Playing the part of a competent woman was easier than dealing with her Pandoran problems. "I'm fine," Teddie lied. "Had blood taken today, results in a week. The Health Department gives you a number. It was easy. Even you could do it."

"Me? Why me? I'll have you know I've learned something in my forty-nine years."

"And to think you used to be four years older than me. Well, take care of yourself. I'll say hello to Howie for you."

"Thanks. He's sweet. Night."

The evening passed in small ways, but, once in bed, sleep was elusive. She unknotted one muscle at a time, but the very moment she was loose and drifting, she jolted awake. The bedside clock claimed that time had passed while her eyes were closed, her mind spinning, but she knew better. She was unravelling, coming apart, pieces hurtling through space, no place to rest. At three A.M. she rose. If she couldn't sleep, she'd work and there were two depositions to transcribe. Wrapped in her robe, she shuffled down the hall. Where was Zach sleeping? Why hadn't she insisted he come home? He said he'd crash at Jesse's house-of-many-people, but she needed to be caring for him, it mustn't be too late.

Soothed by words, in the eyes, out the fingers, she slept heavily from five through another Sunday dawn.

o o o

Howie hadn't finished his weekend on the tennis courts, but, yes, Teddie should visit Thea. Family is important. Howie's only half-sister lived in the California desert with a dog and a grizzled man. When Howie and Teddie had first met, he'd once or twice mentioned a father and a stepmother somewhere in Alaska. "Your family is my family," he finally announced. As usual, Teddie shared.

Now she was treading thin ice on the edge of black water.

The ad in the Yellow Pages confirmed that Securimed was open Sundays for the convenience of churchgoers, but the Carleton came first. Thea's unlocked door framed three heads: curly red, silken blonde, and white. "Is is a party? Am I invited?" Teddie asked.

Jesse threw her arms around her mother. "Mom! We decided to visit like at the last minute. Thea's showing us pictures." Zach winked and waved. Teddie planted the obligatory kiss on her mother's forehead, but Thea was not to be disrupted.

"Come back, child. You asked about your grandfather. Here. It's our wedding."

"Where were you?" Jesse asked.

"Who took it?" asked Zach.

"Oh," Teddie breathed. Adorned with a crown of flowers and a clinging gauzy dress, a maiden perched on a gnarled tree branch high above long grasses shaped by the wind. She was lovely and serious and appeared to be searching the cloudless sky beyond the leafy branches for omens. He stood beneath, both delight and confusion on his round face, hands raised as if to seize her before she soared away—or perhaps to catch her if she should fall, for her slender body seemed anchored by a melon-shaped swelling. "What's he saying?" Teddie asked.

"Oh, Theo. The man with the beautiful name. He made up doggerel. Let me remember." Thea's eyes focused somewhere far behind her as she chanted,

"My Maude,
My God,
My Wife,
My Life."

"Who's Maude?" Jesse asked.

"I suppose there's no reason you shouldn't know. Once my parents called me by that name. Maude Slote, but she was vanquished that day. Here you see Thea Waterford."

"Do I see Aunt Aurora's profile?" Zach asked impertinently.

"Theo was so conventional—he insisted the child have a name. I only wanted his." The round-cheeked, curly-haired man under the tree reminded Teddie of Zach and someone else, who was it? Did her father look like her? "He wanted to take you children when I needed to move on, but I insisted children must have mothers. He argued, but naturally, I won."

"Why didn't we ever hear from him? What happened?"

"He tried to stay in touch, but I lost him. It was easier. Aurora was so upset after her afternoons with that plain, dull man. You were too little to remember, Theodora. Still, you remind me of him." Zach asked where the bride's and groom's families were. "Heaven knows," Thea answered. "His couldn't stand me. I left mine in South Dakota dust—haven't thought about them for centuries. We were married in California, Jesse. Theo wanted to see the country before we settled down. Poor, narrow man. A friend took the photo. He had a studio in San Francisco. Showed me the city while my husband searched for old books. Theo called himself a bookman. Not an interesting occupation." Thea sat back, closed her eyes, and snored softly. Teddie beckoned her children into the extra bedroom to tell them about the day's plans.

When Thea woke, Zach had stashed most of the liquor in the trunk of Teddie's car and tea was ready. Thea took the cup from Jesse, and when she drained it, they all left together, the cane abandoned by the door.

The Securimed parking lot was filled with customers in search of substitute body parts. The Sunday sales force smiled and scraped like undertakers.

"What is this place?" Thea demanded before a display of suspended bags and tubes. "Marvelous." Her gnarled fingers framed images only she could see. "I need my camera. I must come back." Imaging as she went, Thea dawdled past feeding pumps and multifingered, blue foam cushions.

Zach and Jesse were circling the riding machines when their grandmother finally arrived. "Know how they work, Mom?" Jesse crowed as the sleazy salesman, perhaps the same toothpick in mouth, slouched out of the back room.

"Young man! Show us how to run these machines," Thea commanded, and the worm straightened, threw away his toothpick, and smiled charmingly at her mother.

"Simple. Even these kids here could figure them out with some help, but a woman of your intelligence and experience..." and he snapped his fingers before sliding easily into the talk Teddie had had to wheedle and threaten for. Jesse and Zach mounted the machines to the left and right of the model the man was demonstrating. "Why don't you try it?" the salesman cajoled when he had finished. Before Thea could say yea or nay, the two vehicles had pulled out.

"Go, go!" Thea cheered. "Come on, Jesse, don't let him get ahead!" The super-safe machines darted quickly, up one aisle, around the pedestal topped by a bed crowned with a stainless steel superstructure, back past the blue-fingered foam, all eyes on Jesse and Zach.

"No, you don't." Zach spun around to block Jesse at the waterproof chucks and adult-sized diapers. Jesse grinned and backed her scooter through a narrow opening between five types of suspended plastic bags, then sped into the clear next to Thea.

"Good girl. Stay on board. Young man, which is best for me?" Without objection, the salesman saw Thea mounted and hastily reviewed the operating instructions before she squeezed the accelerator handle. Eyes sparkling, she chased her grandson around the braces and whiplash collars only to be cornered by the canes. Thea's sudden reverse sent the display flying, but she scooted into the clear, and without stopping, raised her right arm in jubilation. Several Sunday shoppers applauded, but the salespeople were clumped together, either for moral support or to work out a containment strategy. Teddie had no option. She had to step directly into her speeding mother's path. Thea's joyous grin became a grimace as she stopped inches short of her daughter.

"Didn't you see me?" Thea exclaimed. "That was dangerous, Theodora!"

"I trusted you," Teddie said, rubbing her icy hands. "The posse was on its way." She waved at the medical salespeople who were abandoning their formation for their jobs.

"Do you need a license for this vehicle, young man?" Thea asked.

Their stunned salesman shook his head. "Got to stay off the freeways—on the sidewalks, that's all."

"Then how do I get it back to the place where I'm presently living?"

"Comes apart. Child can do it." Zach had parked neatly, but Jesse abandoned her vehicle in an aisle where she now twiddled her nose ring. "Come here," the salesman ordered. Jesse looked behind her. "No, you blondie, come here. I'll help you take it apart." Jesse rolled her eyes and Teddie stepped next to her. Thea could handle him, but Jesse was young, fresh and green. "Is this the model you want?"

"This *is* your recommendation, isn't it?" Thea said.

The salesman nodded. "Yes, ma'am. Only top of the line for you." The padding, the leather seat, the artful trim all spoke of luxury and expense, but never mind. Teddie had not dreamed it would be so easy.

"I want this one. Add an extra battery. My work is very demanding. Of course there is a discount for the floor model. Dismantle it, Jesse." Teddie's hovering prevented the salesman's hands from landing on Jesse's pale, firm flesh while she turned a screw here and twisted a bolt there, then the scooter sat in three pieces. "One of your men will help my grandson put this in the car. Remember the battery. Jesse, you're in charge of assembly, unless you want this good man to accompany us." Jesse nodded, then shook her head. "Take care of the paperwork, Theodora."

Had Howie made the deposit? Teddie pulled out her check-book. "No good," the salesman insisted. "Credit cards or cash. I told you, insurance is up to you." Thea departing, now he deigned to acknowledge their previous meeting.

"I'll make a down-payment, and you will bill Thea Waterford for the remainder," Teddie said firmly. "She lives at the Carleton. You know the address. I'll give you her apartment number. She will sign your papers." Thea had neither savings nor cash, but Teddie held her tongue. In her need to convey the fine points of truth she had been known to babble about inadequate funds and overdrawn accounts and would they wait a day or two to make sure everything would be all right. As a child, Thea sometimes had sent her off to buy her own underwear or shoes, not with cash, but with Thea's store charge card which Teddie would hand over after making her embarrassed, cheap choices. Then she, an eight- or eleven-year-old child who blushed easily, would be called to the business office and have to relinquish her shoes or underpants—once a bra for her eleven-year-old breasts—because Thea had neglected to pay her bills. Teddie would turn red and stammer and flee. More days than not her shoes pinched and her underwear had holes. "I would have told them the payment was in the mail," Thea said.

"Was it?" Teddie would ask wide-eyed.

"That's for me to say and them to find out," Thea would say.

Teddie paid her own bills by check or cash. Howie had the credit. She handed the man the VISA.

"Is five hundred okay?" he asked meekly.

"Fine," Teddie said.

CHAPTER • 14 •

The memory of Michael was a stored treasure. Her mind explored his loft, tasted his cherry vanilla ice cream, felt his concern for her, her, her. She could see him today, tomorrow or any other day, for he was tucked away, Michael safe from the world, safe for her. Why did danger surround her?

Zach had returned to his students and Bob was better, although he could not go back to teaching even if the school would have him. Jesse had reassembled the three-wheeled scooter, now christened Hermes and parked in Thea's second bedroom. Thea did not mention Teddie's subterfuge as she navigated through doors sized for mechanically assisted living. Zach and Thea rode to the basement darkroom, Zach balanced precariously on Hermes' back, to give Teddie directions for remodeling.

Teddie and Howie never had remodeled. Their house was a contractor's speculation Howie had bought hook, line, and white living room with concealed wet bar.

Head spinning, emotions dislocated, she pulled into the Olds's driveway for the seven-thousandth time in twenty-five years and realized that, like Thea in the Carleton and unlike Michael in the Beekman, never had she belonged to this space. Only in the yellow house with the garden had she been at home even with her father lost.

She must tell Howie what she needs, how she feels, who she is. The night sky was cloudless, but she was lost, no longer able to see. Her trembling hand rested on the door handle. What was it? Suddenly the latch gave way.

"I *did* hear you!" Howie reeled her in. "I thought that lock had been fixed. Never mind. I've got something." She allowed him to tow her through the dining room. The beige and cobalt medallions in the thick sky-blue wool carpet repeated and repeated. Were they what she needed? Her head was clearer and most certainly she knew where she was, passing through their impossible living room and into Howie's overstuffed brown leather study.

"It's not a surprise, is it?" She could not stand another ritual. Oh, he tried, the jewelry, pleasing as objects, but hardly in concept. And flowers, once five enormous pots of blooming orchids. Too bad they'd blackened and withered from a midwinter blight.

Midwinter, that was the key. Travel brochures covered the desk. Coffee-tinted children, flowers tucked behind their ears, stared into the camera; barnacle-coated whales frolicked with a people-packed black rubber boat; coconut palms, white sand beaches, and beautiful men and women watching brilliant sunsets from their beautiful hotel/yacht/mountain-top. "Looks like I can get away next month after all. Where do you want to go? How about Cancun?" and he dangled a picture of a white tower that stepped down to a beach dotted with palm-roofed shelters.

Her turn at their game. "How about the Galapagos?" she should say showing him a brochure displaying two women kneeling in the sand before an enormous, infinitely aged tortoise. "No fun," he'd counter, "how about this Mardi Gras cruise?" "Too much fun-fun," she'd argue, so the game went. She knew neither why she should play nor why she could not. She lived like a trusty caged animal, always fed, allowed out for exercise, but trapped. She should cry for help, beg for release, but her throat was sealed. Silent tears drizzled down her cheeks. The silvery trails switched Howie from marital to professional.

"Rough time for you," he said softly. She did not respond. He went on. "Only hormones. A few pills, replacement, you'll be your old self." Teddie frowned. "Aurora told me about your doctor's appointment tomorrow. Good idea, Ted."

She had forgotten, too involved with new lives to cancel the menopause doctor. With clarity she understood she could not return to the old life, did not want to return to the old, and the barriers had little to do with hormones. Her tears went dry.

"Thanks," she said but she could not say for what.

"You know, it's expected at this time of life, the depression, the mood swings. Natural. All women go through it," Howie declared. Was he right? Had this entire week only been the consequence of deficient hormones? The shadowy impression in the crook of her elbow from the blood-sucking needle spoke otherwise. "I'll pick some of the best trips," Howie said soothingly. "We'll plan later. We need a break."

"You're so understanding," Teddie said in a vile combination of Aurora and Marla. "I'm not up to getting dinner—not hungry," she lied as her stomach began its clockwork growling for food. "Why don't you order take-out? Whatever you want. I'll lie down."

"Who do I call? What do you want? Get it delivered or what?" Howie was a stranger to this domestic responsibility, although Zach and Jesse, in turn, had become experts by the age of nine.

"I'll show you," Teddie said through gritted teeth and flipped the Yellow Pages. "See? There's the Dragon's Kitchen," and she stabbed her index finger into the heart of the ad, "or pizza," and she stabbed again. "Call when it's here," and she lowered her head to dab at angry, dry eyes. Howie patted her shoulder, and she recognized Lisa Greenstein's fear in her own husband's eyes. Her dark powers were ripening, enhanced as they were by Jack Sullivan's wandering leg and Michael Henderson's soft lips. She scratched her scabbed knee and left Howie to his own dinner devices.

Climbing the stairs, Teddie considered her jewelry collection, mostly antique. Howie understood her longing for roots. She'd open the box, they'd admire the workmanship, and Teddie would wonder who it was this time. Perhaps Howie first found the pin or earrings, then the woman. Would that he had been that prepared with sex. She'd know Saturday.

Off with the shoes, onto the bed, close the eyes, and Bob's face rose behind his thicket of tubes. Zach's Bob. Her tears welled, flowed.

She lay damp and crumpled when Howie shook her shoulder. "Ted, food's here." Dutifully she rolled over.

"Need a minute. What did you get?"

"You'll see. Feeling better?" He watched her strip off her wrinkled suit, clean her face, and slip into a wine-colored kaftan thing Aurora had provided. "Sleep did you good," Howie announced. "Knits the ravelled sleeve—better than tranquilizers. We've got Chinese."

An army formation of red dragons waited on their white counter. "What happened?" Teddie asked.

"I couldn't decide." She would not go hungry tonight. The kettle on for tea, she transferred the cartons to a tray for their march into the dining room. Howie brought plates and utensils and his half-filled glass, a travel brochure sticking out of his pocket. He was prepared. She was not, although the greasy smell of American Chinese food was comforting.

The phone rang while Howie was explaining how he had ordered. "Hello," Teddie said warily.

"I've informed the desk and now I'm telling you," Thea announced. "It's fair warning. The contract said it was safe, but the Carleton has thieves."

"What are you talking about?"

"They broke in while we were out. A roving band of drunkards, that's what I told them. Dangerous."

"I'm having dinner, Thea. What's missing?" Teddie asked, although the answer was in the trunk of her car next to the box of photos.

"I was going to entertain. You'll have to shop for me now. Scotch, bourbon, gin, vodka, especially vodka, get the best. All that's left is a little cheap vermouth and sherry. I need it tonight."

"Drink the sherry. I can't tonight." Teddie said.

"Can't or won't?" Thea exploded. "Do I have to take care of myself?" The phone banged. Outside fresh snowflakes floated earthwards. The image of Thea riding Hermes to a strip mall liquor store in the dark night made her shiver. She punched in Thea's number and counted rings. After the twelfth she hung up, then slowly, carefully repeated her motions. Thea answered in a trembling voice after the ninth.

"What's wrong?" Teddie asked.

"Who are you?" a shadow of her mother answered.

"Thea, it's Teddie, your daughter. Are you all right? What happened?"

"I'm weak, Theodora. I was going out. Couldn't. Had to sit

down. Don't tell anyone."

"What's happening? Are you dizzy?"

"Too much excitement. I'll take a nap. You eat with your husband. I'm fine."

"You're sure?"

"Of course I'm sure," a suddenly vigorous Thea barked and banged the receiver down once again. Reassured, Teddie told Howie nevertheless.

"Trust her, Ted," he insisted, but Teddie could think of no good reason. "Trust me. Come on. Food's getting cold."

Why should she worry? Howie was right about the food. Teddie heaped rice on her plate and spooned up glistening sweet and sour pork, some general's chicken, even unfamiliar dishes. Thea would have to take care of herself.

o o o

The rattling mail jeep announced itself this Monday. She and Howie nearly collided by the front door, but gallantly he let her dip into the box ahead of him. First out was another Galapagos brochure followed by a handful of envelopes larded with larger stuff. His hand licked the mailbox clean and sorted the findings.

"One for you. Funny envelope. Is As You Like It some dinner theater?" he asked.

"I thought I told you. It's Aurora and Marla and Dick—the bill. I'm not sure I want to see it."

"I'll open it for you," and Howie slipped his shining fingernail under the flap.

"No!" Teddie snatched the pink envelope. "I pay for this," she insisted, but she didn't know why she'd started paying for her Eva Martin specials. Perhaps it was about being owned, with not wanting to be owned, which did not mean that she did not want to be be wanted. Not unlike Thea, she thought, at least the owned part. Thea always had been desired.

She ripped the pink flap. Howie was studying Galapagos when she made a strangled noise.

"What's wrong?" She was breathing too rapidly, she would hyperventilate. "No, really. Are you okay?"

"No need for 911."

"Let me see."

"No." Teddie shoved the pink paper into her pocket. "They

added a 50 percent commission. I'm a very well-dressed woman."
Was their verbal contract binding? She only had wanted those
two females out of her hair. Yet aside from the bank robber, her
new wardrobe may have contributed more to the last week's
events than her fluctuating hormones. Would the menopausal
doctor believe in wardrobe therapy? What did she believe in? Her
bank account did not hold five thousand eight hundred and ninety two dollars, and the thought of taking another deposition gave
her a headache.

"Now, how about the Galapagos?" Howie held up the new
brochure.

"You know I've always wanted to go. You decide. You realize I'll
have to clear my calendar." Of Liz drinking chicken noodle soup
with Michael, of Theodora having a soiree with a carpenter in the
Carleton basement, of a follow-up appointment with the
menopause man if there was no more pressing business with an
AIDS specialist. All will have to be postponed while Ted packs for
a visit with those sad-eyed tortoises. Teddie smiled. Hormones for
tortoises. Charles Darwin observes bright-eyed, surgically
improved tortoises with baby-smooth, sunscreen-slathered skin.
What are they adapting to?

Howie looked puzzled. *She* was doing that to him. Panic, concern, fear, puzzlement, passion—power. Not bad. "I'll see what's
available," he said. "When's your appointment?"

"Two, I think. I have to work now. I'll tell you about it tonight."

Howie pecked her cheek nervously. "Tonight," and he neither
waggled his eyebrows nor leered.

o o o

Five minutes early, Teddie pushed into a gray and mauve waiting room. Instead of supermarket schefleria, Dr. David Summers's
staff was growing orchids, not a black spot in sight. Two pairs of
eyes rose from their magazines. The younger was not young. A
spotlight aimed at the orchids illuminated shiny pink skin beneath
the elder's sparse white hair. Light years less alive than Thea,
Teddie thought. Clearly she was not one of them, but she remembered her horrifying mirror image after she'd stopped the bank robber. All of us are me, never them. Others grow old. The receptionist handed her a clipboard with its empty spaces waiting for patient
information.

No questionnaire was simple to Teddie. Questions might seem straightforward and answer blanks orderly, but the one and only accurate truth, if it could be found, seldom fit its allotted space. She was here to consult about her condition and she should be able to describe the condition about which she was consulting but she could not. Loss of identity. Adrift from the knowns. Excited. Sexually aroused. Angry. Adventurous. Profoundly afraid. Perhaps Liz could fill in the blanks for her. No need to mention that Teddie was losing her self and mind as well as hair pigmentation, skin elasticity, and menstrual periods.

"Your first time?" the younger elder observed, her nose like a needle. "Not everyone is able to get appointments with Dr. Summers."

"My sister made it," Teddie explained on automatic, while the older elder was summoned into the inner chambers.

"Of course, not everyone can be helped," needle-nose stage-whispered behind her hand. "Especially when you wait too long."

"Mmm," Teddie nodded and returned to the forms. "Have you reached menopause?" she read but could not answer. Liz, what's the answer? "When did your periods stop?" was a logical conundrum. Each time she was convinced she was done, another would come along. When would you know?

"Theodora Olds," Teddie heard. She rose to jealous looks from her companion. "He'll be right with you, dear," the nurse said softly, holding her hand out to Teddie. "Did you get through the paperwork, Theodora? My, that's an unusual name."

"Sorry." Teddie's eyes filled with tears. "We didn't have time."

"It's all right, dear. I'm Lorna. What do you like to be called?" The question implied choice. Liz Gutleben was her first and only conscious choice in the arena of names. Liz would confuse Lorna. "Teddie," she said.

"How cute!" and Lorna opened the door into a pink room, walls, ceiling, desk, couch and chairs, all shades of pink. "Make yourself comfortable, Teddie. I have to take care of the poor dear in the waiting room. Would you mind spending a few minutes more with this?" Lorna returned the clipboard now stripped of the insurance information, so simple to supply. "Dr. Summers likes to know his patients."

"Fine." Teddie wondered if Dr. Summers knew his menopausal women in the biblical or literal sense. The door closed. The pink walls wrapped around her. Hadn't she read that pink has the power to calm both explosive prison inmates and enraged mental patients? She did not want to be manipulated by paint or anything else. She had earned her anger. She'd leave. She'd tell Howie that she was too upset for probing questions and a cold speculum. The door opened before she could drop the questionnaire on the pink desk.

He, too, was pink—pink and smooth and blonde, hair perfectly cut, face perfectly shaven. Her fingers wandered to the stiff black bristle that had taken to sprouting from her chin. "David Summers," he said, holding out his hand. "May I call you Teddie?" His hand was boneless, warm, and impersonal. "Have a seat."

She fell into a chair while Dr. Summers sank into the couch. "You need not lose your youth, Teddie," he said, staring into her eyes. "May I?" and without permission he pinched the skin on the back of her hand.

"Ouch."

The pucker lingered a moment in the air. "A small sign of your deficiency disease." He retrieved the clipboard. "You still have your uterus and ovaries, I see," information Teddie had been able to provide without Liz's help. She nodded. "You came into this world with your lifetime supply of eggs, your potential children. Ah, I see you have two. Good. Now, your number's up," and he chuckled. "No more eggs, much less estrogen, female advantages cancelled. But today, now, we can reset your clock with modern medicines, with hormone cocktails. Almost a miracle. Of course you won't conceive, but everything else will be the same. Your bones, your heart, your skin, especially that sensitive vagina, will stay strong, but I'm getting ahead of myself."

Clouds were gathering around her. How could she respond? He seemed to think he had the power to stop time, to halt death.

"Lorna told me you were having trouble with your history." You would, too, if Thea had been your mother, Teddie thought. "Take your time. Lorna will be back to draw some blood and help you get ready, then I'll check you out. Just relax." He patted her shoulder. Without pinching, she knew his rubber skin bounced back. Alone, her held-in breath escaped.

No one had told her about this phase of life. Surgery had ended Aurora's fertility ages ago. Thea's facts of life were simple—you get what you want. Her mother had been delighted when a teenaged

Teddie had to struggle with gushing menstrual blood, a white swim suit, and a swimming party, but her glee was at her own condition, not her daughter's crisis. "What a relief!" she'd gloated. "No more for me," and she'd tossed a tampon over her shoulder like a pinch of salt. "Freedom!"

A tap and Lorna's head popped into the pink room. "Can I come in, Teddie?" she asked.

"Why not," Teddie sighed and she slipped out of her clothes in preparation for Dr. Summers's latex-covered hands.

CHAPTER • 15 •

She now possessed five handsome informational pamphlets, a self-published book by David Summers, M.D., and promises of prescriptions. Hot flashes she could do without, although her night in the snow was nothing to scoff at. She'd have to return for a sitting-up appointment when the lab work was completed. No one had suggested HIV testing, nor had she flaunted her marked arm. Dr. Summers would not need to poke and palpate her interior again. "Couldn't tell your age from this end," he announced as his brown eyes rose over Teddie's sheeted knees.

Needing deodorant, she drifted into the pharmacy, a mini-Securimed conveniently located in Dr. Summers's building, and found what she wanted among the bags and canes. Film hung behind the counter. Impatiently she tapped a candy bar, creamy coconut filling inside a chocolate shell, while she waited for attention at the cash register.

"Your name?" a painted mouth asked. The white coat did not hide the fact the girl was the store clerk. "For your prescription? That's like what you want?"

"No." She was tired of all of them. They called her Teddie, and he was *Dr. Summers*, for godsake. "Deodorant," she said angrily. "And these." She added two candy bars. "And what are those?" Cardboard boxes claiming to be cameras hung next to the film. She knew nothing of cameras.

o o o

The evening after Thea had reclaimed her daughters from Georgio's mother, Teddie had decided she must understand her competition. The little girl's fingers slipped into Thea's canvas bag until they touched cold metal. They closed, she lifted, and heard footsteps. "Theodora!" At its master's voice the heavy camera jumped out of little Teddie's hands and fell to the floor. She ran, escaped into the safety of strangeness. Under the porch was a hole, a hiding place where she stayed hidden until her new home was completely dark, although you never could tell about darkrooms. Only then her fingernails scratched window glass and woke Aurora.

"You're back?" Thea observed the next morning. Teddie nodded. "Why?"

"I had to."

"Never touch my equipment." Teddie shook her head.

o o o

Teddie lifted the little box the clerk placed on the counter. "How light!"

"Works real good. You know, color prints? You like send the whole thing back and buy another? Disposable?"

The cheerful little box claimed to be fun and easy, something Teddie had earned. Fun and easy, she'd take the indoor-outdoor 35 millimeter, the portrait, and the panoramic view, but left the underwater for another day, perhaps for the Galapagos. Short of cash, she pulled out her check book, then shrugged, and dug out Howie's credit card, which the relieved clerk accepted.

The thin gray winter light was spent when she'd stashed her acquisitions in her car. She was exhausted. Howie must be home, nursing his first drink. Dr. Summers asked how much and how often she drank alcohol, and she'd told him she had a drink most days—didn't everyone? "When?" Before dinner, maybe wine with dinner. "How much alcohol?" Was this a trick question, not how many drinks but much more specific? She manipulated her mental calculator—eighty-six proof was forty-three percent alcohol by volume and three drinks. . . . "How many ounces?" he interrupted her calculations. Let's see, eight ounces in a cup, how much pure alcohol in scotch, add in the wine, so that was what?

"Four, maybe five ounces," Teddie announced, shaving the total.

"Are you sure? That's all?"

"Pretty sure." Had she failed the test? She'd had no time this week for the routine ingestion of pure alcohol.

"Wine? Drink or two?" She nodded, unsure of the question. "Well, you don't sound like an alcoholic," he'd said before going on to other blanks. Of course not! Her proof, Marla's photo album, was safe in her kitchen. With the tiny exception of that photo of Thea in the park, she remembered every single moment of her life.

They said she had no imagination. But she'd learned if you don't look forward, you won't be disappointed. Perhaps the threatening sensation hovering over her head was her captive imagination straining towards freedom. She conjured up an image of herself behind a barrier of tubes in a hospital bed. Thea was reaching out, reaching through the barrier, reaching for Teddie. Impossible.

She had no trouble making schedules. This week, blank until Saturday's return to the Public Health Department, demanded a schedule now she'd dropped off the depositions and seen Dr. Feelgood Summers. There were clothes to be cleaned, her Pandoran wool and London Grill silk, because nothing As You Like It had purchased was washable. Five thousand three hundred and ninety-two dollars plus expensive upkeep. Would they repossess?

She yearned for Michael but headed for home. Tomorrow she would show him Zach's darkroom sketch and ask remodeling advice. Meanwhile, she had to stop at Shop and Save. Supermarkets took credit cards.

o o o

The Olds's outdoor lights were shining as if they expected guests. Howie had opened her car door before the engine was silent. "You're so late! How are you? Let me help," and he grabbed the two biggest bags. "I'll get the rest. Go ahead. Take it easy."

"Thanks. I'll change." Wedged into the suit selected for the menopause man, she wanted freedom. Let Howie tote bags, she'd shower long and hot.

His eyes were fixed on the living room TV screen when she returned to the untouched grocery bags. Growling wordlessly, she stored the melting-soft boxes of frozen foods. "What did you say?" he shouted.

"You could have put them away!"

"Can't hear you." The television was blaring.

She brought a carton of melting ice cream to the doorway. "Why didn't you put the groceries away?"

"Aw, Ted, simmer down." Her face burned. "You never let me help. How am I supposed to know?"

"You are supposed to be an intelligent man," she said through tense lips. "Use your supposed intelligence." Sweat beaded her nose and trickled down her temples. Howie stared. Alarm. Good, she thought, and the phone rang.

"I'll get it!" Howie yelped, but Teddie was faster. Her hello held hatred.

"Teddie? Is that you?" Aurora sounded like a mouse hiding in its hole. "Can you talk?"

"Of course I can talk," Teddie answered. "I've been doing it for years. Now, do I want to? No." My God, I sound just like Thea.

"Teddie, Teddie, I need to talk to you. I've got a problem. Only you can help."

"How can *I* help you? Lately you have all the answers."

"What? Help me."

"Make it fast," Teddie relented. She was swaggering down Main Street at high noon. Quick-draw, that's me, she thought.

"It's this way," Aurora lisped childishly. "I need money. I didn't tell you. They'll take my car."

"You don't need a car in Chicago," Thea's voice blared out of Teddie's mouth. Well, Thea could speak truth, especially injurious truth. This personal power business was not simple, definitely more to it than falsehoods. Aurora snuffled wetly.

"How much do you need?" Howie's voice boomed through the line.

"For what? It's complicated. Teddie, you've got to pay us. *I* used *my* credit cards and I made a mistake." Aurora's voice trailed into sniffs.

"You should have known before you started," Teddie said. "Businesses have to be capitalized. Dick should help you. My bill isn't due for a month. Or you can repossess before I take them to the cleaners."

"TEDDIE!" Aurora shouted. "What's wrong? Help me!"

"I think she can't help it," Teddie heard Howie say. "It's the change. She'll be her old self on medication."

"Not me." Teddie hung up. Everything had to be put in its place before it was too late. She hurled the leaking ice cream carton across the kitchen and followed up with melting macaroni and cheese. The broccoli ricocheted off the wall and settled on Marla's album in the breakfast nook. The milk carton ruptured splendidly on the oven handle, but the corn flake box hit the ceiling and fell to the floor undamaged. Teddie stamped the box with one foot, then jumped. Both feet landed squarely on the famous athlete's face; the cereal crunched like small dry bones. Some performance, she thought, repeatedly stabbing the five-pound bag of flour before heaving it into the dining room. Cheddar cheese and crackers she set aside before shredding and then tossing the lettuce like confetti. The ripped grocery bags were far from empty when she'd had enough. With a sharp knife she speared the cheese through its plastic wrap, then salvaged two green apples and the wheat crackers. She would dine in Jesse's room. How did her kitchen performance measure up to Jesse's young tantrums? Never too late to learn, like daughter, like mother, except who was going to soothe her, calm her, understand her?

Despite Jesse's absence and the weekly cleaning service, her daughter's chaotic bedroom spoke of energy, disorganization, and, what were they, yes, pheromones. Sexual energy in the clothes on the closet floor, in the scrambled dresser drawers, the intermingled books, the scraps of paper, and the cosmetics. Teddie stashed her dinner on the bedside table and shut the door. The radio was set to Jesse's last station. From the mysteries and gothic romances her daughter consumed like popcorn Teddie extracted a real book, *The Awakening* by a Kate Chopin. She opened the crackers, sliced the cheese, and carved the apple. The house was quiet, except for her radio music. Good. Howie could talk to Aurora all night. Jesse's pillows comfortably arranged, she settled on the bed opposite a poster of a naked man's glistening, muscled body. She studied his contours as she nibbled cheese.

Jesse had taken her telephone with her. Teddie was off duty. No responsibilities. Irresponsibility was expected at this time of life, her husband said. Why fight nature on this safari through the jungles of the unknown? Her teeth pierced the green satin skin of the second apple. Juice spurted and ran down her chin. Her tongue was searching out the drops when the door opened.

Howie's pointed beard framed a frightened face. Teddie

punched a pillow, the better to hold her book, then punched another for the fun of it. "Ted, Ted, it's n-nothing to worry about," he stuttered. "Do you w-w-want something?"

"Nothing," she said dishonestly. What if her imagination chased her needs? Where would they find themselves?

"I couldn't find you. I thought you'd left," Howie said in an unprofessional voice. Did she want to leave? She didn't know. She fixed him with her eyes, a snake and its prey. A telephone sounded and Howie ran. She shut the door firmly, then sank back on the bed.

Howie returned before she'd finished the first chapter by this Chopin woman. "I have to go out. Will you stay here?" he asked. "Promise you'll stay here?" Teddie shrugged.

The house was quiet except for faraway telephone rings and her music. She sliced more cheese and crunched three crackers, but couldn't read with her head so full. Observing her mental state, eyes closed, she slept soundly. Minutes later Howie was shaking her shoulders. "I've got something to help you, to calm you. He says take two now and check in the morning."

"Who says? Take what? I was sound asleep." Teddie's gun-slinging hand moved towards her weapon. "You called Dr. Summers, didn't you. Do you have a tranquilizer dart gun? Something for wild animals?"

Howie pressed her shoulders back into Jesse's bed. "Only two little pills, Ted." Terror in his face, even in his whiskers. With her strong legs Teddie pushed her upper body deep into the soft pillows and mattress, then twisted free of his grip.

"You call this civilized?" Thea's voice. "Howie, look. I need time alone. You know what it's like, when you've been working too hard. You have to unwind. You're so thoughtful to get tranquilizers for me." Teddie reached out to take one of his hands in her two. "Leave the pills. I'll take them when I need them. Trust me." She patted his captive hand. That should do it.

"I've got your glass of water. You haven't been drinking, have you? It says not to take them with alcohol." Howie's eyes were bright. Excitement was good for him, too. Crises cleanse the blood.

"Only the juice of the apple," Teddie said. "Leave them here. I'll see you in the morning. Trust me. Quiet time." Teddie rose to usher her husband out of Jesse's room. "Good night, Howie," she said, closed the door, and pressed home Jesse's lock. If there had been a keyhole, she knew she would have found Howie's eye on the other side. Teddie flushed the pills down the toilet and drank half the water before sliding into Jesse's bed and turning out the light. Good night room, she crooned.

Pure panic brought her bolt upright. She was awake, but where was she? Her sweat was pouring into Jesse's pheromoned sheets. Jesse's room, but why, what had she been doing? She remembered the physical sensations of her knife plunging into a bag of flour, then the vision of spiralling white flying through the air, trails of white on the blue rug. Oh. What had she been thinking? She would have to clean.

Tiptoeing downstairs, she followed the fuzzy flour path into the kitchen.

The grocery bags were empty. Anything that needed cold seemed to be in the refrigerator; everything else waited on the counters. Of course he hadn't, the work of minutes. She vacuumed the kitchen while Howie slept above, working her way towards the dining room where Housekeeping Howie had tried to wash the flour from the rug. The resulting paste would not be sucked away. She fell to her knees and scraped with her fingernails. Flakes of dried dough collected in drifts. Yes, the carpet could be its old self. She scraped and vacuumed again and again, then sat on her heels, tears running down her face. Stop. She stored her cleaning equipment and glimpsed the flashing answering machine, calls her husband had not cleared. The first weak message: "Get here early, Theodora. Not much time." The voice gathered strength. "Don't be late as usual." Thea was back.

The second: "Just thinking of you, Mom. Call when you can." Tinkling clicks followed as Jesse's receiver brushed against her metal earrings, then silence.

The dark hours, dawn distant. Teddie piled living room pillows onto the breakfast nook cushions, and wrapped in her robe, settled where she'd found Jesse grappling with that boy.

CHAPTER • 16 •

At first light she slipped into the bathroom Zach and Jesse had shared with sibling acrimony. Another long shower, but too many doses of therapeutic water were turning her skin into sandpaper. She rubbed the old baby oil from the children's medicine cabinet onto her flaking self, rerobed, and tiptoed into the bedroom she'd always shared with her husband. One eye on Howie, she collected clothes and crept back to Jesse's room. Dry cleaning would have to wait, but being understood, being cared for gently, tenderly, would not.

Fortified with frozen orange juice, her heart rat-a-tatted as she set out for the Beekman Storage Tower. He was waiting. For her. Well, to be honest. He was waiting. For Liz. Today she'd take his portrait.

Thea's combination still worked. The elevator rose as she read her cardboard camera's directions. A pause to test Thea's lock, then straight to Michael's home. No sounds, no smells, no signs of life came through that metal door. Her tiny taps expanded and echoed in the empty corridor.

"Michael," she whispered. "It's me, Liz." The name, Liz, sounded like a hissing cannon shot.

"Shh," she heard, followed by the whisk of moving fabric. The door lifted.

"Hi," she said cheerily. Michael jerked her inside. She bent double to avoid being bisected by the half-open door. In a flash the door and the curtain were back in place. In the dimly lit gloom, his finger rose to his lips, then pointed at the clock. She heard approaching footsteps, the clink of metal on metal. Michael drove home the bolt; they were locked in. She opened her lips to speak, but he clamped his hand over her mouth. By what right? She tried to bite him, but her teeth merely scraped his fingers. The footsteps halted. The door shook.

Michael mouthed a silent word that looked like, "God." God's at the door? This man must be insane, although perhaps he'd said, "Guard," for she didn't want him to be crazy. The footsteps resumed, then faded. Five fingers aloft, he pointed again at the clock. If she read the clues, he wanted five minutes more of silence. She was terrible at charades. While Howie and the others shouted fanciful interpretations of Marla's mime movements, Teddie could only watch in clueless silence.

Michael motioned her towards a chair. She could stand or sit, and, it was true, she was shaking, so she sat, clutching her purse and her cardboard portrait camera. From the opposite chair, his eyes pinned her in place, and there they remained for five inter-minable minutes. She slipped her arms out of her old coat. She yawned. He put his finger to his lips. Silent yawns only. She yawned again, and uncontrollably again. She tried to suppress one, to swallow another, but they were irresistible. Under Michael's gaze, she put her purse and camera on the table and covered her gaping mouth with both hands while her eyes streamed.

Her chest heaved as she struggled to reach this yawn's, ulti-mate, tension-relieving climax. "You couldn't have picked a worse time," he said.

The final yawn aborted. "You were unspeakably rude," she replied.

"You are unspeakably thoughtless. Why do you think I gave you the surveillance schedule? You endangered my entire future! What were you thinking of?"

"You," she said. "I couldn't sleep. I wanted to see you."

He turned on lights and opened the window curtain to yet another painted sunny day, then retraced the few steps to her seat beneath his sleeping platform. "Whatever happens. Fate," he mut-tered. "What's wrong?"

"So much." She paused. "I mean I just moved, and this big assignment came out of nowhere and I couldn't turn it down. I thought of you while I was fixing a temporary darkroom, of how you've used every inch of space here." Teddie pulled Zach's drawing from her bag and thrust it at Michael. "Is this the best I can do? Do you have any ideas?"

"Hmm," he said and sat down. "You drew this, Liz?"

Teddie hesitated. "Yes. What do you think?" While Michael studied her son's drawing, she opened the cardboard camera's flash reflector and estimated her distance. She needed a yardstick to ensure the prescribed six feet. Take a chance, she thought when the battery light came on. She wound the film and contained his head in the view finder. "Michael?" she said and triggered the flash.

"What is that?"

"Someone wanted my professional advice on this contraption," Teddie said blithely, although why anyone would want a court reporter's opinion about a cardboard and plastic camera was beyond her. Take more than one picture, its box had insisted self-servingly. "Let me take another." This time she checked the background—books, good—and pressed the button.

"Let me take you. Over by the window," he insisted. She snapped his smart, boyish face again, surrendered the cardboard box and let him have his way. "Clever," he said after two shots. "Now, stand sideways. I want your lovely profile." Teddie swiveled on command. Mug shots finished, Michael lunged. "Take off your clothes," he said breathing heavily. "I need to see the rest of you." He pulled at her suit jacket.

"The plan," Teddie stammered. "What do you think?"

"I think the plan was your little excuse. You know what you're doing. You said you're a pro." He gripped her tightly.

"You're right," Teddie half-shouted. "That's why I need to go. My appointment." He would not let go, indeed, his right hand was inside her bra kneading her bare breast. She quivered. Innocence turned lust. "I'm sorry I came at a bad time," she pled. Footsteps returned out of silence.

He released her. The clock read eight fifteen. The feet sounded jaunty, not the shuffle of a guard. Teddie put her finger to her lips, checked her buttons, and reached for her coat. The feet passed. She took up her camera and purse. Suffocating, she bent to unfasten Michael's bolt. Not what she'd planned. What had she planned?

"Did I do something wrong, Liz?" he asked, suddenly shy.

"No, I don't know. I'm late," she muttered as his hand stroked her back.

"You'll come back soon? I have so few pleasures."

She squeezed under the partially raised door. Michael bent double to wave. She stroked the air in return. With the bravado of freedom, she blew a kiss, then quick-stepped away. Her nervous wait ended with the swoosh of closing doors, and Teddie was behind her steering wheel before she remembered she had left Zach's drawing. Taking a pad of paper from her briefcase, she drew what she remembered, except that she couldn't remember much, and her trembling pencil-holding hand traced weak wobbles.

Her hand shook as she turned the ignition key. She could not, did not want to think. Thea had insisted *she* needed her, but this morning Teddie needed food more than her mother needed her. A brilliantly lit family restaurant was only two stoplights away. Breakfast all day, the sign said. She would eat breakfast all day. And then something would happen. She would not provoke it.

Teddie ordered the one-two-three-four. One bottomless cup of coffee, two eggs over easy, three table-sized pancakes, four strips of bacon. The pancakes she slathered with butter and syrup. For ten minutes she concentrated on eating until the waistband of her skirt burst, but she rescued the button before it could escape under the table. He had wanted her naked. She'd dreamed of him undressed, or was it the shining torso in Jesse's room? Pheromones. Sexual attractants. The unknown. Fear. Disease. Go, go, go, go, STOP. And she had. Michael's eyes were the most remarkable blue. He wanted her.

Three times Teddie signalled for her bill until the waitress pointed it out, translucent with butter, sticky with syrup, close by the pink packets of sugar substitute. Four dollars and eight cents total, and a tip of course, that's all. She tossed Howie's credit card onto the bill, but the waitress ignored the plastic. "Sorry, love. No cards. No checks."

Teddie stared at her blankly.

"New management rule. Cash only. See the sign?" and indeed, the sign also sat next to the sugar substitute. "I didn't know," Teddie mumbled, green eyes round as marbles. "What if. . . ." she started. "I'll look," she finished. The waitress left. A search through her wallet and all the pockets of her purse produced two dollars and six cents. The bottom of her bag contributed a large safety pin, a shredded tissue, a Shop and Save receipt, a pencil. From a deep corner, she fished up six pennies. Surely, only experts washed dishes in modern restaurants; she couldn't operate machines, but she could wait tables. How long would it take? Thea would be very angry. Her left coat pocket produced a crumpled dollar bill which she smoothed and anchored with the heap of coins. Taking her coat and purse, she stood, nodded to no one, and mouthed, "Right back." No one stopped her as she cheated the family restaurant of ninety-six cents.

Soon Teddie was knocking on her mother's door. "Stop scratching." Perched on Hermes, Thea swiveled and rose. "Watch!" and she spun the machine in a slow circle, then reversed, stopping several times to snap finger-framed photographs. With a warmed Fun and Easy in hand, standing an estimated six feet from Thea, Teddie raised her camera. Her mother ignored the impossibly bright flash.

"Stop playing around. Hand me my camera," Thea ordered. "We'll be late."

"Do I need my coat?" Teddie asked as she struggled to pin her waistband.

"Am I wearing a coat? Think. Exercise. Give me the little camera." Shocked by the privilege, Teddie raised the small Nikon in both hands. It was heavy. She might drop it. Thea snatched when her camera was in range and slipped the strap over her neck. "Open the door."

Confused, carrying her cardboard thirty-five millimeter, Teddie chased after her mother. Thea, one heavy camera hung around her neck, another stashed in Hermes' basket, maneuvered her machine with complete disregard for the eggshell white walls. A new black mark scored the entry to the elevator. Thea punched number one.

"Howie said you had a personal trainer. Why are you going to exercise?" Thea's look was withering.

"So gullible," Thea said, shadowing Teddie's thoughts. "To capture their courage and degradation." They hurried past meeting rooms where women knitted without watching, where white heads circled bridge tables. Exercise class members lowered themselves stiffly onto functional waterproof chairs. A child Jesse's age, perfect body and legs encased in electric blue spandex, torso in a skimpy layer of neon stripes, counted foam balls and oversized rubber bands. A husky woman Teddie's age stood beside her. A bent man waved at Thea. A woman with a bitter, deeply wrinkled face (cigarettes and sun, Teddie thought) followed his gaze and brightened.

Thea aimed her camera at the sun-smoker. "They like you," Teddie said, but Thea ignored her. She shot a sleeping dormouse with sparse, fluffy hair. She spun her seat towards the blue spandex and shot while the girl stretched and twisted her agile young body, then turned with a bright, empty smile to the class of elastic-stockinged, hearing-aided, movement-impaired.

"Good morning, everyone," the matron shouted. "This morning we have a treat. Suzy, my niece, is visiting. She has her own aerobics studio and knows everything about movement. Give her a welcome." Scattered applause.

"Good morning, class," Suzie sang. "What a beautiful day!" Their gymnasium-like meeting room had no windows. The elderly were forbidden to smash glass with their foam balls and canes.

"Good morning, Suzie!" two front-row women answered.

"Raise your arms and stretch. Good morning, sun. Good morning, world." Suzie followed her own directions while half her students approximated her motions. The rest watched Thea. "Now, let's do our routine." Teddie watched Thea focus on two women in the second row whose heads were touching. One had just passed the other a color snapshot when Suzie's throbbing, booming music filled the room; the women clutched their ears, faces masks of exquisite pain. Thea's camera caught their anguish as they dialed their hearing aides into silence.

"Left, right, left, right, arms up, arms down, all RIGHT!" Suzie shouted. "Now legs, show me what you're made of, left, right," and in amazing movements she touched her forehead with her electric blue knees. Her seated students shuffled their feet. Watching, observing, shooting, Thea rolled around on Hermes as if she were stalking game. Do not frighten the animals. Sun-smoker coughed, a deep wrenching bark, and keeping her eyes on the woman, Thea reached into the basket for her second camera. Teddie moved swiftly to help. Heavier than the first by far, how were Thea's scrawny arms going to support the weight of her art? Teddie slipped the strap over her mother's head. If Thea dropped this camera, she'd be dragged to the floor, but she did not falter.

Teddie could not keep up with her mother's eyes. Randomly she snapped the plastic shutter of her Fun and Easy. Teacher Suzie ignored them, although the two women, one with a safety pin holding up her skirt, the other, circling the class on an electric scooter, might have distracted anyone less committed. Suzie danced and tossed multicolored balls into the class. The students fumbled and dropped instead of catching with grace, although a pink sphere plopped directly into the surprised dormouse's lap. The music's driving beat shifted and slowed. The coughing smoker retrieved an inhaler from her handbag and breathed in a draught of medication.

"Everything okay?" a middle-aged, blue-blazered security man shouted into the din. Thea swiveled Hermes and snapped him. "What are you doing?" he barked like an ex-cop expecting wrong-doing. Implied guilt riveted Teddie to the spot, but Hermes rolled forward to catch a better angle. "You got permission?" He approached Thea threateningly.

"Theodora, come here! We're finished. Take the cameras." Teddie sprang free, unlooped the straps from her mother's neck, and returned the cameras to the basket. Suzie exhorted and pranced while her students watched Thea drive Hermes at the security man who was standing his ground, legs apart, arms akimbo. "Don't dawdle, Theodora." Thea stayed her course until the guard jumped out of her motorized path. "We'll be late for tea with Daphne."

CHAPTER • 17 •

The security guard reached into his coat. "Stop!" he ordered. Thea turned Hermes hard right. Teddie trotted after her mother. Another gun? "Halt!" he shouted, but they did not halt until they were safe in the elevator and Teddie found herself giggling.

Thea chuckled, then they both laughed recklessly. "Africa all over again. It was a ceremony for women. You remember, the girl who'd killed a chicken. The witch doctor claimed I was sucking power from him and ordered me to leave."

"You were, weren't you?"

"What? Oh, yes, sucking power. Of course."

"That poor man's authority will never be the same," Teddie observed. "Now, do you have enough power to make this thing rise by itself, or should I push a button? Where does Daphne live?"

"Daphne?"

"Tea with Daphne. You said we were late."

"Let's go home. I was lying," Thea said. "I decided to sound civilized. Tea is so civilized. Daphne is not. We'll see her. Later."

In the apartment Thea dismounted, and Teddie asked what should be done with the cameras.

"Put them next to my chair," was Thea's amazing answer.

Was this teamwork? Teddie raised the larger camera to her eye.

What was she looking for? Gently she placed Thea's tools on the table, then drove Hermes to rest. When his power source had been joined to the Carleton's, Thea was back in her chair. That weakness, her spells, only bad dreams. She's eighty-five, she can tire, but she won't fail.

The door bell tinkled, a sound Thea claimed made her taste saccharine. "Well, open it," she ordered. A nervous boy pretending to be a man in a suit and an oversized bowtie waited.

"Is Thea Waterford in?"

"Whom may I say is calling," her mother's aging gatekeeper responded.

"It's only Frank." Teddie stepped aside. Frank's eyes took in the photos, paused at Georgio in the garden, and came to rest on Thea.

"Director Olson told me to apologize."

"That's very nice, Frank. For which of her transgressions?"

"About today. Security hadn't been briefed about your project. There's been talk. You're colorful. . . ."

"Euphemism for troublemaker."

". . . a colorful troublemaker, but he didn't know you were an artist doing a story on the Carleton."

"Not the Carleton. Age, the people who live here."

"What about permission? Do they *want* to be included in a Rossotti's book?" The famous picture of despairing Aurora on a doorstep wearing a hat of twisted cotton underpants flashed through Teddie's mind.

"My daughter, Theodora. She works with legal things."

"Ms. Waterford has permission to take what she likes photographically speaking. It's all included in her contract, a clause our lawyers drew up. And we are allowed to use four pictures, her statements, and her name on one promotional brochure. Our tenants sign releases with their leases, although photos of the few who refuse will be eliminated. Her fame. Her artistry." Teddie shook her head and grinned at Thea who was doing something to one of her cameras. The Carleton would not want to print any of Thea's pronouncements about her current residence.

"I wonder where I'll live when I do the next book, the one on adolescent rituals," Thea mused.

"I'm sure Jesse would be glad to have you. Did you know her house is purple? They must have been giving the paint away."

"Director Olson wants to know if there is anything she can do for you, anything you need," Frank said hurriedly. "Can I help you? Hold your cameras? I would be honored to load your film."

"Thank-you, Frank. My daughter is a perfectly good assistant—ignorant, but trainable. You tell Director Olson I'll remember her offer. Theodora, take a portrait of him, your little camera." Teddie powered her Fun and Easy, framed and snapped, then saw Frank to the door. Before leaving, he pumped her hand and told her how lucky she was.

"I make my own luck," she said. "I'll see you get a copy of your picture. I was afraid that man was going to shoot us."

"I'll talk to him right away. I know Director Olson already has," and Frank crab-walked down the corridor.

Thea opened her eyes. "You thought you'd caught the old woman asleep, didn't you? Wrong again. Sleep." She waved her hand. "I've never needed more than a few hours a night. Never napped. For babies."

But these days drifting off in the midst of swirling activity was to be expected.

"It's cold. Get my shawl. That's a good girl," but Teddie was suffocating. The thermostat read eighty-one tropical degrees. Clothes littered Thea's bedroom. The greasy fringe of the Spanish shawl reeked of aging lamb, but Teddie pulled a fleecy sweater from a drawer and hurried to sleeping Thea. Gently she tucked the warm wool around her mother's shoulders. Thea murmured plaintively, as if to herself. "What's happening? I feel, I'm. . . ."

"What's wrong? Should I get a doctor?" Teddie's fingers remembered what it felt like to touch those bones.

"No. . . hope. . . ." Thea's blue eyes were filmed.

"You're fine. Just tired. You worked hard this morning. You've never been afraid of a little hard work." Gut watery with fear, she could not allow herself to think that word, the final one. Would she be guilty if Thea died here? She should do something, but she could do nothing. Helpless, she knelt on the carpet and wrapped her warm hands around her mother's icy fingers. The heavy, hot air was quiet. Thea breathed on—shallow, bird-breaths, but she was alive, again unconscious. Teddie lay her head on her mother's lap and joined her in sleep.

Her left leg was numb when she woke. Her neck was stiff. She was being watched.

"Do you know how heavy you are, Theodora?" she heard,

though Thea's imperiousness had lost its sharpness. Teddie struggled to stand, but her leg collapsed. Her safety pin popped. "I can't
remember what we were talking about," Thea said. "Oh yes, Frank
was here to apologize. I have an errand for you."

The anguish of sensation returning to her foot brought Teddie
to herself. "Errand?" she asked.

"Do as I say. Take this to PhotoPro." Thea handed over two
rolls of film. "In Ann Arbor. Ask for Walter. No one else. Tell them
Thea Waterford insists. He was my darkroom assistant—you don't
remember—attractive young man, ambitious but no imagination,
you know the type, you married one. He knows what to do. Insist
on proofsheets tomorrow."

"What about your darkroom? The stuff in the basement."

"I'm in a hurry. Now go. Leave me alone."

Dismissed, Teddie stumbled into the bathroom, washed, reset
her skirt pin, and ran a comb through her hair. She looked
disheveled, but fresh somehow, like a child after a nap.

No one answered when she called home. Howie was gone. The
place was hers.

Thea's naked rolls of film frightened her. She'd trip. She'd fail.
With great care she slid them into an envelope from her mother's
desk. Napping Thea's mouth drooped, her breathing unchanged
while Teddie collected the rancid shawl and closed the blue door.

o o o

The previous night couldn't have been real. Had Howie actually held her down to force tranquilizers down her throat? She'd
made that bed, Jesse's bed, this morning. Back in the master bedroom, she collected the cleaning, stripped off her Eva Martin suit
and put on a full skirt and a comfortable top. Good. How much
would Howie send Aurora? She didn't care if he paid for her sister's
shopping services, but eventually she had to take care of her own
affairs—five thousand three hundred and eighty- two dollars. And
today she'd stiffed a family restaurant. She wanted a new coat.
She'd take Jesse shopping.

No human answer in the purple house, but she left a message.
PhotoPro and Walter were waiting.

o o o

Walter fawned over Theodora Waterford's fifty-year-old messenger daughter. He insisted she inspect his facilities, the enlarging machines, the personalized trays of stinking chemicals, the flowing waterbaths, the dark-lighted rooms. This combination of high-technology and sorcerer's art is what she had taken upon herself to reproduce in the Carleton's basement. What had she been thinking of? And yet, and yet, Walter was only preserving a slice of visual reality, just as she, as a professional, preserved spoken reality; neither made judgments; both relied on accurate input for their truths, for sand-shifting, ever-drifting truths. The experts would search their products for flawed imperfections or shining revelations, but she and Walter were only technically-adept middlemen. Dullards both, not Thea Waterford, not even Jack Sullivan.

Such imaginative stirrings were not pleasant.

o o o

On the library's icy wall the homeless still swore and smoked. Strange to think that across town her blood was being assayed for lethal intruders. She was disintegrating, scattering. Perhaps she should visit Bob, but she needed her father.

"I want to find someone, but I don't know much about him. What do I do?" she asked the information librarian.

"Thea Waterford's husband? Let's start with *Who's Who*." Somehow those editors had uncovered Maude Slote, listing her under Thea's entry as having married Theo Waterford some fifty-four years ago. "Maude Slote," the librarian mused. "I never would have known. No divorce mentioned. He was a rare book dealer." Teddie nodded. "They cherish rarities." Thea fit that category. "Let's try something else. Come on."

Perhaps he was around the corner, the father who'd given her Tiger Poo, a man she'd never known. He would make her whole. Her love was primitive, formless, without a single memory.

"Now we're cooking!" The librarian's finger held a page. "In 1965 he had a store in Detroit, the Gray Wolf. I bet our director knows the place. Too bad, he's at a conference this week. Well, you can talk to him later."

"Nineteen sixty-five," Teddie wailed. "What about now? Where is he?"

The librarian eyed Teddie. "I know it's none of my business, but why do you want to find him?"

"My father," Teddie said. "I'm named for him, never knew him."

"Do you think he's alive? His bookstore's gone. See?" Neither his name or the store's was in the most recent edition of *American Bookdealers*.

"But it doesn't say he's dead. They say he and Thea are married. They have children."

"Make a copy of the page. Take that. Try cross-referencing his name with newspaper obituaries. Bookdealers seldom retire." The librarian was finished. "I hope you find what you want."

She copied the two entries, but couldn't bring herself to do the obituary part. Putting *American Bookdealers* back on the shelf, a threatening, unpleasant sensation prickled the back of her neck. A nearby man, jeans and down jacket, old, her age, leafed through one book, took up another, but his sideways glances were for her. She shoved the papers into her bag and escaped.

It wasn't surprising that the purple house's door was unlocked. The living room was cluttered with television, sound system, mattresses, uncomfortable chairs. With no desire to enter the kitchen, Teddie switched on the television and arranged pillows on a mattress. The talk show host cheered her guests on to reveal their personal degradations and abuses in their searches for, for . . . something. The sad-eyed woman with the failed breast implants said she had been enhancing her self-image. "I loved my breasts," she mourned. The tattooed eyeliner of another had become so infected that her lashes had fallen out. "Take off the false ones, honey, so we can see what you look like today. It's okay. You're with friends," and the hostess winked at the audience, which gasped and applauded the naked, scarred eyes. Teddie turned off the sound and closed her own eyes.

"Mom? You okay?"

Jesse was reassuringly herself, blonde hair gleaming silver, gold nose ring reflecting the dancing light of the television tube. "Tired. Thea sent me on an errand. You weren't in."

Jesse joined Teddie on the mattress. "Last night I dreamed about you, you were lost, I was trying to find you."

"Strange. I was safe and sound in your bed, well, almost safe. I had a tantrum and threw food around the kitchen, just like you used to. Your room seemed right."

Jesse frowned.

"Do you have time to go shopping? I need a new coat, have for years. You must need something. How about some bright colors?

You look funereal."

"Oh, Mom. Like I said, I'm fashion. How's Thea?" In the car Teddie told her daughter about the photography session and shared what she'd learned about her daughter's grandfather. Their route took them past the Health Department.

"Did Zach tell you he brought me in for testing?" Teddie said. "Thank God he's negative. I'll find out on Saturday."

Jesse's eyes widened. "Are you worried? I thought you did it because of the police. You been sharing needles or something?" The girl hesitated. "It's Dad, isn't it? I mean, he's never been exactly a one-woman man. Is he okay?"

"He's the way he's always been, except I scare him. Healthy. Of course he looks healthy. He claims he'll get tested, but only as a favor. Can I spend the night with you? Thea's proofs will be ready in the morning. It would save a trip."

Jesse threw her arms around the tweed coat. "Sure. One condition. Tell Dad where you are."

"Okay. You do it. You don't talk to him enough." Teddie wondered what he'd think if she said she'd bumped into an old friend, one who'd always found her irresistible. Jack Sullivan. Or she could say she had to pay back the trucker who'd paid for her one-two-three-four breakfast—her body being the price. No. Let Howie think what he wants. "We both will, if he's home. Now help me find something life-transforming."

CHAPTER • 18 •

The skies would remain leaden and chill for weeks, but the best stores already had sent their winter coats to places summer reigned. "If you won't try surplus, Mom, I know a great secondhand store. That's where I shop. The Salvation Army always has coats."

They strolled past mannequins disporting under umbrellas in bright cruise wear. "No more secondhand. Never again." Teddie shuddered.

"When did you ever wear used clothes? You never talk about growing up. It's like you and Aunt Aurora were born full-grown."

Teddie faced her daughter. "We weren't. I remember everything, but I'd be much happier forgetting. It's a miracle we survived. Maybe we didn't. I learned how to be a walking zombie."

"Hey, what's happening?"

"I don't know. I don't know. Can we sit down? Did you have lunch?" Jesse shook her head. "Me either," Teddie said. "It's almost dinnertime."

"Tea. I know a place. We can get little sandwiches and cakes. Very elegant. Like us," Jesse said. She linked her arm with her mother's and tugged. "Come on, Mom. I'm hungry."

"So am I, but what do I want?" Teddie wondered aloud. "Tea's a place to start."

At the combination bakery and tea shop at the far end of the mall, they ordered the regular assortment for two, then added extra cream puffs, raspberry tarts, and slices of devil's food cake. Teddie wondered how Jesse's sylphlike body could contain the calories. She looked like a modern copy of Thea running through the park. And until two days ago, before being shown her father's wedding photograph, when she'd bothered to consider images, she'd known only that she was unlike her mother. When Zach had come along, she and her son were a pair. Jesse was simply a beautiful child. Now they were matched up, links to earlier generations. And of course Thea complained often enough that Teddie was just like her father, whatever that meant. Yet she needed to find the source of so much confusion, their shared names, Thea, Theo, Theodora. . . .

"Mom? What's wrong?"

"I was thinking how beautiful you are," she replied slowly, "even with that thing in your nose, and how much you look like Thea."

"You look like your father, at least that picture Thea showed us. Had you seen it before?"

"Never. I know it's impossible, but Thea's mellowing. We weren't allowed to mention his name. In private Aurora told me stories about what he was doing and when he was coming to get us. To me it was play."

"Was Grandmother jealous? I mean it sounded like Aunt Aurora wanted to be with him if she cried and cried after she came home." Jesse used a teaspoon to extract the cream puff filling she licked like a lollipop.

"Thea with human emotions? To me she was an ice goddess who lived on a higher plain. I got frostbite whenever I approached."

"Is that what you mean about growing up? She must be changing. I mean she's so weak and old. Sometimes she's nice." Jesse poured herself another cup of tea. Teddie gestured for her daughter to refill her cup. Both took sugar and milk.

"She'll never give up her power. Remember how it hurt when she dismissed your life as adolescent rituals? She has some instinct to climb over others, to rise to the top. What she destroys doesn't matter. 'Why are you so upset?' she'd ask us. 'You know it was for the best. It's not personal.' And you're demeaning the goddess by suggesting she could be jealous of her little daughter's love for her husband? Really. You may be right," Teddie finished.

"Old Dr. Freud would say, 'Mmmhmmm.' We've been studying him in Modern Thought, only I think he's not really modern. The unconscious. I mean everyone knows about the unconscious. And all that Greek myth stuff." Jesse stroked her nose ring.

"Jes, what does Modern Thought say about lying? Is it evil? Is it okay?" Two questions without answers.

Jesse's eyes widened. "I don't remember that subject coming up. What are you talking about?"

"Me. My lies. I decided to, last week, for the first time. Now I'm doing it without thinking. I told a man my name was Liz, Liz Gutleben, and let him believe I was a professional photographer. I've lied to Aurora, to strangers, to Thea, of course never to myself, sometimes little lies to make my life easier, but now they're growing. Today I cheated a family restaurant. I pretended I'd paid the bill, but I didn't have enough money. I left a pile of change, said I'd be right back, and walked out." Jesse was a good listener. "There's more. Do you want to hear it?"

"I don't want it to get too sordid."

"Do you remember having tantrums? Zach was so calm, but you screamed and yelled and threw anything your little arms could lift. You kicked, too. Last night I was so mad at your father. . . ."

"You told me you had a tantrum. You, the great calm one? You really blew up at Dad? Why?"

"I don't know. Everything, a lifetime." Teddie chased a nugget of devil's food around her plate. "They say it's menopause. All I know is that exploding felt fine, even wonderful. Should we get something more?" Mother and daughter surveyed the battered remains of their tea.

"Did you see those strawberries?" Jesse asked.

"Better, I smelled them. Like summer. Unreal. Let's share." Teddie signaled a gray-haired waitress, made sure they took credit cards, and ordered.

Jesse popped the first into her mouth whole. Teddie held the frill of green leaves in her fingers and bit into the sweet, dimpled fruit, then sucked the red juice before it could run down her hand.

"Good decision, Mom. Now tell me, what happened when you got mad at Dad?"

"Which time? Once I threw groceries all over the kitchen. I stabbed a bag of flour and heaved it into the dining room. It was wonderful, spirals of white powder filling the air, covering that dumb rug I've always hated."

"You hate that rug, too? It always seemed so self-important. You worried about our dropping food on it, as if it would criticize you if we did something wrong."

"Not surprising. Thea's wedding present. Howie picked it out. And I protected it. No more. Maybe it can go in his study and I can start fresh."

"Might have to cut some off, but that could be fun," Jesse added.

"Tell me why you had tantrums, Jesse," Teddie pleaded. "I hate the hormone answer, but I'm coming apart."

"How do I know? I got mad, still do, and you were so calm and Dad kept saying he understood, but no one knew what it was like to be me. It was so frustrating. Finally I'd explode."

Teddie licked her fingers and put her hand on her child's arm. "I'm sorry, thanks. I promise to be less calm. We could be partners in rage."

"Are you telling the truth or lying, Mom? I mean, before last week did you always tell the truth? Not me. Never. Impossible! At least I always could trust you, which is more than I can say for other people."

"Too many questions. No answers. No toothbrush, either. Let's get going. We should call your father. I feel better." Her interior furniture had come to rest, rearranged but mostly undamaged, after an emotional earthquake along unknown fault lines. Perhaps it didn't matter whose fault it was. If she could accept this moment of peace she might be able to plan a future, but her mental earth shook at the very idea of a future. No, only now.

They returned to the purple house with a toothbrush and expensive lingerie—underwear, Teddie insisted on calling it—for both, all silk and lace and rich colors. "If you have to wear mourning," Teddie told her daughter, "next to your skin you'll have your true colors. No one has to know." But someone is most likely to find out. She wished she could hold her daughter safe, but she also wanted Jesse to explain why the man she'd lied to had lusted after her mother. Would Jesse have been as frightened, saved only by footsteps from. . . .

A soundless game show was on the empty living room's television when Jesse shouted down the stairs. "Aunt Aurora answered," she announced. "She wants to talk to you. Dad's there, too. Take that extension. I want to listen."

Teddie's face flamed. Sweat dripped into her eyes as she switched on the cordless phone. "What are *you* doing there?" she snarled into the mouthpiece.

"You're so right, Howie dear," Aurora's voice said. "But I don't think she's dangerous. Not enough imagination. I flew in this afternoon at your husband's request. He's sitting in his study, very worried about you. He says you're irrational and a naughty. . . ."

"For godsake, Aurora, 'naughty'? I've been grandly, wonderfully angry. That's mad. As in fed up. With you, with Howie, with my job, with Jack Sullivan. . . ."

"I knew I'd get to the bottom of it. Sisters always do," Aurora laughed. "Jackie. Say no more." Teddie felt herself split. Her calm, rearranged self coolly observed the angry, frustrated child who saw red—bubbling molten lava, spurting blood, a witch's cauldron.

"Dad, are you there? I guess everything's been so busy you didn't get her message. I mean we planned this last week, shopping and tea and everything."

Jesse is so good, Teddie thought calmly, but she kept her eye on the red, roiling cauldron. "Yes," she chorused. "I left a note in the kitchen. You must have lost it when you put away the groceries." Oh, that's nice, blame squared, Teddie thought, admiring her growing talents. Instead of a court reporter, she'd be a professional storyteller.

"When are you coming home, Ted?" Separated from his handsome body and beard, Howie's voice sounded like a scared teenager's.

"I had to do an errand for Thea, too, bring film to a lab here in town. It'll be ready tomorrow. Jesse suggested I spend the night. The weather forecast isn't particularly good, you know." Teddie hadn't read a weather forecast since Thea's reception and Zach's first safe return to Kalamazoo.

"Hah. Thea would never let you touch her film," Aurora said. "Howie, she's having an affair!"

"Don't be silly," Teddie said. "She trusted me to take her film to Walter, maybe you remember him, Aurora. He showed me his darkrooms. I'll pick up her proofs tomorrow." Nyah, nyah, nyah, so there. "I wouldn't accuse anyone of having affairs if I were you."

"What time will you be home?" Howie's wide-eyed voice repeated.

"Late afternoon. I'll be tired. You get dinner. Thea and I are working."

"I could call the Red Dragon. Do you want hot and sour soup?" Teddie had to admit her husband had learned something this last week. With practice and study he still might be able to pass Order Out I.

"By the way," Aurora's disembodied voice inserted, "you can stop worrying. Your husband's paid your bill. He's so sweet." She'd known it would happen, but still she felt shamed. Just when she was breaking free, Howie had locked her in debt.

"We'll see," Teddie muttered, then added brightly, "Good night you two. One of Jesse's friends needs the phone, so I'll hang up," and she did in the deserted room, feet rooted to the same spot she'd stood when she first picked up the cordless phone. Freed by technology to roam where she willed, habit held her fast.

Identical housemates wearing jeans, parkas and backpacks swept into the living room, and froze as if they'd come upon a nasty surprise, the police, or a rotting carcass. "Jesse let me in," she said. "Guess I'm intruding."

"Don't mind them, Mom. They never learned manners." Jesse at her side, Teddie stuck out her hand and introduced herself. Automatically they shook her hand and escaped.

"Sure it's okay?" Teddie asked. "I can go to a motel or something." She did not want to go to a motel with a brown paper bag for luggage.

"We're not the Hilton, but I'm game. We'll have to share my bedroom."

"Is there space for both of us? I didn't bring a shovel and after last night. . . ."

"Yes, you were in my room," Jesse remembered. "Why?"

"I told you. I was falling apart. I hid out after I threw the flour. Some interesting books you have, Kate Chopin, for one. Never heard of her."

"Yeah. She was a Women's Lit course, but what was Aunt Aurora talking about? What bill?" Jesse walked into the kitchen. Like a duckling, Teddie followed. Jesse's housemates might be afraid she was from the Health Department. Teddie explained the shopping service, the fifty per-cent markup, her need to pay her own way. Could Jesse understand the latter? Weren't husbands supposed to take care of their wives, to love and cherish and feed and clothe til death do them part? But her daughter did understand. "You want to pay Dad back? Like six thousand dollars or so? How much can you get on your own credit cards?"

"Nothing. Never had any."

Jesse shook her head. "That's dumb. You always could get one, but right now you could use a loan. How about that man at dinner, Thea's lover? He was into money."

"Georgio! I have his card." Her living substitute father. The man with pheromones.

"So do I," Jesse said.

"I'll call," Teddie said as she rummaged in her purse. "Here it is." More residents of the purple house returned, but with her daughter's protection, they only passed Teddie as if she were a shadow. Did they wonder why the phone was floating in the air?

A woman answered. "Is Georgio Aponopolis there? This is Theodora Olds." Teddie sounded small and shy, as if forty-two years had slipped off her. The voice said she would see, and then he was there, unlike Howie, with competence and strength in his voice.

"Twice in a single week!" he exclaimed. "The gods bless me. Where are you, Teddie?"

"With Jesse, here in Ann Arbor, just tonight. I'm helping Thea."

"I'm here, too," Jesse said into another phone.

"Wonderful. Can we get together?" Georgio asked. "I'm not far away and free tonight. How about you?"

"What time?"

"Whenever you get here."

"Yes." Jesse said. "Give me directions. Mom has a car."

CHAPTER • 19 •

Jesse navigated them through the rolling hills shaped by melting glaciers, their headlights picking out street names until the signs ran out. "Not far," Jesse claimed, but it seemed as if they'd been driving through night dark forever before they turned up a graveled road to a fenced yard on a hilltop. Georgio's frozen garden was crusted with snow.

"A woman answered," Teddie said. "He wasn't married last week. But if we find him so attractive, why not others?"

"Would he be unfaithful to us? Come on. Remember, you need financial advice." Jesse's voice sounded hard.

"It's your Dr. Freud at work, I suspect. Not mine, you notice. I wonder if I should tell the truth. Why should I object to my husband paying my bills?"

"Because you do. It's something to do with integrity, with self-ownership. We'll play it by ear." Jesse's boots crunched down the path. Georgio stood framed in light before they could ring.

"I saw your headlights," he said. "Welcome." His house glowed with firelight and warm colors. Had he done his own decorating? Artwork was everywhere, groupings on the wall included those photographs, not Georgio in his garden, but the well-known weeping Aurora on the stairs and another Teddie couldn't remember. She patted her cardboard portrait camera as she strolled around the living room until she reached the picture of a sturdy child, curly hair and too-short coat blowing in a punishing wind, coat sleeves ending inches above her thick wrists. The girl seemed emotionless, solid, immovable. "I look like a rock," Teddie said. "That was in the park, wasn't it?"

"Yes. Near our house," Georgio said. "When we were together."

"Over forty years ago!"

"You looked trustworthy back then, too, Mom. Someone you could count on." Teddie opened her mouth to speak, but Jesse silenced her with a warning headshake. "I needed that when I was growing up. Zach, too."

The fire hissed and threw sparks as Georgio put on another log. In this beautiful room with her daughter and almost-father, Teddie felt encased in a transparent bubble, able to see and be seen, to hear and be heard, but alone, beyond being touched. So she had moved through life, duty after duty, transcribing word after word, her frozen existence preserved by the slivers of ice beneath her rosy skin.

"Thea's working again," Teddie announced. Her mother's unwanted downtimes had been painful for everyone. Her productive life was over, Thea would insist. Pity me, pity me, she commanded. Those within hearing range were obligated to nurse her ego until she announced herself cured, her powers replenished. Only then could Thea take on another assignment. "She sends her love," Teddie lied, or perhaps she did not.

"I worry about her," Georgio said. "Even surrounded by people, she's alone." White hairs curled upwards from the confines of his shirt collar. Was he white from head to toe under his clothes, a civilized ghost?

"Not so alone," Jesse said brightly. "You should have seen us Sunday. We terrorized a medical equipment store and Thea bought an electric scooter."

"She needs it. Her body is, well, is, she's getting weak," Teddie finished in a rush. "She can get around to work with the scooter."

"The machine could not have been her idea. Come, sit down, tell me. Would you like a drink? Something to eat?" Warm cinnamon cookies and a glass of milk flashed through Teddie's mind, but she followed her daughter's example and asked for white wine. They sank into the leather couch. How long since she'd eagerly gulped her first strong drink of the day as the sun sank low in the afternoon sky? Her new life allowed no time for the ritual dosing that had marked her married years. A silent servant brought their wine as well as a plate of crackers, cheese, and cookies. *Those* cookies.

"What happened to your mother?" Teddie asked, for the girls had accepted the hospitality of strangers without backward looks or thank-you notes. "She was so kind to us."

"She'd be ninety-five today, ten years older than Thea, years unimportant in midlife, but counted by months and minutes at the far end. One morning she wouldn't get up and finally she faded away. She always remembered your short stay with her. I'm afraid I did my best to forget. Thea. How she hurt me when she left."

Teddie passed the plate, then nibbled her second cookie. Good with wine, who would have thought, and with the cookie came questions about the magic Thea had wrought to get others to take care of her offspring. Did she speak lies? Or did she provide the cruel truth, that she lived for her work and her misbegotten children were an interference. Teddie neither lived for recording the words of lawyers and witnesses nor did she expect her adult children to defeat her loneliness on more than the rare occasion.

Jesse was describing their medical supply slalom. "Bet they'd get a lot more customers if they made it a competition—kind of like those Monster Big Wheel Rallies." Georgio and Jesse laughed and looked at Teddie. "Like you said, it was Mom's idea. She did it, but Thea doesn't know."

"Georgio, what would you say to an old friend who needed maybe six thousand dollars. A sure investment?" Teddie asked, she hoped with innocence.

"If he or she were a genuine friend, I'd say there are no sure investments, only gambles with weighted risks. I'd have to evaluate those risks."

Embarrassment reddened her face. A burning log popped and spit a red ember on the brick hearth.

"Was Thea worth the risk for you? Aurora and I had no choice." Teddie rose and ground the fire out of the loose coal. In the dancing light she spied a dark wood mask with shark-sharp teeth and hollow, round eyes, a cousin of her scarified familiar.

"Weighing monetary risks is possible, but difficult. Measuring human risks is elusive at best. What good are my regrets? She's embedded in me. Part of me."

Good. "You know working agrees with her. She hasn't been

shopping for ten or twenty years, but now she wants some new clothes." Teddie stumbled. "She's never had money, but you know her financial situation better than I. She never tells me anything." Careful. Don't whine.

"Aunt Aurora loves to shop. She'll buy what Grandmother needs, but money's the problem. It's no good asking her." Jesse stopped, frowning.

"You flatter me that I'm familiar with Thea's financial situation. Once I invested a windfall for her. Still, it would give me pleasure to contribute to Thea's future." Georgio refilled their wine glasses. "I'll be right back."

"What's he doing?" Teddie asked softly.

"Getting his checkbook," Jesse answered. "What now?"

"Leave it to me."

"What are you whispering?" Georgio returned, leather-covered folder in hand. He sipped his wine. "One thousand should be enough for now. I'll make it to Aurora who does the shopping. It will be our secret surprise."

"Not to Aurora," Teddie ordered. "To Thea."

"Of course. To Thea. You deposit it in her account. Tell Aurora to buy strong, bold, beautiful things, nothing artificial, no pinks, no pastel flowers."

"Thea would make Aunt Aurora eat pastel clothes. That's all you see at the Carleton, that and blue and green polyester pantssuits."

"Exercise clothes, too, pink and gray sweats, but you didn't see the exercise class we photographed today. Thea took on a security guard who didn't know how important she was. She drove straight at him. That's why I'm spending the night in town, to bring her proofs back tomorrow."

While he wrote the check, Teddie powered her cardboard portrait camera, brought it to her eye, and framing Georgio in the plastic loop, snapped. After the flash he smiled and posed and Teddie snapped again. "Let me take you two, wise mother and most beautiful daughter," he said. "On the couch, heads together." Jesse grinned, then adjusted her smile to ravishing. "Another." The camera flashed three times while Jesse and Teddie mugged and Georgio laughed. The bubble wall was thinning. Teddie almost was feeling. "Now take us," Georgio said. The arm he put around Teddie's shoulders radiated comfort and warmth. They smiled into

the camera and at each other. Georgio's rich brown eyes were fading, his sixty-seven years melting the black outlines of his irises
into circles of watery blue.

She raised her glass. "To us! Long may we prosper!" Teddie
toasted. The trio touched glasses and drank. "Can I ask a favor,
Georgio?"

"Of course, anything."

"I need seven thousand dollars as soon as possible, really tomorrow." She spoke without wavering. "I don't want to explain what
for, although I guess it's a kind of an investment, an investment in
my future." Five thousand would pay off Howie, and the other two
would make her feel better. Only sounds of burning wood could be
heard in the quiet.

"That's a great deal of money at short notice. Are you in trouble? Can you tell me about it?" Teddie's face fell. "What's wrong?"
That was three questions. "I know I'm asking a lot. Especially
after all these years. I'm sorry. It's personal."

"Mom always pays cash. She doesn't even have a credit card,"
Jesse explained, "and this she has to do on her own."

"Your husband shouldn't know?" Georgio asked.

"In a way, it's *for* my husband, and me, too, of course." Teddie's
face burned with embarrassment. "No, he shouldn't know. I don't
know when I could repay you," she blurted nervously, honestly.

"I could give you the amount of Thea's gift tonight, an indefi-
nite loan. But we must discuss the rest. Not tonight. When can we
get together?"

"Oh, I don't know. . . ."

"That would be wonderful," Jesse interrupted, "wouldn't it,
Mom?" Teddie agreed she'd phone for an appointment. She could-
n't ask him to give her Thea's money, to ask that the check made
out to Thea be rewritten to her, but two thousand was a start. One
thousand would not. The evening wound down. Her almost-father
did not ask her to stay with him in warm luxury. Teddie left with
Jesse for a night of student squalor.

∘ ∘ ∘

Her daughter wore her nose ring to bed. Teddie rose early from
her side of the double futon after sleeping surprisingly soundly and
made her way to the horror of the communal bathroom. She
should scrub the sink, the tub, the toilet, the floor, the walls,

impossible, what's more she did not want to be a cleaning woman for aging adolescents. She splashed, brushed, sponged and dressed in yesterday's clothes. In the dim hall, she glimpsed a middle-aged woman walking towards her in a wrinkled rose-colored skirt. Had those wrinkles been set in while she slept at her mother's feet?

Jesse sat up blearily. "Where are you going?"

"Out. For breakfast. Do you want to come?"

Jesse shook her head. "Got to study. Call if you need me."

"You too." Teddie kissed her daughter's forehead. "Stay in touch."

o o o

As if she were knowledgeable, Walter insisted she study Thea's work, and, it's true, she had been there in person. The anguished women clutching their hearing aids. The cooperative hands struggling to catch a ball. The lively eyes of Thea's admirer. The smoker spraying her lungs. Susie touching her forehead with her knees before a row of frozen, arthritic legs. Images isolated from the fabric of life, images with their own power and lives.

While Walter discussed compositional strengths and details, Teddie could think only of the real people frozen in time. Was this what they wanted from life, this exercise class? Not Thea. Her own head was spinning. The question hung like a multifaceted prism. Who was she?

Lost in minutiae, Walter talked while she took out the cardboard camera. "I know this is a silly thing, but I'm trying it out. May I take your picture?"

Walter glowed. "Why not?"

"Go on talking, just don't move too fast," Teddie said and she snapped and wound, snapped and wound. With the portraits added late last night, the camera and film were finished. "Walter, do you know what I do to get this developed?"

"Leave it to me. I'm better than those factory machines."

"Remember, it's not very important, only an experiment." Swamped by inadequacies, Teddie handed over the plastic and cardboard camera. "Can you have it ready by Saturday? I have an appointment then."

"What time?" Walter asked. Before or after, Teddie questioned herself. How would she feel? Ridiculous. Howie couldn't be her lethal instrument. After was fine. "I'll be here at three."

CHAPTER • 20 •

R evisiting the bank to deposit her check was mere routine. The secret door was invisible behind the fully peopled loan desks. Without the scar on her knee and her Saturday appointment, the ski-masked robber would be a dream.

At ten sharp she was at Thea's with Georgio's second check, a clean shawl, and proofsheets. Thea, who shouted her in, looked expectant, one camera around her neck, another in Hermes' basket. With a camera pointing directly at her, Teddie pulled in her neck turtlelike, reconsidered, produced her version of Jesse's ravishing smile, then her own aging coquette. Laughing aloud, Thea shot again. Teddie was familiar with Thea's laugh, but always at a distance. Now this mother was laughing with pleasure at her clowning daughter.

"You're out of character," Thea observed. "Something agrees with you."

"Didn't go home. Spent the night with decadent youth, scouting locations for your next book." Loathe to leave her transformed mother, even to enter the bedroom to hang the cleaning, she draped the plastic-wrapped shawl on a chair. "Walter sends his love," she said and placed the large envelope on the round table. "He says some are very good. I think they're wonderful."

"No time. We have work," Thea commanded, then paused.

"Why are you looking at me?" Two red rouge points dotted the old woman's unevenly powdered cheeks, a lipstick trail slid towards her chin, yet her gray-circled eyes gleamed.

"I see someone who wants to get going," Teddie either lied or spoke truthfully. "How did you sleep? You look tired."

"Another spell, that weakness, last night, but never mind. At least you I can trust. Not your sister. You call them as you see them. Of course it's my doing. I brought *you* up to be honest. Truth is greatly overrated, but sometimes useful, occasionally irreplaceable. Simply put, you are my safety net."

All that she had condemned her mother for, the ice, the terror, the rejection, was nothing next to this offhand boast. A safety net. She was her mother's safety net. Her lifelong absolute truth, her very own decision, had been turned on its head. Her honesty was Thea's, a utilitarian creation of her cold-blooded mother.

You did this to me! she screamed in silence.

"This is news to you?" Thea asked with a lopsided grin. "Aurora wasn't sturdy enough, but there you were, unusually strong and still a malleable child."

"How?"

"You want to know?" Thea looked pleased.

Teddie nodded.

"It was inspiration—love and fear. My love was real, of course, but demanding—interfered with work. If my work interfered with love, you children were too small to notice. The fear was harder until I realized you were terrified of being alone. You lied and I left. You were a quick learner. Didn't I do a good job?"

Suddenly, horribly, Teddie recalled that childhood lie. Had she been five? They were together, mother and daughters, in their own apartment. Aurora dressed for school while Teddie pinched her face under the dark of her blanket. "I'm sick," she whined when Aurora peeled back the bedcovers. "I need her," and Thea had been fetched from her work.

Wreathed in those mysterious chemical smells, the mother sat on the blue blanket and clucked her tongue at her daughter's mottled skin. "Didn't you have the measles?"

"No. I'm awful sick," the child replied and for beautiful minutes they were together, the two of them, until Teddie's healthy skin paled and a thermometer proclaimed her normal.

"You lied. No one loves a liar."

Dispatched to kindergarten late without an excuse, when she returned the darkroom door was open and the red light extinguished. She searched, but Thea was nowhere. She woke only when Aurora tripped over her, curled as she was in a ball on the darkroom floor.

Night had filled the rooms before a babysitter pushed open the apartment door. Teddie truly believed her mother was gone forever, but it was only a photographic safari to Mexico to film subsistence living. Two weeks later Thea was back.

Monster mother! What was best for *her*, for Thea, for Maude Slote! Even my own thoughts belong to her. Thief!

Thea pointed at her camera. "Pick it up. We have to get started."

"What are you saying?"

"Can you change film? That cardboard thing you had made me think." And so Thea moved on.

Teddie quickly mastered film loading, and stored the ready cameras in Hermes' basket.

"Help me aboard."

Teddie's arms shook as she levered her mother onto the scooter, although she couldn't locate the source of the tremors. Was Thea shaking with rage at having to ask for help or trembling with age? Or was Teddie, herself, stricken with fury or quivering in empathy?

Breathing roughly, unevenly, Thea settled into the leather seat. "Where are we going?"

"Follow me. Close the door." Again she scrambled after her mother, the indoor-outdoor 35 millimeter hanging around her wrist. "Private spaces today," Thea said as they traversed the basement tunnel that shot beneath the frozen garden and paths. It was warm, too warm. Suffocating walls pressed in. Teddie would be trapped underground while her mother drove away. "Don't daydream, Theodora. They don't like to be kept waiting. Fame spoils people, you know," and moments later both arrived at the fourth floor. The navy blue door swung open and Teddie was introduced.

There they were, plump gray shoulder next to plump gray shoulder. A mirror copy of Thea's apartment, Simon and Ruth Edgerton's rooms not only were book-lined but book-covered. Foothills rose from the floor. Mountains crowded overstuffed chairs. The massive dining table, for holding food once must have been its lot, was blanketed with books, drifts of papers, and a blinking, flashing computer.

Ruth followed Teddie's astonished gaze. "Moving here wasn't easy," she explained. "We had to give up..."

"Almost everything, but our books," Simon added.

"Our books are our blood," Ruth continued. She waved Teddie towards the chair next to the computer and settled beside her marital twin. "You have your own seat, Thea. How clever! We wonder. . . ."

"Do you know what your mother wants of us?" Teddie heard her mother's shutter click.

"Capture age, that's what she said," Ruth answered.

"Strange concept. How many?" Simon mumbled to himself.

"One hundred and seventy. That's between the two of us."

"Eighty-seven are mine. But she's a child."

"Bragging again. I'm only eighty-three."

They still lived, this couple who had authored volumes of history, not narrow, parochial history, but sweeping, multidimensional world history, the world as seen through multicultural eyes, so much more than one lifetime could accomplish.

Elbow on armrest, Thea shot again and again.

These two people, this man and this woman had merged, now separated only by their thinning skins. Teddie's years of marriage had worked differently.

The computer's screensaver danced on. Teddie asked about their current project.

Simon chuckled. "A timely one. . . ."

". . . for us," Ruth continued. Thea's wheels whirred, but her progress was blocked by books. "Death. Attitudes towards life's endings through history, across cultures. Look." She held out a picture of a tranquil woman who appeared to be sleeping in a coffin of flowers. "A Victorian funeral. Would you do the honors for us, Thea? When the time comes, of course."

Thea coughed. "What is the answer?" she asked.

"What's the question?" Ruth inquired.

"So dense, Ruthie dear. To death, of course. The great leveler. We can't escape. . . ."

". . . so we might as well understand. . . ."

". . . understand its virtues."

Thea appeared to be sucking a bitter lemon.

"Look at her, Simon. Death may not sell."

"Does it matter, dear? We're truthseekers, like you, Thea."

Teddie snapped the trio with her Fun and Easy.

"We're historians."

"Up-to-date historians. See that machine, Theodora? Ruth uses it. Show them." Teddie relinquished her place. The old woman played the keyboard like a virtuoso. Teddie snapped, Hermes' motor whirred.

"Here it is. What I was looking for. *Ars moriendi,* the art of dying, Simon, a concept in need of renewal."

"'The long habit of living indisposeth us for dying,'" Simon read. "Sir Thomas Browne said so, creates a conflict, doesn't it?"

"Stop!" Thea exploded, but the Edgertons ignored their guests. The Waterfords had to see themselves out. Teddie scampered after Hermes.

"Their book will be shunned. Terrible. Ah, we're here." Twining vines had been painted on this green door, images so real that Teddie touched the surface before she photographed it. "Daphne's idea." The green door swung open.

"We meet at last! Your mother often speaks of you." Daphne's deep voice caressed the hanging vines, the potted trees, the blooming violets, orchids, even roses that covered all surfaces, a personal blossoming jungle inside an anonymous Carleton apartment. The multiplying, moisture-loving growth created a perfumed tropical atmosphere. Daphne's strong-jawed face was surrounded by electrified strands of gray hair. Her plant grow lights illuminated several long white hairs sprouting from her chin and throat, as if age had put her in competition with her brother.

Did Thea actually talk about her dull daughter? She must have meant her own mother. "I saw you in the garden last summer," Teddie said.

"My poor tomatoes? This year I'm planting kudzu. Watch them try to pull out those suckers. Kudzu will stop them in their tracks."

Thea looked through her lens. "I've seen fields, trees, houses smothered. Destructive vine. Amusing. Close your mouth, Theodora. Reload."

Gaping at the Garden of Eden, Teddie took the camera. "How do you do it?" she asked. "I mean, I can't keep plants alive and here you. . . ."

"Yes. My friends live forever. See this fern? My great-grandmother's favorite, and these, too, all from her plants. Slips, shoots, plants don't have to die even if their tenders must, eh, friend?"

Thea ignored Daphne's attempt at inclusion while Teddie covetously eyed the youngspring of the century-old fern, plants to pass on to Jesse and Zach along with her quilt.

"Pretend we aren't here," Thea said. "Do as I asked, Theodora."

What was she supposed to do? Teddie took the camera Thea held out and raised it to her own eyes. "Are you ready for the basics?" Thea asked. Daphne puttered while the old woman cast a handful of camera truths upon her angrily blessed daughter. Why now? Why not forty years ago when she needed it most? "Now. Take one." The scooter swiveled in a patch of plant-free space, and Teddie framed her mother and shot, wound, readjusted, and shot again, then gently lowered the camera.

"We're leaving," Thea announced. Daphne did not stop dusting leaves, but Teddie needed a fern baby. Would Daphne part with one of her children? Teddie should not be rude but she should be honest. The child hostess at a fourth-grade birthday party had asked who wanted the last piece of cake. Everyone else had chirped, Not me, I'm too full, You take it, and Teddie said, "I do!" As she alone savored the chocolate-frosted morsel she felt the atmosphere turn to ice, almost as if Thea had come into the room.

I want one, she thought, but tempered her words. "If you could bring yourself to part with one of your great-grandmother's ferns, I'd be honored to be considered."

"You want one of these?" Daphne clapped her hands. "Why didn't you just say so? Most people run when they see me coming with greenery. I can't stand killing them, but there are limits."

And so, laden with two ferns and a blooming begonia, they retraced their route back through the tunnel to the elevator to Thea's own apartment. Teddie fetched a footstool to elevate Thea's swollen feet, plugged Hermes into his electrical socket, and would check the bottle-hiding places when her mother was safely napping. She would imitate Thea's spidery signature on Georgio's contribution and deposit it in Thea's account. Her own thousand would buy time and space.

CHAPTER • 21 •

"You could help me."

Aurora's eyes remained glued to the kitchen mini-television, but Howie took the heavy carton of photos from Teddie's arms.

"Dinner's ready," he announced unexpectedly. "Where do you want this?"

"Coffee table," Teddie commanded.

The smell of chili filled the air, the cupboards, the curtains, the cushions, the clinging fragrance of Howie's Fourth of July treat for the Olds's annual Independence Day party was shocking, cloying on a winter evening. Her grocery-tossing, moreover, was a model of cleanliness compared with the aftermath of Howie's cooking—chili-stained sink, pots, counters, even the floor. Wasn't it fortunate she was abdicating kitchen responsibilities.

"I'll get you a special."

"No," Teddie snapped. "Not a manhattan. Scotch and water, heavy on the scotch."

He turned to Aurora. "A special for you?"

"I don't know, but it's easier, isn't it? What she's having? Pretty please?" The sisters had staged a cocktail hour revolution.

"Do not put it down. Not here. The living room, the coffee table." Howie left with his load.

"You're different," Aurora commented. "Rumpled, but different. Radiant, I'd say. Jackie boy must be better than he seems. Don't tell me he's got an imagination."

"I won't," Teddie answered. "Yours is pretty good. Howie's calling."

Glasses iced and waiting, he embraced Teddie. Like a mannequin, she neither resisted nor assisted, her head being full of childhood lessons, f-stops, and trust. No departures, no nostalgia. This was not the time for arousing kisses. "I've been waiting," he breathed hot in her ear. One arm around Teddie, another wrapping Aurora's waist, he pressed both women to him. The chili stench was overwhelming. Teddie pulled herself free.

"To family!" Without further explanation, she raised her glass to Thea and Theo, and downed half.

"Hear, hear!" Howie followed.

Aurora drank and then poked the box. "What's this?"

"From storage. Know about family photographs?"

"Wait!" Howie returned with more scotch and the silver ice bucket, already slightly tarnished.

The sisters were digging in the cardboard box. "Do you recognize anyone?" Teddie asked. "These could have belonged to him." She knew Aurora knew who she was talking about. "Did you know his bookstore was named The Gray Wolf?"

"Of course. Daddy had a corner there, just for me. My own desk and chair. We worked together. He read to me. I had my own bookcase, my own books, the best books, my own bookmarks, my own paper, crayons, pencils." Teddie had heard this before, a made-up tale like Thea's, but perhaps Aurora did have a father who'd loved her even if Thea dumped him.

She smelled burning beans.

"Howie! Your dinner."

"What? No!" and he was gone. Teddie refilled. No reason to abstain. The last search of Thea's apartment had uncovered a bottle of white wine, no replacements, no empties although she'd rather over-indulgence was the source of Thea's dissolution instead of the morbid alternative. Tomorrow her mother would be fine and strong and her make-up would be applied with bewitching skill. Teddie jumped to answer Howie's telephone. Travel brochures still littered his desk.

"Mom!" Zach exclaimed. She visualized his round, eager face, always open, not sly like Jesse. "You haven't changed your Saturday appointment? Still meeting me?" It hadn't occurred to her that she had a choice.

"Don't worry. I'm not worried," she lied. "I'll be there."

"I need to ask—see what you think."

"Yes. I'm here."

"See, they want to send Bob home on Saturday. Hard to believe, he looked so terrible. He can't come here. They barely tolerate me, but never him." She knew the scenario. In their sterile suburb, Zach always lured home strays: dogs, kittens, a young raccoon, even a pocketful of baby possums whose mother had been flattened by a delivery truck. "I could bring him on Saturday. Until we work something out, a week or two."

Teddie hummed noncommittally.

"If you say no, I'll see about Jesse's place."

Teddie imagined a person with impaired immunity surviving in that bathroom. "No!" she exclaimed. A defeated groan came from her son. "That's not what I meant. Not Jesse's. He can stay here. I'm not busy. He can have your room. I'll talk to your father." How much did she, much less Howie, want to know about Zach's relationship to Bob, the young man who gave her son joy? "Aurora's back. I've been bad. Tell you later."

"You're a life saver. I knew you'd help, Mom. See you Saturday." Her world was rocking, crumbling, dissolving either from the earth's movement or from alcohol consumption. Perhaps both. She knew she could care for normal young people but not those marked for early death. And Zach, Zach. Those intellectual historians never could provide the words to make things right for them all.

Yellowed newspaper clippings, dusty photographs, the shadowy smudges of history, littered the white couch. Aurora's wide eyes were tear-filled, her once-tightened facial skin folded and shrunken like the dried apples they'd once used to make dolls. She was crying without reservation. "What's wrong?"

"Daddy's dead!" The voice was hollow, her hand clutching a scrap of newspaper.

The words neither made sense to Teddie nor stirred feeling. The alcohol anesthesia was beginning to take.

"Didn't you hear me? Look, Daddy's dead!" Aurora shook the crumbling newsprint. A date, twelve years back, was scrawled on the obituary in Thea's black spidery hand. Thea knew. She knew even while Teddie searched the library. Aurora's arms clung like a drowning child's. "There, there," Teddie crooned. "How sad, how hard, but he would have been very, very old, ninety, couldn't expect. . . ."

"Come and get it!" Howie shouted. Red-brown footprints followed him from the kitchen into the dining room. Possibly he was wondering what role-reversing magic had made his wife so calm and drunk while her sister was dissolving. Looking at Aurora, he lowered the steaming kettle toward the polished dining table.

"Stop!" Teddie screamed. The kettle wavered. Greasy red gravy splashed on his head-of-the-table chair.

"Daddy's dead, Daddy's dead," Aurora moaned.

"The kitchen." The voice was Thea's explaining an obvious truth to a slow-witted child. "The kitchen." Howie stumbled. Eager, anticipating, Teddie watched him teeter. A chili tidal wave would sweep them out of this house, a clean sweep. She hooted expectantly, but Howie and his burden disappeared leaving only traces of desired disaster. Aurora had forgotten her drink. Teddie drained both glasses.

On his return the professional comforter's greasy hand reached out to pat Aurora's thin back. Play-acting or real, with Howie's touch Aurora cleaved harder to Teddie. "He's gone. He's gone. Don't leave me!" she cried. For thirty years Aurora scarcely had mentioned the man, although, considering her three husbands, perhaps she'd always been looking. Hollow, cored, Teddie had just begun the search. Howie was forced to refill glasses. Teddie poured scotch into her emptiness while Howie riffled through photographs.

"Recognize anyone?" He held up a shot of three old-fashioned men, arms linked around shoulders. Teddie shook her head. "Aurora?" Aurora shook her head. "How did he die?" Howie asked. Teddie handed her husband the brittle obituary. "Heart failure," he read aloud. "Hey! You're mentioned." Aurora loosened her grip on her sister. "'He leaves two daughters, Aurora Waterford Simpson of Chicago, Illinois, and Theodora Waterford Olds of West Bloomfield, Michigan, and two grandchildren.' I wonder if this got into the New York Times. More famous Waterfords."

"Tell me about him," he asked gently, again in charge.

Dry-eyed and in no pain, Teddie dug down to a lower layer until she remembered the plants. She must rescue the baby ferns and begonia from her car before the cold killed them. Aurora was blathering on about her little desk next to Daddy's desk when she added Daphne's heritage to the coffee table's load.

Teddie's desk was on loan from her son. Where would she work when Bob took Zach's room? Perhaps Thea would let her set up next to Hermes, but why would she need any desk? It wasn't as if she did anything useful, although she should send Georgio a receipt. Or she could wait until he asked for repayment. Casually her fingers flipped over another cardboard rectangle and she'd found it. She had him. He was in her hand. Her father's loving eyes twinkled behind steel-rimmed glasses. A charming five-year-old who was flirting with the camera embraced one of his hands while a sturdy, frizzy haired toddler, mouth a surprised O, clung to the other. He was looking with love at the toddler, at Teddie, love to *her*. She was wrestling with the ramifications when the picture jerked. She held tighter.

"Daddy and me!"

"No!" Teddie held fast. "Me!" The cardboard twisted, ripped. Little Aurora and the bottom half of their father cleaved to Teddie's hand; Aurora possessed toddler Teddie and their father's smiling face. Thea probably had taken the photo to memorialize her plan to assure he'd never see his children again. Something to remember him by. "Give me!" Teddie grabbed and switched fragments with her sister. Of course there might be others in the box. Of course copies could be made, but this piece was hers. Teddie rose. She had to look for her mother.

Nor had she confirmed the birthday party truth. Marla's album still waited in the breakfast nook. At last she opened its musty pages. What satisfaction, what vindication awaited! She'd make Aurora eat her words, carve them from blocks of butter, from terrines of gooseliver, force-feed and fatten anorexic Aurora. Confidently, arrogantly, she flipped the pages. The girls making faces. Aurora in front of a cabinet pleading with her baby sister. Aurora waving a bottle. See? Teddie was right. Aurora drinking wine. Everyone clutching glasses. Everyone drinking wine. Teddie finishing one bottle and waving another. Teddie drunk. Teddie a pie-eyed, wine-bottle baby. The picture lied. No. No. Was it so? She had lived a lie. That girl who was her was drunk and they were right to blame her, her mother, her sister were right, for she had lied to herself, to them, to everyone. Shame licked her body. Melting with shame, she thrust handfuls of cubes from their ever-replenishing ice-maker down her front, inside her slip, into her bra, but her dizziness did not abate. How many drinks, how many ounces of pure alcohol, had she swallowed tonight, on other nights? Any court would find her guilty as charged, sentence to follow. She was her own judge, her own jury. She awaited punishment. Move out, leave, but she had already served her sentence, thoughts like smoke. She rubbed ice on her temples. The room swirled, turned, spun in sickening loops. Her stomach heaved. Braced on the counter, she inched towards the grease-splattered sink, where she fought the upwelling, but her body was stronger than her will. Teddie was sick, horribly, copiously sick, again and again, and she went on heaving after her vomit had smothered the chili. Her As You Like It garments were stained, her damp hair plastered against her face.

Something terrible had happened, some revelation, but after the eruption, now, right now, can't think, can't remember.

She crawled up the back stairs. In the dark she washed her mouth and hands, rinsed the face she did not wish to see, and undressed. Wrapped in Solomon's Judgment, Teddie passed out.

CHAPTER • 22 •

Running, escaping, fleeing from, fleeing from something, from nothing, she rose to consciousness, although her eyes remained sealed. The twisted black nails of wailing devils were scraping and scratching her brain, their hairy hooves beating against her white bone skull. Her devils. She had lived truthfully, but her righteousness was ruptured. Pain was her punishment. Punishment for sin.

Stop it, she told herself. So childish. Take care of yourself, a Tylenol or two, maybe one of those tranquilizers. A bundled lump was snoring on the far side of the bed. A sign of power. Howie was keeping to his side. Shuddering, she swallowed a pill, gulped water, and, still spinning, rolled back into bed. She must leave, remove her deceptive self, self-deception, the worst kind, but how could she? You have to wait for morning, her old practical self explained. It's not as if you have a choice. This house where you have lived so long is a mere island in suburban seas. Only marathon swimmers or those mounted on wheels can escape. You are full of poison. You know you cannot drive. No more scotch. Not like that. You don't need it. Repentance. Resolution.

o o o

"You sure hung one on, Ted."

Beaming with affection, Howie seemed proud of her. For what? For getting stinking drunk? If one photograph proved she had lived one lie since her thirteenth birthday, how many self-deceptions lay in waiting? One had changed the world.The outlines of the familiar bedroom, of Howie, were sharp but quite distant as if seen from the wrong end of a telescope. Her husband was the size of a tree frog, a sleek, shiny, wet amphibian with enlarged, sticky toe pads. "Stay in bed. You've been working too hard," he instructed her. What is hard work? How about a multiple choice question? Hard work for Theodora Waterford Olds is (a) throwing groceries, (b) understanding pheromonic behavior, (c) eating illicit oyster lunches, (d) burying her father, (e) all of the above. Among Howie's skills was an eerie ability at making the correct choice from a multiple selection. "Want some breakfast? I'll tell Aurora."

If she were quick she could catch him in her hands, put him in a terrarium—she'd have to ask Daphne about plants. She closed her eyes and imagined doing the same to Aurora. "No," she said aloud after consideration, "not Aurora."

"Anything you say, Ted. I'll be late, but I'll bring your juice and coffee. Stay warm."

Howie might be easy, but she had things to settle with her sister. The pain was gone when she woke next. The orange juice from her bedside helped cleanse the evil taste—she would wish her devils' hairy-hoofed feet on no one—as did the cold coffee. Almost nine. Time to move. Where? To Thea's, of course. Work to do, living to learn. Working too hard is coexisting with your mother. You missed the question, Howie.

o o o

"Why am I here?" Teddie asked her steering wheel as she stopped outside the Beekman Storage Tower. "I don't want to see him." Yes, she would look for more photographs, for a complete picture of her father with his children. Liz wouldn't disturb Michael. Today she smirked into the surveilling cameras. Thea's storage room was messy, unsettled, just as she had left it last week. She rearranged boxes like a child pushes toys. A functioning darkroom in the Carleton was folly, a pipe dream. Bending forced something from her stomach to bubble into her throat. What if Thea had stashed more than her father's obituary in a box, what if that big one, there, the coffin-shape in the shadows, what if it was his, what if?

No reason she shouldn't walk down the corridor and look at Michael's door, drop in, say hello before she left. She'd checked the schedule in her glove compartment. This was a safe time. She wouldn't bother him, just bring a friendly greeting from the outside world.

Room locked, Teddie and Liz hurried. "Have fun," Liz sang sotto voce, "in 751." Approaching, almost there, she saw a black space, like a giant missing a tooth. Had the neighbor retrieved the dining set? She passed 745, 746, almost there. No. Inside the dark opening was the shadowy form of his sleeping platform. He'd fallen, injured himself, opened his door, and collapsed, his magic blue eyes were closed in pain. She'd help him, nurse him back to health. She flicked on his light. An empty sleeping platform, a painted window, and trash—crumpled papers, a greasy can lid, dust. He was gone, moved out, books, papers, carpet, refrigerator, and microwave. She had lied to him about who she was and what she did. She had lied to him about everything and he had left her.

On her way out she needed to ask a real person a real question. "I rent a space on seven and noticed 751 was empty. Is it available?"

"Let me check."

The clerk had a broken front tooth and a bad permanent. "Oh, that one! You wouldn't believe. A man was living there. Security tried to catch him, but he escaped. The police will find him."

Empty-eyed, without sidetrips, Teddie steered the Saturn to Thea. "About time," her mother observed. "You look terrible." No surprises from Thea's bad mouth. Teddie had scrubbed her aging body but the filth clung.

"Awful. Bad. Last night."

"Have you eaten? Food always settled you." Thea creaked upright while Teddie sank into a chair. Supporting herself on furniture, the old woman made her way to the kitchen. The refrigerator opened. "They keep bringing these things." Glass clinked on the counter, liquid was poured, something plopped. "What else?" Cupboard doors creaked. "Langues des Chat. If you want wine, you'll have to open it yourself. White wine." Teddie groaned. "Don't bother to speak up." Box under her arm, glass in her hand, Thea retraced her uneasy steps back to the round table. Her carrying hand was so steady that the milk scarcely rippled—she could have been supporting a camera. "There. Eat."

Under her mother's strangely calm eye Teddie consumed the offering and heard, "When you're ready. What happened?"

Teddie yawned. "Tired."

"Lie down. Sleep."

Teddie stumbled into Hermes' room and fell onto the bed. A soft covering drifted over her and she was floating face down in tropical water.

o o o

A city beneath her, a coral reef perhaps or a simple reflection of the everyday, its brightly colored inhabitants going about their business. She is the keeper of this world. The life-saving bubble will stay strong and whole and she and they will live only if she holds absolutely still. Children play in the sun and the dark, flashing their colors, Zach and Jesse, Aurora and Teddie. Marla. Georgio, Daphne. A pale plump shape slides into the shadows. Little Aurora and Teddie chase Daddy. Daddy wants to sell Michael's book for him. Where is Michael? Thea braces her camera against her shoulder and aims. "Look out, Daddy, she'll trick you," little Aurora pleads. "She'll steal your soul. You'll disappear." "Hear her warning, but only I can help you," little Teddie answers back. "It's my magic." I stay still, quiet. I am pure, truthful, and never change. I keep us safe. I ignore my itching foot. It is only a tiny mosquito and I am strong. But it is an evil mosquito! Its needle nose has punctured my most tender sole. It pierces my heart. Oh, it itches, I must scratch, I must move, but the responsibility is mine. Torment, but I will not, cannot, stir. I smile, suck a cooling breath. The gases explode from my lungs. The torment stings. The air I gulp fans the flames. My resolve weakens. Why must I bear such a burden? I have earned freedom. The fire consumes me. I will die if I cannot scratch my sole. I thrash on the warm sea surface, ripping, tearing, and when I have destroyed that devilish itch, the world collapses in darkness.

o o o

Teddie's tongue lapped the warm drops on the corner of her mouth. Sweet salt. Water was streaming down her face. She would drown. Her sentence.

A feather or a bird's wing brushed her forehead, but the tears were brutal forces of nature. She was motionless deep inside a padded box. Dead. Only her eyes could wander. Feathery strokes. She would see a raven perched beside her, if she could raise her eyelids.

"You've come back," a rusty voice said. "About time." Thea's voice, her mother's voice, her mother next to her, stroking her brow. "There, there," Thea murmured.

"My ears are wet," Teddie said. She could lift neither head nor hand.

"Take your time. This is serious. It's not an Aurora frivolity. My Theodora."

"Why are my ears wet?"

"You have filled them with tears. That is an accomplishment. Perhaps I haven't been fair to you. For you life is so serious. No fun. No play, but how could you after I wedded you to truth? I am a perfectionist."

"I destroyed him." Her voice was distant in her wet ears.

"We like to think we're that powerful, Theodora, but it's rare, truly rare. Tell me about him. Surely you're not talking about Howie."

"Not Howie. The other, Michael in the storage tower. He lived there. Only a painted window." Thea said nothing but lifted strands of wet hair from Teddie's cheeks. "He disappeared. I lied. My fault."

"Strange. You always claimed responsibility for others' actions. A god-complex." Thea sounded introspective, her voice less harsh than her words. "Do you want to tell me more about him?"

Teddie rolled her head from side to side. Her tears were slowing. They settled in silence. Teddie closed her eyes. When she reopened them, the light had dimmed, the day far gone and her face not dry. Thea was perched with an open book on Hermes beside the bed. "He's not important," Teddie said.

"The one in storage?"

"Yes."

"What else is wrong?" Thea asked. Her voice was not unkind. Those sourceless tears came again.

"I was tested for AIDS."

A quick intake of breath. "Well?"

"I don't know. Saturday. Zach's friend is in the hospital."

"Why?"

"Pneumonia. AIDS. Zach wants him to stay with me, with Howie and me, and Aurora's living there again, Jesse's too sexy. She's piercing herself. . . ." Teddie's words drifted, her forehead wrinkled, her mouth grimaced.

"Why were you tested? Is Zach in danger?"

Two questions. She applied the old rule. "The police. The bank burglar's parents want to know. We both were bleeding. I held him until the police came. He's negative. Howie isn't, isn't exactly faithful to me, you know. Oh, he's too faithful and dull and sleeps around like an alley cat." Mournful mewing accompanied new tears.

"You needed time to learn. I thought you were a good match, but I underestimated you. He needs reflected glory. What do you need?" Sobs punctuated Teddie's mewing as she explored her tarnished self.

"I lied," she moaned. "To myself. To everyone." A wail joined the sobs, but Teddie's body was frozen. Only her voice had movement, her voice and her tears.

"You're raving, Theodora." Thea sounded incredulous. "You? Explain."

"No!" She lifted her hand to her mouth. Her warm lips searched until her tongue embraced the tip of her thumb.

"You can't get up. Too soon. It happened to me in Africa, too much, could not move, would stay on that mat in that dark hut forever."

"Why?" Teddie asked around her sucking thumb.

"That girl—you remember—said it was the witch doctor. He seized my life force as I slept and he'd hold it until I died or begged for his mercy. I would not die, never will. I refuse. I couldn't ask that stupid little man to save me. But for the girl, I was alone. She had a sister, made me think of you and Aurora. My work was meaningless, built on deception, snatching fragments of lives, never the whole. One day I was full of excitement and the world held promises and the next I was spent cinders. Like you, I cried and slept and cried a day and night and. . . ." Her voice ever fainter, Thea faded into silence. Round-eyed, sucking, Teddie watched her mother close her eyes. She could move, yes she could, and she swung herself upright on the edge of the bed to pat her mother's nearby knee. Thea did not waken.

Did she dare? It was too dangerous, but she wanted to. She wanted to hug her. Equally, she wanted her mother to hold her. Teddie slid her wet thumb from her mouth and reached out. Fearsome eyes snapped open. Her hand froze in an arrested embrace. Their eyes locked, not in anger, not in love. Teddie saw only naked confusion.

"What are you doing?" Thea asked sharply. "I left you at home. It's not healthy for children in the bush. He was sentimental. Insisted you two be born. I knew better. I don't have time for children. Work to do."

"Who was sentimental?" Teddie asked quietly.

"Theo. Your father."

"He's dead." Teddie fell back onto the bed.

"When did it happen?"

"You know. You didn't think to tell us, his own children. Twelve years ago."

"If you say so."

"IF *I* SAY SO! It's you! You say whatever you want, you live, you breathe, deception!" A flush spread from her face through her body. She wanted to rip out that woman's lying liver. Sweating, Teddie would have torn her mother from her perch but for the ringing phone.

Thea rolled away. Teddie teetered on her feet at the edge of the bed. "She's here," her mother said. Silence. "She has every right, Aurora." Silence. "Yes he's dead, has been for years, what matter. Your place is here." Pause. "Don't argue. Take a cab." Silence. "I'll pay. Now!" The receiver rattled. Teddie rocked unevenly towards the bathroom.

"That African girl saved me. She stayed until the tides turned. We will do the same for you."

"I don't want Aurora."

"She didn't want you either. Most of my life I could have done without you both, although there were moments and times change. I need to call Daphne. Can you look after yourself?"

"What choice did you ever give me?" Teddie snarled. Muttering, in the bathroom she did what was necessary. There was a stranger in the mirror. She was not unattractive. Worn, but might travel well.

"Are you all right?" Thea demanded from the other side of the door.

"Why do you care?"

"I don't know. I do."

Teddie pulled down an eyelid and studied one red, irritated eye, then the other. Not pretty. But the face wasn't bad. She should take a portrait photograph of that face, wrinkles and all, but Walter had her camera.

Clean tears overflowed the eyes in the mirror. The deceived eyes. Was that the face of a lush? Who was she, the woman in the mirror?

CHAPTER • 23 •

Distant explosions pierced the dusk of her hiding place. "She's my wife!" Bang. "Let me in!" Thump.

An electric whir. "Aurora, are you there?" Thea, calm.

"Yes, mother." Aurora, failing.

"Go home, Howie." Thea, officious.

"She's mine." Howie, sulky.

"Home!" Medean Thea commanded. Teddie shivered. "We'll keep in touch."

"In touch," Teddie repeated in the back room.

Outside whispers.

"I'll be back."

The door banged shut. "Tomorrow. Someone will call."

"Tomorrow," Aurora sighed.

"These things take time. You look ghastly. Fading." Who was Thea to talk about fading, Thea of the touchable bones, a bag of bones. In the dark Teddie smiled. Her sucking thumb was dry. She's pretending to be a mother, poor thing.

"Where's Teddie? If it hadn't been for Howie, I don't know. . . ," Aurora's tiny voice tinkled. "He's dead! Daddy's dead!" she keened. "He didn't say good-bye."

"Aurora," Thea said disparagingly. "A child's dream world! When did you last hear from that little man? I threw him out a half century ago. Fifty years."

Another exaggeration, or name it, a lie. *Not* fifty years. Less. Forty-eight? Forty-nine? Accurate details make all the difference. "We stayed in touch. I talked to him."

"IN YOUR DREAMS!" Teddie called out. "I heard you," she muttered.

"Oh, you. He sent *me* birthday cards. Until I was ten. More than *you* got."

Thea would soon announce her imminent departure for Tanzania or Ecuador and the girls should pack their brown paper bags. But instead of doing her mother's bidding, if it should come, Teddie decided to stay put. She'd never been so comfortable. She'd stay in the Carleton Retirement Home forever, sharing Hermes' room, although there was scarcely space for Aurora unless she could be encouraged to speed her dissolution, finish her fading. Thea would be hers alone.

Teddie sensed a catlike presence staring at her in the dark. "What are you doing?" Aurora asked.

"I don't know," Teddie said softly. "It was the only place."

"Move over." Teddie did not want to share. Yet if Aurora truly was fading, she always could squash her and her dumb daddy birthday cards.

"You always bossed me," Teddie observed.

"Someone had to. Who else did we have?"

Teddie's tears trickled. They lay together in silence.

"You took care of me," Aurora whispered.

"You made me," Teddie answered.

"No, I didn't. You wanted to."

"That's what you say. You ordered me around. Like that birthday party."

"Marla's pictures. Why do you have those? I looked at them, but you didn't come home."

"You made me get the wine. I got drunk. I don't remember being like that. All my life, I've known who I was, what I've done. But I lied. To myself, to everyone. People disappear when I lie."

Aurora giggled, rolled on her side and propped her polished head on her hand, face even with her sister's, toes ending at her sister's mid-calf.

"I thought you were playacting, but then you got sick. Like last night. It was terrible."

"I don't act, that's lying, and the pictures. . . ."

". . . the pictures aren't everything. Marla passed out, remember? No more pictures that night. You could have had the flu. Everyone makes up stories."

"Not me. Never. Not before now." That's it. That's what telling the truth is, accurate, perfectly clear, like a photograph, no mistakes about meaning.

"You're so obscure. As far as I know you never touched the stuff again, not until you were trying to catch Howie. You did what he wanted."

With certainty Teddie remembered the catch-up courtship. "I lied about that night."

"Maybe. So what? What a prig. So righteous. You should do something about yourself."

"Look where your fancy clothes got me." This morning Teddie had thrown on the Pandoran dress, the first garment her hand touched.

"Good wool resists tear stains. Better late than never. You've always been a crybaby. Now you won't have so many spots." Aurora placed her thumb on her sculpted nose. Her three diamond rings sparkled in the gloom as she waggled her wrinkled hand back and forth. "Cry some more. Go on," Aurora demanded before flopping onto her back.

Teddie's eyes went dry. Year after year, squabble after squabble, her sister had reduced her to a sniveling swamp, but tonight Aurora's taunts were stingless. "I may have been a prig, but you're promiscuous," Teddie sneered. "Three husbands, never satisfied with your own green pastures, you chase anyone's husband into bed, even mine, even Howie, you slime!" Teddie sat up to glare through the dusk at the slight figure who deserved her comeupance. She would jump on that fading body, she would hear those hormone-laced bones crunch like dry cereal. She had raised her arm for the first blow when strong, artificial light flooded the room. Thea and her machine filled the doorway. They'd been shouting. Unseemly emotion, their mother had called the outbursts she would not tolerate.

"I'm leaving," Thea announced. "I have a job to finish."

"Why are you bothering to tell us? You said you'd stay. Of course you're running away. You always run away from us!" Teddie exclaimed, bitter but not shocked at Thea's latest betrayal. "What happened to 'we'll stay with you?'"

"Even *I* know that's not how to handle children!" Aurora said, popping up next to her sister, two improbable oversized, middle-aged dolls with legs straight before them. Teddie's fist still was poised for the sistorial strike when an insight assaulted her. "You're afraid!" Her accusing finger uncoiled towards Thea. "You!" Lit with discovery, she swiveled towards Aurora. "She's afraid! Of us! She's afraid of us! Afraid of us!" Insight became playground chant, and Thea fumbled her knobbly red-tipped claws over the controls of her machine. The scooter refused to let her retreat from her children.

"It's not working," Thea said.

"You're out of power, Mommy. Now you'll have to go it on your own. That's what you made us do." Aurora shone with vindictive glee.

"Aurora!" Teddie reprimanded, newly protective of her mother-in-name-only. Thea's head drooped, her chin on her dried, flat chest. "Your fresh battery is somewhere under your seat," Teddie said. Thea was motionless. "I could look for you," Teddie added, but she did not budge.

"What did you do to my daddy?"

"He was *my* daddy, too," Teddie inserted. "You don't hear me whining."

"Why should you? You didn't know him."

"He held my hand. The picture said he loved me!"

"Photographs. Fragments." Thea sounded as if she were speaking from an empty well beneath a rock. "Never the whole. Love changes." The last two words tolled like abandoned bells. Teddie absorbed the mournful sound.

"You didn't send him away, did you, DID YOU? Our father escaped! He was too strong for you. Don't you see, Aurora, he left her. Isn't that right, Mother? Father left you!"

"I told him to go away," Thea moaned. She rotated her seat. First one useless swollen foot, then the other slid onto the utilitarian-gray carpet. Too weak to push herself upright, escape was forbidden by both body and battery. "He said no matter how many moths flocked to my flame, my heart was ice. I wouldn't let him take you when he left. You were all he wanted of me." Thea glared at her daughters in-a-row.

Indignant warmth suffused Teddie. The source was weakening,

the mother-implanted ice slivers melting.

"I was alone. I *needed* you." Thea's cracking voice was barely audible.

"*You* needed *us?*" Aurora cawed indignantly. "Why, that's evil! Children need mothers, not the other way around."

It was a mirage, a vision in the desert. A spring was flowing from dry, hard-shelled Thea. Teardrops joined the food stains spotting the ancient gray silk her mother had chosen for this day's work, a day she had given to her younger daughter.

"You're disgusting, evil, evil!" Aurora roared from her stiff perch. Emotion lit up her hidden surgery scars, road tracks tucked behind her ears, under her chin, around her eyes. Teddie listened to her sister. She watched her mother's tears. Feeling each muscle and seeing each nanosecond as if it were forever, she raised a flattened hand, and slapped her sister across the face. The shadow of Aurora's cheekbone tingled in her open palm.

"Of course. That's what she did to you." Teddie nodded. "You were kept from love—never learned mothers need children, oh, they do—never learned how to give, how to take, only to beg and to whine and to manipulate." It was pity she felt for her bitchy sister. "It's not too late for me. I can drop my burden of truth, but you—too late, much too late."

Aurora howled and grabbed Teddie's curly hair. Teddie struggled to break her sister's grip. The bedsprings beneath them wheezed.

"Stop!" The sisters froze like statues. In the silence, Daphne asked Thea to move, but there was no reply. Aurora plucked at the strands of graying auburn hair caught in her diamond rings. Teddie walked unsteadily to Thea where she placed her mother's limp arm over her shoulder, half-squatted to grip the puffy legs, her own arm about the foreshortened waist, then heaved the surprisingly heavy body meager inches back into Hermes' seat. Thea blinked. Teddie may have heard, "Thank you."

"Her battery's dead. How do we switch to the fresh one?"

"Personally, I'd use herbs," Daphne said. "I brought a potion, but I thought it was for you."

"See if *she'll* take a sip if it would help her. I'll work on the battery." Perhaps she'd try Daphne's harmless brew herself. Kneeling, Teddie reached for the battery boxes behind Thea's seat. The seams of her expensive dress weren't complaining, but she was stymied by the machinery. The unsavory salesman's instructions had flown. She needed Jesse.

"No." Thea complained. "Smells like death."

"Woodsy, but scarcely death, dear," Daphne said. "Blackberry, mushroom, leaves of colewart, very healthy." A jumble of arms and legs waved like seaweed about the motorized scooter. Teddie would have to crawl over the stalled machine to call Jesse. Thea's windy bones had no balancing substance. She would have to be careful where she put her weight. She had started to climb when Hermes vibrated. His motor purred.

"And you thought I was worthless," Aurora cackled. "A simple switch."

Aurora jumped clear of the wheels as Hermes towed Daphne and Teddie into his room. Thea slammed into reverse, knocking Daphne to the floor, then, like a dog shaking off water, Hermes went into a spin and Teddie flew free. "Unnh," she grunted, then stared.

All she'd had to do was wish and pale Jesse, nose and earrings shining, was standing before her. "I knocked, but the door was open. I hope it's okay. Dad said I might be needed, but really," the girl announced. "Where should I start?"

Daphne dabbed the dank, stinking spot on the carpet, Aurora crawled back onto the bed, Teddie struggled to her feet, and Thea dismounted to throw her arms around the young newcomer. "A vision. A vision from the past," she cried.

"Hardly, Grandmother. Not much past, just now and maybe some future, but you never know. Do you want to sit down?" Jesse propelled Thea into the dark green wing chair.

"We have a fresh chance with you here, child. Call down and tell them to set a table for five. Daphne, you are free? Your plants will let you go? I know you two," and Thea nodded towards her daughters who had straggled after her, "have no immediate commitments."

"You gave Mom your grandmother's fern? She told me all about your place. I'd love to see it." Jesse turned to Aurora. "I didn't think I'd see you this trip. You should know how fantastic those clothes are, the things you bought for Mom. She never appreciated shopping, not like you. Dull, that's what she bought." Teddie marveled at her daughter's seamless joining of veracity and fiction. So much to learn. Jesse winked at her. Children are to learn from. Does Thea know?

CHAPTER • 24 •

The Waterford women prepared themselves or each other, according to temperament, for the evening, while Daphne hurried home to care for her least forgiving plants and to search out a special wine. "Real wine. Nothing dandelion," Thea said. "No parsnip, no parsley. Grape only." Jesse and Aurora turned Thea's closets out to improve themselves for a dinner gathering in the Carleton Commons. A hanger and a steamy bathroom resurrected Teddie's expensive wool, but, as she'd complained, everything of Thea's was on the edge of tatters.

"Cool!" Jesse exclaimed as she pranced around in one ancient garment after another. "Totally cool."

"Look at you! I feel reborn!" Thea mused. The generational resemblance made Teddie shiver. Thank God Jesse possessed her own solid mind and soul. Short Aurora had to make due with a hand-painted silk scarf—a Picasso, Thea claimed—artfully draped over her stylish Chicago suit. Tear stains persisted like grease on Thea's gray silk, so Teddie helped her mother into the ceremonial red that had done London Grill duty. Jesse finally decided on a blue and white floral rayon dress from, Thea said, 1940, the year before World War II. "Keep it," Thea ordered. "It goes with your boots. Now, Theodora, get the cameras." Aurora watched Teddie retrieve the sacred canvas bag and place Thea's close-up camera in her

mother's lap. "Right. Check the settings. We need to shoot Jesse."
Teddie moved her hands over the camera body while Aurora gaped.

"Don't you have an automatic focuser like Marla, Grandma?
What will your camera say about us?"

"Only frozen fragments," Thea said as the shutter opened and
closed.

"No," Jesse contradicted. "Your pictures open minds, change
the way people see."

Teddie's hands were under the camera as soon as Thea's began
to tremble. "Take another, Theodora. The cameras will come to
dinner. How do I look?"

"You look wonderful, as always," Aurora said hastily.

"Not you. Theodora?" Teddie closed her eyes. Only Jesse
looked healthy beneath the high power overhead lights. Aurora
was outlining her lips with a color barrier; her lipstick would not
ooze into wrinkles to create a blurry red hole in a death's head face
as Thea's had done.

"Jesse's beautiful, well, maybe not the nose ring," Teddie
observed, "but the rest of us look, um, ah, careworn." While she
paced her words, Teddie switched on two floor lamps and turned
off the overhead light. "No need to look as if we're about to go
under the knife. You haven't had time to take care of yourself
today," she continued in evasive approximations.

"Let me fix you up," Aurora offered. "Stay there," she added as
Thea struggled to stand. Surprisingly, the old woman let her older
daughter dab color on her face. Teddie guessed at the light, reset
the camera and attempted to record the scene. This particular present felt ephemeral, no, fragile, that was it. It could not last, but
they were together, four women, connected by webs of truth and
lies to this time and to this room and to each other.

Daphne returned with two bottles just as Aurora stopped her
fussing. "Is that better?" Thea asked.

"Aphrodite lives!" Daphne cried out.

"Not you, old woman. Theodora?"

"You look fine," Teddie replied, for Thea did. Jesse helped her
grandmother mount Hermes, and the party departed.

In a setting where, on a weekday winter night, fifty-year-old
daughters are as rare as hen's teeth, Thea's collection of two aging
children and one radiant grandchild was exceptional. While Jesse
helped Thea into her dining chair, Daphne asked Carlotta, the

Spanish-speaking server, to bring glasses and open their wine. The residents were looking familiar to Teddie, individuals instead of the undifferentiated "old"—those embarrassingly identical faded people who push nearly empty carts around supermarkets and fumble for exact change at the head of impatient lines. The man from exercise, the one whose heart beat faster at a mere glimpse of her mother, winked and waved. The picture-sharers with hearing aids glanced at the group with the sharp frowns of house critics, and the identical Edgertons toddled to the table and asked to join the party. "For now," Thea said.

It was like being on stage. Each word, every gesture was larger than life. "Are those two actually the famous historians? Those historians?" Jesse whispered into Teddie's ear. "How rad!" she exhaled. "What a place. All this knowledge, all this life under one roof."

That was, Teddie had to admit, a different perspective. More like a living library or museum than a warehouse for the near-extinct. Jealousy stabbed when Thea handed Carlotta a camera to shoot the entire table. Aurora smirked, but Thea caught her younger daughter's naturally green eye and shook her head. "Don't worry, Theodora. Years of experience, an expert," the old woman said, but who would trust Thea's word?

"Is it a family celebration?" Ruth Edgerton asked.

"More like a coming-out party," Thea answered. Teddie felt herself blush.

"Ah, a ceremonial occasion!" Ruth exclaimed.

"Our specialty. Final days, death, funerals, grief, that's what we're studying. We were inspired by. . . ."

". . . by a nature program, an inspiration. Elephants. . . ."

". . . an elephant cemetary and those enormous beasts reverently carrying, stroking fleshbare ribs, leg bones. . . ."

". . . leg bones, tusks, the tusks. . . ." The Edgertons seemed not to have noticed the silent chill at their table. Walking brains might have as many social problems as people who cannot lie. But no. Feelings can't touch those for whom only ideas are life. The images of huge beasts cradling comrades' bones, of an elephant mother drawing wisdom and comfort from sparse earthly remains, made Teddie's eyes fill with tears. At least the Edgertons had each other.

"I didn't know you were writing about nature," Daphne remarked. "How fascinating!"

"Not that kind of nature. What human nature hath wrought,

that's our territory, isn't. . . ."

Thea intervened before another duet struck up. "Never would I photograph the morbid scenes you delight in. It's a principle. Only life." Thea lifted her glass. "To life! Everyone say it."

"To life!" they chorused while Carlotta waited to serve the soup.

Teddie was comfortable, relaxed and supple. She could ride out any storm, enjoy it, never resist, never insist on order and control. She saw herself sailing through the skies on her broomstick, at one with the wind and air and universe.

"You're smiling, Mom. Do you like the soup? What are you thinking?"

"Soup?" Teddie asked. "Like it?" Now she'd stopped to consider, she realized she'd been spooning up salty water with a few floating vegetables. "Hardly. But pleasant thoughts."

"Where are you and Howie going on vacation?" Aurora asked abruptly. "He has beautiful brochures. A cruise to somewhere, he said." Trust her sister to break a mood. No, she wouldn't allow it. Teddie relaxed her shoulders, focused her mind, and imagined herself traveling. Howie was not in sight. Those tortoises again. And spiky lizards barely discernable on a background of black volcanic rock—perhaps that is where her devils went.

"I'm going to the Galapagos Islands," Teddie announced, for she had a great deal to learn about adaptation.

"A dream of mine," Daphne said. "Have you been there, Thea?"

"Never, never. Can't stand animals. Like children, all demands and unpredictability." Thea's rehearsed response was burnished with the patina of the years.

"Grandmother, I don't believe you." Jesse said. "Besides, you had to like children a little for Mom to turn out the way she did. That's what I think."

"Daughterly praise." Daphne smiled, but Aurora did not.

"What about me?" Aurora whined back.

"You, too," Jesse added hastily. The soup bowls were removed, and the vegetarian pasta primavera placed before Daphne, Teddie, and her daughter. The Edgertons probably could eat Galapagon lizards or boiled book covers without noticing, but they had chicken breast along with the rest.

"When we were little, Mother, all those times you left, did you ever go on vacation?" Aurora questioned.

"What is a vacation? A carefree period, perhaps, but I never was free of cares, and my eye always was searching, alway working." The edge of Thea's long red sleeve was wet with soup.

"Yes, you were punishing me when you left, punishing me for my lies, so I must have lied, even if I can't remember," Teddie said.

"So self-centered, sister. What about me?"

"Self-centered, me?"

"Why not?" Daphne interjected. "Children are self-centered. That's how they survive."

"That's what I mean about animals and children. You understand," said Thea. Teddie couldn't control this looping conversation, couldn't prevent it from smashing their fragile comfort.

"You left when I lied to you about being sick. I remember. You sat on my bed, but my measle spots went away and I had to go to school and you left," Teddie persisted.

"Yeah, you pinched your little face, all right, but come on. She was always leaving. You weren't always lying, just sometimes, you righteous control freak," Aurora spluttered.

Only Jesse bothered to eavesdrop on the Edgertons' continuing conversation. Teddie twisted a strand of linguine and considered her sister's logic. "That's right. You always were disappearing and I felt so responsible."

"Do you think you had that much to do with my schedule, with my work? Your training took no time at all." Thea laughed. "You two may have tried to be little anchors, but I was too strong. I did what was necessary, my work, splinters of time to share with others. Photography. Common man's art."

"Not common the way you do it," Jesse said. Thea had returned the conversation directly to herself. Me, me, me. Who was the most self-centered and childish? Not little Teddie. Oh, no. Still, what did it matter? Now she could float, if only she freed herself from this clinging debris, from the illusion of control.

"I know. We all should go to the Galapagos together," Teddie said. "Thea? Take pictures of us and them. Another book."

"Oh no," Ruth said.

"Definitely not," Simon added. "Count us out, although I can't speak for anyone. . . ."

". . . for anyone except me," Ruth finished.

"I don't think so, Mom. I'm kind of like Grandmother. I outgrew that nature stuff, but I wouldn't mind going to France or

Cambodia or India. Somewhere interesting."

"When are you going?" Daphne asked, struggling. "No, I can't leave my plants, not now. Next year I'll train someone to take over."

"Count me out," Thea stated firmly, but she was looking wan. "Rossotti's is interested in my next project. You remember, Jesse, you and your friends, rituals of youth." Jesse winced. Carlotta cleared and asked about dessert. Thea had eaten little.

"That leaves us, doesn't it sister?" Teddie imagined traveling to those volcanic islands with Aurora and her thirteen cases and trunks. She'd open her make-up box to bring out the youth in a hundred-and-fifty-year-old tortoise. Those big reptiles took forty years to develop the maturity to reproduce. Do they take turtle hormones to stave off the onset of tortoise menopause? Do cold-blooded animals have hot flashes? "Those tortoises may have the secret to eternal life, Thea. I read none have been found dead without good accidental cause. Nobody knows how long they actually live."

Dishes of ice cream were handed around. Thea tapped her glass with her spoon. "Does everybody have wine? It is time for dessert toasts. To my first daughter, to Aurora, whose glowing light always brings joy and hope!"

"Hear, hear," came from the Edgertons.

"Quiet," Thea ordered. "Next, to my second born, to Theodora who has passed through her ordeal. Welcome!"

The Thea-ordained silence was broken by Aurora's whispered, "What's she talking about?" as glasses clicked and touched lips.

Teddie felt the eyes of the room on her as she rose. Her mother was slumped in her dining chair. "A toast to the source, to Thea, without whom we would not be! To Thea!"

"To Thea!" and everyone at the table stood, even the Edgertons. A sprinkling of applause rose from tables within earshot. Teddie and Aurora watched Jesse throw her long arms around the old woman whose 1940 rayon dress she was wearing. Thea's answering smile was lopsided. Teddie felt limp, but limp with the deep relaxation of a child being carried into the house after a day at the beach. "Good night, everyone," Teddie said from stage center.

The Carleton diners now could return to watching television, or writing books, or painting pictures, or making discoveries, however they spent their evenings. The party was over.

CHAPTER • 25 •

The soft morning air promised rain when Teddie stepped onto Thea's balcony. Soon purple and yellow crocuses would dot the future home of Daphne's kudzu. Soon Teddie would phone to thank Howie for sending Jesse and to tell him Aurora and she would find their way back today.

Last night, after Thea was bedded and Jesse had departed, they'd nestled in bed like two logs, reminiscing amiably about generalities and arguing over details. Had Teddie thrown her second-hand nylon sweater into the garbage or was it her first and only angora that had been stolen at school? After forty-four years of believing herself a victim, Teddie reluctantly remembered a square child's hand surreptitiously lift a metal garbage can lid and slip in a stuffed paper bag. "You hated it!" Aurora said. "It was so ugly! You had good taste back then."

"A frozen six-year-old, how pathetic."

"We were, we were. And everyone thought our lives were glamorous."

"She created us, even our images," Teddie said.

"Noohhhh," Thea groaned from the other bedroom where the nightlight cast its glow. "No!" The sisters rose as one. Thea rolled restlessly. "Get away! No!" she shouted. Teddie put her hand on her mother's clammy brow but stopped short of stroking, afraid the paper-thin skin would peel off.

So she rested her hands on her mother's shoulders and pled, "Wake up, please wake up. Only a bad dream."

"Could be her bad conscience," Aurora sniped as Thea groaned. Without surfacing, the old woman slipped into a deeper sleep. Only her hand twitched like a dreaming cat's paw.

"She's been so strange," Teddie whispered. "Sometimes she's herself, like tonight, but then she has some kind of spell or something, doesn't know where she is."

"It's horrible, like her skin is draped over her bones." Aurora shuddered. "I don't want to get old, not like that."

"Consider the alternative," Teddie said flatly. In recent days she'd had more contact with her mother than in her entire life. A new beginning. It sounded like a political slogan. New Beginnings! Life Without Fear!

"I hate her! She has to suffer. She has to know what she did to me!"

"Always me, me, me." Teddie's voice started a whisper, then roared like a furnace on full.

"Oh shut up, Miss Righteous!" Aurora shouted.

"Silence!" a hollow voice commanded.

"Is it her?" Aurora mumbled.

"Hope so," Teddie answered. "Shhh."

o o o

They breakfasted and Thea dressed for an appointment with her editor. Over Thea's objections Aurora had fashioned a head-covering from the Picasso scarf for no one could expect her to go in public with hair looking like a porcupine's nest. She promised to return the scarf, one of Thea's favorites, a lover's gift, but that would not happen. Teddie had no idea what revelations lay in wait at the Olds's suburban house, but she didn't think she'd be living there long, certainly not the rest of her life. "Thank you, Thea," Teddie breathed as she bent to kiss the painted face. "You understood when I needed you. Call if you need me."

"Naturally. A mother's duty," Thea said. "Now hurry. Don't clutter up my business life." Dismissed.

Rain spattered the windshield as they passed the Securimed mall. "What about Howie?" Aurora asked.

"I don't know. Are you waiting for a handout? The scraps?

Might not be worth it. Tomorrow I find out about my HIV status."

"You're cruel."

"Oh, yes." Her possible viral future was terrifying.

"It's not fair," she sighed.

Approaching headlights were bright points in gathering morning darkness. Thunder rumbled. No more protective bubble, nothing held her safe. Forked lightning streaked towards distant rooftops; seconds later the crash shook the car. Aurora closed her eyes and covered her ears.

Teddie took the first exit. They'd get coffee at the family restaurant and she'd pay her bill, leave a few extra dollars, and that would be finished. She could do nothing about Michael but buy his book when she saw his name on a cover, but there was no guarantee that the blue-eyed man living in storage was named Michael Henderson. Or writing a book. "We'll stop!" Teddie shouted over the drumming rain. Sheets of water flowed over the parking lot. Only a few cars this morning, no lights inside, another power outage. Teddie took the Saturn up close, expecting the flicker of candles, but a heavy chain sealed the doors and a sign said, CLOSED.

Aurora opened one eye. "Looks out of business, probably bankruptcy. Let's stay here until the rain lets up."

"No!" Teddie jerked the wheels into a skid on the cushion of water. "We'll go home." The clouds began to lift as she threaded her way along a car pool route. Perhaps the house had been struck by lightning, but she wished in vain. The house was there. Howie was not. He had her messages. He could have spent the night being comforted by a stewardess, even another court reporter.

Two hours later Aurora emerged, dressed for professional shopping. "You should know. Where do old people shop? Not the Special Shoppe for Thea, not her size." Teddie drew a blank. Not the malls she knew. The old Detroit department stores where other people's grandmothers took young ladies to tea and bought their own ageless garments had long since disappeared.

"Your problem. Remember, eight hundred, maybe a thousand tops—and that includes your whopping fee. How about second-hand stores or estate sales?"

"Oh, divine justice," Aurora said gleefully. "But seriously, where do they shop?"

"Your fifty-fifth birthday next month and it's still 'them.' Look at a calendar." Today her freshly painted sister could pass for forty-five, but what did that matter. While Aurora had been recreating herself, Teddie had been phoning agencies about affordable travel to Darwin's islands of natural selection. Those tortoises weren't afraid of wrinkles, but travel wasn't cheap.

She would clean the rest of the day as if she were readying the house for inspection by realtors. Her weekly carload of giggling cleaners had glided over the surfaces in less than an hour last Monday. What with her tantrums, Howie's chili, and other erup- tions, today's filth would silence their laughter before they had crossed the threshold.

Kitchen gleaming, she took the call on the third ring. Zach's worried voice asked where she'd been.

"Out. With your grandmother. You didn't leave any messages."

"I didn't want to talk to Dad. It's about Bob."

"Is he worse? Is something wrong?" She bit her tongue. How stupid.

"He's so relieved you're letting him stay with you. I've told him all about you." Someday she'd have to ask Zach what he'd said. Bob, too. She jotted "latex gloves" on the shopping list next to the phone. Perhaps he, too, would bring self-understanding, as Thea's pictures had. "But they don't want him to leave the hospital yet. I wanted you to know. He can't come tomorrow." Teddie did not approve of her relief.

"Thanks for letting me know. You're thoughtful. I was cleaning. Do you love him, Zach?" she blurted.

Silence stretched. Eventually he spoke. "Yes, Mom. In every way. I can't imagine living without him." Teddie could hear her son sniffle.

"How awful for you," Teddie started. "No, that's not what I meant, or maybe I did, let me start over." A kaleidoscope of images whirled through her mind, the little boy who'd taught her to be a mother, the young man with a frizzy beard glowing at the sight of his love behind a tangle of tubes in a hospital bed. What would his children be like? His children.

"I'm sorry, Mom. It's nothing you did, really."

"No, that's not it. I'm happy for you, no, that sounds all wrong, it's so complicated, but you're able to love." Teddie had to swallow hard. "That's why I'm crying. Life's so hard. You love him." Teddie heard the shouts of children in the background.

"Got to go. Glad you asked. See you tomorrow."

"The library, at eleven. Will you come with me?" Teddie asked.
"Sure, Mom. Count on me."
"Count on me, too. Bye." Teddie listened until she heard him hang up, then lowered the receiver.
Carefully she completed every blank on the credit card application that had come in the mail. Time to bring credit to her name. Non-thinking work did not still her mind. The power vacuum had inhaled most of the spiraled flour, but the carpet still spiked, like miniature adolescent hairdos. Howie's chair would need professional attention. She lugged it into the garage. Photographs and papers were shoved back into their storage box; of course no one had moved them. Some day she'd search seriously, maybe, if she ever felt like it. Her cleaning skills could not eradicate black smudges on the white couch. Another job for professionals. She shut his study door and took her cleaning equipment to Zach's room. Today she'd straighten. Later she'd move her office to Jesse's room, or why not, the guest room. Aurora could sleep in Jesse's bedroom. She'd like that shining, muscular, nude torso, but as hard as she tried, Aurora was shy on pheromones. Aurora was a pheromone-free environment. Was it too late for a transplant?
No answer at Thea's. One of the cave dwellers in the purple house claimed Jesse would get the message that her mother had returned home. Telephone wires connected them all, like strands of a spider's web.
She had given the house her best when Howie arrived clutching an enormous bouquet of everything from red roses to yellow and white daisies. Once upon a time Teddie had played "he loves me, he loves me not," with daisies like those. What simple, outmoded questions. He thrust the blossoms into her arms. "You're home. Sit down. We need to talk," he said.
Arms filled with flowers, she watched Howie mix the manhattan. "I don't want it," she stated. "Haven't for years. Remember? People change."
"Of course we do. Tell me what you want."
"White wine. There's a bottle in the refrigerator. And put these in water." Teddie frowned as she perched on their black-shadowed white couch. What was their future? Her own? Her mental crystal ball was clouded, but she could wait.
Howie reappeared. "There, Ted. Is it all right? I'll bring an ice cube if it's too warm." He sat, his knees touching hers. She retreat-

ed an inch to consider what she'd say about the last twenty-four hours, about her life of lying, about her drowning tears, about her mother's gift of milk, cookies, terrible truths, and love. "Here, I've got something for you." Howie pulled a box from his pocket.

"Why?" she asked.

He looked puzzled. "Why not?" She sighed but lifted the lid. A tiny frog looked back at her from its hiding place, a green jade tree frog whose toe pads clung to a darker leaf which in turn hung from a heavy gold chain. "It's perfect!" she exclaimed in spite of herself. Howie reached out to fasten the necklace around her, but Teddie rose and shot the clasp home on her own. She was heading for a bathroon mirror when the doorbell rang. Aurora had returned, arms filled with shopping bags.

"More for Ted? Good. I'll pay for them."

"This is Thea's order," Aurora said. "Hard work. We have to go back tomorrow."

Tonight Aurora's presence was an unfamiliar pleasure. "Oh, yes, Howie. Tomorrow I find out if I'm HIV-infected, well, there will have to be other tests, but . . . if it's only all right tomorrow. . . ."

"You're fine. Stop badgering me. I'll do it. Tennis tomorrow." Her sleep would be uninterrupted tonight.

CHAPTER • 26 •

Teddie's calm, no, *joy*, eroded as the message tape rewound, rewound, rewound. Broken, she thought, can't last forever, but who called? Lost. The machine stopped and reversed.

She was studying the brochures the public health department had pressed on her not an hour before when the first recorded voice spoke. "Teddie, this is Daphne. Thea's under the weather. She needs to see you. Come when you can."

"Mrs. Olds, this is the Carleton. Your mother's been in an accident, not injured, but knocked down two residents. Call as soon as possible." Which two, Teddie wondered, probably not the Edgertons, more likely the critics with hearing aids. AIDS, no AIDS for her. HIV-negative! On the way home she'd purchased a box of latex gloves and, from a collection of amazing possibilities, thrown in another box of goldfoil-wrapped latex condoms. For whom? Why not stuff a cookie jar in the kitchen? After dinner mints. A few in her purse.

"Ted, Thea's making trouble. My answering service found me on the courts. I only got in two sets, but I'm going right over. Let you know if you're needed."

"This is the Carleton. Director Olson insists you come immediately. There are papers to sign." Probably money. Thea shouldn't use the residents as bowling pins.

"This is Director Olson, Mrs. Olds." Their names are so alike, but actually it's Howie's name. Is it mine after all these years? User's right. Or am I supposed to be his. That's un-American. Waterford is an elegant name. Thea knew what she was doing when she got rid of Slote. What's she saying? Director Olson sounded very angry. Teddie pushed rewind, then let the tape go forward. ". . . rector Olson. Your mother is ill. She won't cooperate, refuses treatment. Come immediately."

"Mrs. Olds, I shouldn't be calling," a young male voice said. "We met at your mother's last week." Yes, Frank's portrait picture was in Walter's envelope. "You should be here. No one tells me anything, but it looks like she had a stroke. She won't go to our hospital. I reviewed her contract and they can't make her. Treatment in her own apartment. Please come."

"Where are you, Teddie?" Daphne's booming voice rang Teddie's alarm bells. "Your mother needs you. Get your sister. Everyone should be here. I've called Georgio."

Only Thea could straighten this out. Teddie began to punch her number, but stopped. It was no good if she was in one of her moods. She tried Marla. The girls were out, Dickie reported, but, yes, he'd tell Aurora. He would remind her to bring Thea's new clothes. Zach she tracked down with Bob at the University Hospital. He said he'd find Jesse.

"It may be nothing, only another tantrum."

"Trust me. It's serious, Mom."

Just in case, she left a note for Aurora, grabbed Thea's new proofs and her own portraits, and climbed into her still-warm car. Yesterday's balmy spring had reverted to winter. Clumps of wet snowflakes exploded on the windshield. Her car was thick with muddy slush when she parked in the Carleton's lot. Reluctant to go inside, she took the outdoor paths. Teddie's face was fresh and cold when at last she stepped through Thea's unlocked door. A gurney waited in the living room, blanket and sheet folded under straps bisecting its middle. Hermes rested patiently next to the wing chair, but his batteries were not being recharged. Unpleasant sounds leaked out of Thea's bedroom. The apartment air was hot, heavy, almost unbearable. Her own internal heat competing, she veered to the refrigerator. She would crawl inside. They couldn't find her there. She dumped ice into the kitchen sink and rubbed her face and neck. Thea's photographs seemed flat in the bright light, even Georgio's briskly curling chest hair looked lifeless. She wished Thea had hung the beautiful scarred girl.

In the next room people were squabbling. An inhuman sound, an eerie cry, part moan, part desperation, joined the voices. Chills wormed across the nape of her neck. She wanted to be gone. She'd take Thea to the Beekman Storage Tower to help find the last supplies and they'd set up the darkroom. Teddie had more proofs to give to Thea, excellent work, Walter said, although her own shots looked like a non-automated Marla's. The cry became a high-pitched scream. The voices went silent.

She hurried to her mother.

"Sedate her! Now!" a heavy-set woman ordered. With Teddie's approach the pitch of cries from the form writhing on the bed lowered. Thea. Bulging plastic bags with tubes hung from a pole above. None were attached to a body.

"I have," a white-uniformed man insisted. "Let it take hold." Half of Thea was tossing and heaving, but the other side seemed lifeless. Howie held the inert hand to his lips. Was he going to eat it? His round bald spot reflected in the dresser mirror. Thea rolled her head towards Howie and screamed.

"Stop!" Teddie demanded. "Let her be!" Howie was wearing white tennis shorts and a white braided sweater with maroon and blue trim. "What's going on?"

"Probably a stroke, Ted. It's bad. She needs to be in the hospital." He lowered Thea's hand. Its owner glared and made those sounds.

"Your husband's right, Mrs. Olds," a dark-haired woman said.

"Who are you?" The woman jumped. Howie introduced Dr. Irving, Theresa Irving. She was young and pretty but not in tennis clothes. How did her husband know her?

"We've done what we can, but she should be in the hospital. Any delay is dangerous."

"The problem is legal, Mrs. Olds," the woman who must be Director Olson explained, although the problems here seemed much more than legal to Teddie. "We have an unusual contract with Mrs. Waterford. We had to agree she had to approve being taken to our hospital, but you can see that's ridiculous. You have her power of attorney."

Thea loosed another cry.

"You didn't tell me that, Ted. Why you?" Howie looked hurt.

Thea didn't seem incapacitated enough to relinquish control. Her right eye issued orders, as did her voice, her body, the parts that worked.

"I'm sure she understands everything." Daphne had appeared from somewhere. "I saw it start, after lunch. She lost control of her scooter, didn't see them, didn't slow down, just bowled Maisie and Veronica over."

"Were they hurt?" Teddie asked.

"Bruises," Director Olson said. "They're resting. We're watching them." If Thea's action had been intentional, what were her responsibilities as her mother's potential legal caretaker. "Afterwards she seemed a little strange, nothing new," Daphne continued, "but then this happened," and she waved her hand towards Thea who seemed to be listening. "She can't talk," Daphne added unnecessarily. Howie was cherishing Thea's left hand again when Marla and Aurora rushed into the room. Thea's cries escalated.

"What happened? Oh dear Thea. Can I touch her? Is it too late?" Marla begged.

Teddie ordered Daphne to take Marla for a walk. "Keep her out." Thea quieted.

Aurora put down her shopping bags.

Teddie pointed at the intravenous equipment. "Why are those things here? Don't you need them?" She should talk to a lawyer. She would sue anyone derelict in their duties.

"I wanted to wait until she was in our hospital," Dr. Irving said.

The shadow of her mother strained to rise from the bed. "You can't get a needle into her veins. She hasn't any veins," Teddie insisted.

"Oh, everyone does, Mrs. Olds."

Teddie rolled her eyes at Howie. He nodded. "They can cut down, go a little deeper," he said as if that made it all right.

"We're trying to do what's best for your poor mother," Director Olson said and held a paper and pen towards Teddie. "She couldn't have anticipated all this." Teddie suspected it might be bad public relations if people died in their own rooms, make them hard to resell, bad karma, and all that. To die, die, die.

"If she told you she's not going to the hospital, she isn't. Thea knows what she wants." Teddie said, relieved that she was not free to make her own decisions. As always, Thea was the eye of the storm. "I have to make a phone call. Come with me, Aurora," and her older sister trailed her obediently. Thea might think her weak for needing to call Jack Sullivan, to establish the legal basis for any actions, but she had spent almost thirty years with the law. Thea might be above it, but she had a life to live.

"She must be happy, center of attention." Another shriek cut off Aurora's words.

Teddie tried to shut out the sound while Lisa Greenstein got Jack on the line. "That's her making the ruckus?" he asked. "Must be in a bad way. Legally she did everything she could. Said she never wanted to go near a hospital. Deathtraps, she called them. We've got the agreement with the retirement home, we've got her will, her living will, you know, you signed those papers." But I didn't pay any attention, Teddie wanted to say. I did as told. "So it's up to you, little lady. She trusted you to do the right thing. Do you want me there?" It would not be palatable to add Jack Sullivan to this human stew.

"Not now, thanks." Little doors opened and shut, cling to a childhood rhyme. She was dizzy, the sound unbearable. Why doesn't she stop, she has to stop, she's driving me crazy. Zach did that when he was three. Night terrors. He'd scream in his sleep, not even wake up, I'd hold him and. . . . "Of course. She's terrified. She told me again and again," Teddie said. "He claims she trusts me. What should we do?"

"What about me? Why you?" Tears in Aurora's eyes. "Shouldn't she be in the hospital? Let them take care of her." It would be a relief. Just sign Thea over to the authorities, leave her to them. Only just. Teddie looked at her watch. Less than ten minutes since she'd walked in the door.

"Look, she signed all this stuff. She doesn't want to go. She knew what she was doing. What do we do?" Teddie asked her sister.

"Don't ask me. What does Howie say?"

"Oh, Howie," Teddie said and waved her hand in Thea's dismissive gesture. The cries pierced her heart. They gnawed her brain. Her mother can't go on like this. It will kill her. Kill them both. "I'm going back. You come, too. We have to talk to her."

Thea was tied down, her sheets firmly attached to the bed posts and bottom frame. A cocoon. Still trying for freedom, her good hand escaped its restraint to grip Teddie like an iron claw. "Thea, we need to talk," Teddie stated calmly, sensibly. "Would you excuse us?" she announced to the room. "We have things to discuss. Yes, please step outside. You too, Howie." The man in white, Director Olson and Dr. Irving nodded to each other and Teddie before they left.

"Hurry," Dr. Irving said. "Her condition's precarious." Thea rumbled.

"Howie, send in Jesse and Zach when they come. And have them take away that stretcher thing. We won't need it."

Howie backed towards the door, his bony knees gleaming in his dark, hairy legs. "Why can't I stay, Ted? I'm family."

"Close the door, Howie. We'll call when we need you." Air was more plentiful with the crowd gone, breathing easier. First the props. Teddie turned to Aurora. "Bring that lamp. Turn off the ceiling light. We need to focus. Thea, I know you'd be happier if you could sit in your chair, but that seems difficult tonight." Teddie forced herself to look beyond her mother's good eye, to the whole face. Thea was grotesque, but present. "I'll stay here. Now let me go," and she pried Thea's grip loose. She'd have bruises tomorrow, part of that thin skin menopause problem. Teddie untied the sheet and pulled the dressing table stool next to the bed. "Look. Walter was pleased. Which do you want him to print?" Teddie pointed and watched the moveable side of Thea's face. Yes, yes, no, yes, decisions were made. "This one of Jesse," Teddie pointed at her daughter in her grandmother's dress, "the end of your age book or the beginning of youth rituals? Or both. What do you think?" With her red nail Thea tapped the picture twice and pointed at the smaller envelope of portraits. Her bad eyelid drooped further. The good eye was wide open. At the sight of Teddie pretending to pull Jesse's nose ring, half of Thea's mouth twisted in a dreadful grin. Thea captured Georgio's portrait so it rested over her heart.

"When's my turn?" Aurora asked as the bedroom door opened.

Howie's bearded face announced that Dr. Irving wanted them to hurry. Director Olson had to leave. "Soon enough. Go away." Thea was listening, understanding, if her cries were to be believed. "Hush," Teddie said. "See what Aurora has for you," and Aurora opened her magic bags.

Like Teddie, she held up the garments one by one, yes or no. The yeses she draped on her mother's four-poster bed. There were no no's, at least that's what Aurora seemed to think. Thea tugged the red rose patterned cashmere shawl over her. By chance its folds framed Georgio's paper face.

Jesse and Zach slid into the room. Zach pulled Teddie aside while Jesse swept up to the bed. "They say she'll die if she stays here," he said.

"She'll die anyway," Teddie whispered. "This is her choice." Zach looked tired even in the Carleton's flattering lamplight. Jesse was stroking Thea's forehead as Teddie had been unable to do when Georgio entered, followed by Howie and the medical help. Thea's cry made Teddie's heart stop, but she swallowed her fear as the crowd converged on the woman in the bed. "Stay where you are!" Her voice could cut steel. They stopped. Zach joined Jesse at Thea's side.

"Stop that noise, Thea. Now!" she ordered and Thea did, although her hand was attached to Jesse's pale forearm. "You're afraid, but there's no reason. Listen to me." Teddie put both hands on top of Thea's clinging claw. "Listen. You are not going to die. Do you hear? You have work to do. You have new clothes, your art, your talents, your contracts. You will never die." The ancient hand relaxed.

Georgio eased himself behind Teddie. "Listen to Theodora, my love." Thea's eye left Teddie to seek out her once-lover. "She always speaks the truth."

"Thea, you are not leaving." Teddie's fingers moved automatically to record the message she spoke. "Believe me. You will always be with us." Teddie paused and heard her two children say, "Yes, yes," in soft, sibilant agreement. Thea's body shuddered as if shocked. Her good eye closed and she sighed, the limp side of her mouth fluttering with the exhaled air. Teddie removed the relaxed hand from her daughter's arm, but did not let it go. Thea took in air with ragged, shallow gulps. Howie found his way back to the bedside and put an arm around tearful Aurora's shoulders. Dr. Irving flashed her penlight into Thea's unseeing eyes. She took her blood pressure, felt her pulse, and looked at Teddie.

"You're sure this is how you want it? She's probably slipped into coma, but there are things we can do. A ventilator, drugs."

Everyone looked at Teddie, Teddie the center of attention. "It's as close to what she wanted as we can manage," she said, keeping an eye on her mother's rising and falling breast, Georgio's snapshot moving with her. "I guess you must have other things to do, patients you can help," Teddie said.

"I'll come any time. Call. I'll be at the Carleton all night," pretty Dr. Irving said. "You realize she's not likely to recover?" Georgio nodded, but for Thea's sake, Teddie refused to change her lie. "Max, you can stay if you like." Teddie read the nurse's nametag. Maxmilian Scholes. Thea would like a nurse named for an emperor.

"You don't have to," Teddie said. If they'd go away, Thea might sleep, be fresh in the morning.

"Push that button if you need help," Max said, pointing at the buzzer within reach of the bed. "There's another in the bathroom. I'll be here in a minute. Leave the door unlocked." They were on their way out when Daphne phoned. She'd had to water plants, but Dick would pick up Marla after she'd said good-bye to Thea. What did they want to eat?

"Is anyone hungry?" Teddie was. She'd like Peking duck in a thin white pancake brushed with that sauce and a crisp piece of green onion. Fortune cookies, too. She asked Daphne if there was a place nearby to order Chinese. "Peking duck for me."

"I'll take care of it. They deliver."

Marla left. Aurora hung up Thea's new clothes, but left the shawl on the bed. The six of them milled from room to room, always coming back to the four-poster center, to Thea, who continued to breathe that awful way. "Don't go, don't leave me," Aurora begged her mother.

"Of course she won't," Teddie snapped. Daphne took charge of the food, but no one could eat. Even Teddie could barely swallow her wrapped morsel of duck. Georgio told Howie about the years he had lived with Thea, and he told Thea how much he loved her, what she always had meant to him.

"Your work, your photographs are important, Thea," Zach said to the comatose form. "Your fame, your reputation will only grow."

Zach was too close to the truth. Thea knew true fame was reserved for the dead. "Just wait til they see your next book," Teddie added hastily.

"She's someone special," Howie said mistily. "Do you hear that, kids? You won't meet someone like her again soon." Teddie wanted to stamp on Howie's sneakered toe, but Zach put his arm around his father and walked him out of the bedroom.

Hours passed as each tried to say important words before being left speechless, and Thea breathed on, in and out, in and out. The air grew increasingly close. Unpleasant odors wafted from Thea's direction. Teddie chose to ignore the stench, as she had chosen to deny death. Instead she repeated again and again, silently to herself, and aloud to Thea, "Remember, you'll always be with us." "Understand, Thea. You will never die." She appeared peaceful, no thrashing, no obvious terrors. Teddie enticed Zach to lie down in Hermes' bedroom, while Jesse curled into Hermes' seat for a catnap. Howie passed out in the wing chair, and Daphne put her head on the round mahogany table and dozed. Aurora and Georgio rested heads on Thea's bed. Thea slept or whatever it was she was doing, but Teddie could not. Under the bedside light, she leafed through the Thea Waterford retrospective volume of photographs signed, what was it, two weeks ago and found her friend, the one who wore scars proudly, beautifully, her friend who had briefly been as a daughter to Thea. She clasped Thea's hand. "You'll never leave us," she whispered again and closed her eyes.

Thea was changed when Teddie awoke. Impossible, but she'd shrunk. Any more and she'd disappear. Her face looked calm, relaxed, but indistinct, sunken. Teddie opened the draperies to let in the light. Georgio said, "She's gone," and Aurora cried out. Zach put a hand on Teddie's shoulder. "Mom? You okay?" She wrestled the window open. Pink clouds streaked the robin's egg blue dawn sky. A rustling came from the open book on the bed. "What's that?" Jesse exclaimed.

"Thea," Teddie said.

CHAPTER • 27 •

"I'm sorry," Jack Sullivan's voice said. "You write the obit? Beautiful." For a fleeting moment, Teddie had been reluctant to have an obituary appear, but that was nonsense. Just because she'd convinced Thea she'd live forever didn't mean she had to feed and nourish the lie forever. Howie was collecting obituaries, bought papers from around the world. It seemed to make him feel better. "Your mother's affairs are complicated, let me tell you. You're her executor."

"Yes, her executor. But right now?"

"Yes, ma'am. You execute her will, make sure things are done just as she wanted. Remember, I'm on your team, every way. You got a big job ahead of you."

"Who is it?" Aurora shouted. The two were staying at Thea's apartment, sorting and ordering their mother's material possessions.

"Excuse me." Teddie put her hand over the mouthpiece and shouted, "Jack Sullivan."

"Oh, Jackie boy."

"What were you saying?"

"How about you and me having lunch? A working lunch. I can explain about this executor business. You could be a wealthy woman."

"I choose the place," Teddie said. No more oysters and flowers in Chez Nicole. "The Garden Grille, you know it, the Lakeside Mall, upstairs." All exposed, tables on the balcony, see and be seen. "Can you make it tomorrow, say twelve sharp?"

"Maggie, you know my wife Maggie, she likes that place. Never been there, but whatever you say. No problem as best I know."

Aurora was at Teddie's heels. "Lunch tomorrow? We could run into each other. Marla and I are returning clothes." Aurora winked. The cashmere shawl and Teddie's photograph of Georgio had stayed with Thea as she, or what was left of her, was rolled out of her Carleton apartment and into a fiery furnace. A heavy plastic box wrapped in white paper and tied with string now rested on the West Bloomfield mantel. Howie clipped his newspapers and magazines on the coffee table below. There would be a memorial service when her publisher, her galleries, and select museums had been consulted.

"I'm supposed to be her executor, but it can't be very complicated," Teddie explained. "She didn't have that much, just this place and the stuff in storage."

"If you don't want that chair," Aurora pointed at Thea's throne, "I could take it. What do you think?"

"Want an idea? Take over her apartment. You're almost old enough to live in retirement, fifty-five it is, think how simple. . . ." Aurora's look stopped the speech in midair.

"You forgot. I'm forty-eight. Much too young."

"She should have a safe deposit box," Teddie said. "Have you found any little keys? People keep birth certificates in them, don't they?"

"Not mine," Aurora said. "Mine was lost in a fire."

o o o

The pace increased after the lunch with Jack Sullivan. Thea's legacy included her art, even those proof sheets, and the final film Teddie had taken to Walter from the cameras. All of it had value. Even on the day Teddie had been learning her HIV status, the day before the dawn when her mother had died, Thea had been taking pictures. There were almost enough for the book, Frederico said, and sales would be helped if they could get it out soon. "Ride the wave," he said with unabashed commercialism. Did Teddie have any ideas?

The day before Bob moved into Zach's room, she rented an office in a Detroit riverfront building. She liked driving into town but always returned to the white house in West Bloomfield, the house Howie and she still shared. Aurora and Teddie were Thea's heirs, fifty-fifty, except for cash left to Jesse and Zach. Bob brought his portfolio with him, pictures taken when he was not leading the Walker Preparatory Academy's Photography Club. Teddie insisted Frederico come to her office. "Sit down and look at this work," she'd said. "No, now. He's good." If all went according to plan— whose plan?—Rossotti would sign Bob to finish the book. Zach and Bob talked about moving to San Francisco when school was out.

Tax authorities, federal and state, were staking claims on Thea's estate, so little of it liquid. Teddie was learning to communicate on first-name basis with museum curators and gallery owners. Georgio brought in balance sheets and long explanations that he said would both satisfy authorities and spare the estate. Neither mentioned Teddie's loan request, for she had decided to accept Howie's charity. Why not? The work was more demanding than any court reporting, even the six-month trial of that lawyer accused of multiple murders, of targeting old women in order to get back at his mother, the shrink for the prosecution had said. That trial had spawned nightmares in which she and Thea were locked in mortal combat. Teddie never won in her dreamworld, but the lawyer was acquitted in the end.

A small refund from the Carleton paid the office rent and provided Teddie with executorial cash, for Thea had insisted she wouldn't be a real resident until she had lived at The Carleton a full year. Teddie's office had a computer and a fax machine, both of which she was learning to use. Howie was collecting Thea memorabilia. He had perfected phoning for take-out and was expanding his culinary repertoire far beyond Fourth of July chili. Teddie was pleased to see him taking pride in keeping his kitchen spotless.

It was peculiar. Thea was dead, but she spent most of her waking hours dealing with Thea's business. She wasn't sure who was worse, her mother's admirers or detractors, but she could sympathize with those who felt they had been wronged by Thea Waterford, nee Maude Slote. A cousin called from South Dakota, a farmer, said he'd heard about little Maudie and now she was famous, hadn't she remembered them in her will? Teddie forged

Thea's spidery signature on the commemorative book she Federal Expressed the cousin.

Jack and Georgio talked about setting up a Waterford foundation, something Thea should have done, but of course refused to think about. All this would take time, years, and meanwhile neither Teddie nor Howie had taken their vacation. Howie was loathe to leave his collections and his clean kitchen, and Teddie did not invite him to come with her.

o o o

And so she flew to Guayaquil, where she was to meet a university group intent on studying the adaptations of the flora and fauna of the Galapagos. The tour operators did not seem to mind that her alma mater was the Eva Martin School of Court Reporting. She did not take many medicines with her. Dr. Summer's tests had not complained about her health, so she decided not to complain about him. She would see what her own system would accomplish without additional hormones, her own experiment in adaptation.

The hotel was old-fashioned, decaying in the Ecuadorian coastal damp. At the hour the tour group was scheduled to gather in the lobby for their first look at each other, Teddie heard a voice. "I'm leaving!" the old woman barked. "You've always been pigheaded." Heart pounding, Teddie peered around a tarnished gilt column, silently telling Thea that she was dead, that she wasn't eligible for resurrection. Clustered around a mountain of a woman were a middle-aged couple and two teenagers. Like a passing feather, a breeze brushed Teddie's cheek.

No one else was keeping to schedule, so she left the family to stroll outside. A camera from Thea's canvas bag hung around her neck. The tropical air smelled of salt and mold sweetened by drying cocoa pods. A ship waited at port. Tomorrow she would set sail for a handful of volcanic islands six hundred miles out at sea.

CLAIRE VEDENSKY KORN has worked as a psychologist, university teacher, middle school founder and director, freelancer and author of nonfiction, including *Michigan State Parks: Yesterday Through Tomorrow* and *Alternative American Schools: Ideals in Action*. Freed from other people's truths, she's written her first novel. After a forty-two year absence, she again lives in Berkeley, California.